Pr

L

A SPORTING M

5 Stars: "A fantastic foray into the genre of cozy mysteries, and I simply loved it! In this engaging and extremely entertaining novel, we are introduced to Eve Appel, a delightful and spunky protagonist.... *A Sporting Murder* is fun, funny, fast-paced and exciting, with several twists and turns that I didn't see coming.... I absolutely loved this book. Any reader who enjoys mysteries, suspense, action, or just a great read would love this book, and I highly recommend it."
—Tracy A. Fischer for Readers' Favorite

"Settle in for a nerve-wracking mystery set in the rural Florida. Lesley A. Diehl's A Sporting Murder may include women from West Palm Beach, but the characters and murderous activities are right out of old Florida.... character-driven and action-packed."
—Lesa's Book Critiques

"An entertaining mix of characters, an engaging setting, and two unsolved murders that baffle the reader until their resolution at the end of the novel. Her intrepid amateur sleuth Eve Appel is reminiscent of Janet Evanovich's Stephanie Plum, with her lively sense of humor, her unresolved love life, and her uncanny ability to get into—and out of—trouble."
—Michael J. McCann, The Overnight Bestseller

"What a fun summer read!.... It's a type of mystery that's not too complex but it keeps you wanting to turn the page and read on. Eve and Madeleine are the main characters

and their boyfriends move in and out of the picture without much romantic involvement. The secondary characters—the mobster backer, the card shark grandma, the bumbling ex-husband—are the ones who provide the boost to propel the story along with wit and flare."
—Tribute Books Mama

"Diehl gives us characters with strength and humor. Eve is a great mix of intelligence, charm and minx, and exhibits the tendency to butt in where it may not be comfortable. She also has a few friends in low places that are there for her regardless of what she needs…. If you enjoy mystery, romance and a little bit of crazy you will enjoy *A Sporting Murder*."
—Leslie Wright, Blog Critics

DEAD IN THE WATER

"A well crafted cozy mystery that has action, adventure and detective work involved through a few interesting and fun characters to read about. While reading the book I got intrigued enough by Eve and her list of quirky friends that I'd like to read more books in the series. Especially about Eve's Indian friend."
—Mystery Sequels

"There is action galore. The plot becomes more convoluted as new developments take place just as answers seem evident. Each twist is followed by a further twist, the action is continuous, and Eve is suitably confused…. Recommended."
—Michael F. Hennessey, I Love a Mystery

"*Dead in the Water* is a laugh-out-loud cozy with just the right balance of suspense, plot twists, romance, and airboat rides."
—Sharon Potts, author of *South Beach Cinderella*

"Lesley Diehl has outdone herself with *Dead in the Water*. She still has her carefully drawn characters you enjoy knowing and the sense of humor that makes you laugh out loud. But in *Dead in the Water*, Diehl has developed her most involved plot. With murder, kidnapping, the mob and alligators, you won't want to put the book down. This second Eve Appel Mystery is a must-read."
—James R. Callan, author of *Cleansed by Fire* and *A Ton of Gold*

"Like the biblical Eve, Eve Appel, the main character in Lesley Diehl's *Dead In The Water,* is an impulsive, curious, and determined woman who doesn't always live by the rules. Those characteristics place her in extremely dangerous situations and add to the intriguing plot in this second book in the series."
—Patricia Gligor, author of *Mixed Messages*, U*nfinished Business*, and, *Desperate Deeds.*

A SECONDHAND MURDER

"Lesley A Diehl is a very clever writer. Most of the time I can figure out the murderer in a book but this one kept me guessing right until the end. The characters all have one thing in common, trying to solve the murder .... *A Secondhand Murder* is a cozy mystery, and is part of a series called An Eve Appel Mystery. Hopefully all the other ones will be just as good as this one."
—Sharon Salituro, Fresh Fiction Reviews

"Fun from Page one!.... Not only is *A Secondhand Murder* filled to the brim with entertaining characters, but the mystery contained in its pages is also well crafted. Everyone, even Eve, seemed to have some sort of secret. I enjoyed peeling back all the layers of this story as I tried to figure out what was related to the murder and what wasn't. I absolutely enjoyed reading

A Secondhand Murder. The web of murder and deceit is well spun, but the characters Ms. Diehl has created are truly the shining stars of this book. Anyone looking for a laugh out loud, fast paced mystery would do well to pick up *A Secondhand Murder* today."
—Long and Short Reviews

"A full cast of zany and dangerous characters makes this cozy mystery a fun read. With laugh out loud scenes and some scary moments, this book is so hard to put down and when the end did come, I found myself wondering what madcap adventure awaits the reader in the next book. I loved it!!"
—Kathleen Kelly, Celtic Lady's Reviews

"I'll have to personally recommend this book to all of my friends who love cozies. It's a great mystery, with a little suspense, a little romance, some slapstick, and most of all, characters who feel like family."
—Ryder Islington, author of *Ultimate Justice*

"Thrift with a murderous twist ... vivid Florida setting with lots of suspense and humor."
—Kathleen Delaney, author of the Ellen McKenzie Mystery Series

"Author Lesley A. Diehl blends humor and suspense into a delightful tale of intrigue. Diehl has created likable, realistic characters that will have you laughing as you try to guess who the killer is. *A Secondhand Murder* flows at a steady pace with some interesting twists along the way. The setting is inviting and the story will draw you in."
—Mason Canyon, Thoughts in Progress Blog

"An extremely fun and wickedly entertaining cozy mystery.

The quirky characters and the complex entanglements each of them have with the deceased and the protagonist is the best part of the book. The author creates a well-plotted, light-hearted mystery that has some really good laugh out loud scenes. Cozy mystery lovers will thoroughly enjoy *A Secondhand Murder;* it is an outstanding read from beginning to end."
—Robin T. for Manic Readers

"Humor, adventure, mystery and romance are all blended together to make this a fun few hours of reading. The book kept me guessing until the end—I kept changing my mind about who the killer was and I guessed wrong. LOL—This was a good thing. I enjoyed this one."
—Yvonne, Socrates Book Review

"[*A Secondhand Murder*] will delight you. It has a little bit of everything that you want in a murder/mystery, complete with romance!"
—Mary Bearden, Mary's Cup of Tea

"I am absolutely in love with this story. Lesley Diehl has created such a fun character in Eve Appel! She was funny, sassy and smart. She's a great protagonist. The story has a great mystery and there's so many different things going on that I was definitely surprised by the ending. I love a good mystery dashed with humor."
—Brooke Blogs

"I really enjoyed the page turning action that even involved getting help from a Mob boss. The story was complex but very easy to follow. The quirky characters including Eve lead the reader through lots of excitement…. I wholeheartedly recommend this cozy for all cozy mystery readers."
—Carol McKinney, Carol's Reviews

"There were so many characters that I really enjoyed everyone from Eve's crazy ex-husband Jerry to Alex the Private Investigator to her grandmother and grandfather. They all had their quirks that I loved. Definitely a great new refreshing series that I can't wait to read more of when the author writes more!"
—Community Bookstop Blog

Mud Bog Murder

Mud Bog Murder

An Eve Appel Mystery

—

LESLEY A. DIEHL

Seattle, WA

Camel Press
PO Box 70515
Seattle, WA 98127

For more information go to: www.camelpress.com
www.lesleyadiehl.com

Cover design by Sabrina Sun

ISBN: 978-1-60381-315-0 (Trade Paper)
ISBN: 978-1-60381-316-7 (eBook)

Library of Congress Control Number: 2016939037

Printed in the United States of America

Acknowledgments

Too often we forget that good writing is really good rewriting, and I have certainly done a lot of that; first, when I submitted my work to the person who became my agent, Dawn Dowdle of Blue Ridge Literary Agency. She certainly put me through the wringer with my first Eve Appel book. How could this perfect work be made more perfect, I wondered. Thanks, Dawn, for being so insistent I could do better.

Over the course of the Eve Appel series Eve has matured and developed into a woman not only sassy, but also one coming to know herself more fully. Eve has taken some surprising turns in her life, changes encouraged and fostered by Jennifer McCord, associate editor at Camel Press and Camel's publisher, Catherine Treadgold. Thanks to you both for helping to make Eve a woman we want to admire for her pluck and love for her generosity to others.

I'm a better writer because of the support of Dawn, Jennifer, and Catherine, but most important, Eve is a better character.

Also by the author from Camel Press:

A Secondhand Murder

Dead in the Water

A Sporting Murder

Short Stories in the Series

"The Little Redheaded Girl is my Friend"

"Thieves and Gators Run at the Mention of her Name"

"Gator Aid"

CHAPTER 1

———

"I THINK YOU should hang one of the pictures on the wall behind the counter." I flipped back several pages in the album and pointed to one of the photos. "This one."

Madeleine and I were going through her wedding album in our consignment shop on wheels, an RV we had converted to hold our merchandise. We still hadn't moved into the new, non-mobile location because the carpenters who were supposed to begin the renovations had been held up on another job. Or so they said. Finding professional crews to do carpentry work and painting on schedule wasn't easy, as I was learning. A crew would show up once then disappear, and tracking them down proved difficult.

"You mean on the wall in the new place, right?" Madeleine asked.

"When we move into the new store, whenever that might be. Could be next week. Could be next year."

Madeleine shook her soft red curls in that ultra-feminine way of hers. She's cute and petite and sometimes makes me feel like a stuffed giraffe standing next to My Little Pony. I'm tall, skinny, and I rock stiletto heels and gel my blonde hair.

We couldn't be more different in appearance, but we've known each other since childhood. We're as close as sisters. "Don't be so pessimistic, Eve," my friend said. "It'll happen soon, and then our only dilemma will be whether we close down this rig or keep it and operate both places."

Madeleine Boudreau—now Madeleine Boudreau Wilson, having married David Wilson, love of her life and owner of a hunting ranch outside our community of Sabal Bay in rural Florida—and I have been best friends since sixth grade. Several years ago we bought a consignment shop that features designer fashions and other pre-owned items such as jewelry and house wares.

If you're thinking we're crazy to be selling and consigning high end merchandise among the cowboys, horses, and alligators of rural Florida, then you just don't know your wealthy West Palm matrons. They relish making a few bucks off their classy worn clothes plus discovering bargains in a shop where their friends won't know they're buying secondhand. Of course, that's a ruse, because those same matrons run into each other here all the time. They just pretend that Ralph Lauren gown wasn't the one worn to the cancer benefit gala—the gown the wearer brought into the store last week. And as we've found, which has only added to our trade, the clientele from West Palm love to patronize the shop. It's the perfect excuse for them to slip off the coast and indulge in activities not found in West Palm, such as spending an afternoon riding an airboat and hobnobbing with the local alligators.

Probably the strongest lure for the ladies to our environs is the cowboys who sing and dance the two-step in our local bars. I have to agree with them. There is nothing sexier than having a long, lean cowboy's strong arms around you while dancing to some country western cryin', lyin', and dyin' song. And of course, I'd be remiss if I didn't say our resident country gals have classy taste too, and don't mind buying Oscar de la Renta or Jimmy Choo for pennies. The best part? Madeleine and I meet some pretty unusual people, and we make money.

One of our customers, Jenny McCleary, emerged from the dressing room in the back of the rig.

"You like the blue lace Diane von Furstenberg?" I asked Jenny.

Jenny, a big woman almost as tall as me—I'm over six feet in my stilettos and I always wear stilettos—but carrying more curves, shook her head. "It didn't fit, which is just as well. I don't think I'm the lace type."

"I'll agree with you on that. And I'd choose a primary color to bring out your tan. And your dark hair. Don't you agree, Shelley?" Jenny's daughter Shelley was as tall as her mother but thin like me.

"Whatever." Shelley shrugged her shoulders. I knew she wasn't being rude, just a young adult trying to look bored while shopping with Mom. Shelley, sixteen and soon to graduate from high school, not only shared her mother's height but also her dark hair. The two of them came into the shop often but rarely purchased anything. Shelley always carried a sketch book with her. She'd look at clothing then flip open the book and draw something in it. When I asked her one day what she was doing, she showed me her work. She'd drawn a picture of a dress on the rack, but so transformed that I hardly recognized it.

"I'd like to be a designer," she said in a quiet voice.

"Well, you certainly have the talent for it," I replied.

She gave me a shy smile. Shelley seemed like a pale shadow of her mother, who was larger, more outgoing, more colorful and had an opinion on everything and liked to state it out loud. And at the top of her lungs. Yet I found something likeable about Jenny. Maybe that was because her mouth was as out of control as mine. Her daughter Shelley I admired for her developing fashion sense. The kid would be a killer designer in a few years.

Jenny handed me the dresses she had tried on, and I laid

them on the counter. As with my first encounter with her, I noticed her unusual eyes—one brown, the other hazel. Then, as now, they twinkled with delight. Jenny always seemed to be upbeat and liked a good laugh.

"So what are you gals looking at?" she asked.

"This is Madeleine's wedding album."

Madeleine moved to one side to let Jenny and her daughter take a look at the book.

"Eve thinks I should put up this picture in our shop." Madeleine pointed out the one of her and David. In it, Madeleine's gaze was turned away from the camera and she was looking up at David. Her gauzy beige dress, whipped by the breeze, billowed away from her legs and the ringlets of her red hair blew across her delicate face. David's hand caressed her cheek, his handsome features stretched into a wide smile. The picture said "We're in love."

Jenny focused on the photo, then bent forward for a better look. "Hmmm. Well, I guess it is a great picture of the three of you."

"Three? What three?" Madeleine leaned over the page, her mass of red curls obscuring my view of the photo. I grabbed the book and turned it around so I could see the photo better.

Madeleine gasped and stepped backward, her freckled hand flying to her chest in a gesture of horror.

"I never noticed that before," I said.

"Yup. There's a damn alligator in the background." Jenny chuckled. "And here I thought you were the maid of honor, Eve."

"I'm sure the photographer can Photoshop the reptile out of the picture, honey," I assured Madeleine. "It's such a sweet photo. Don't toss it out."

"Where was it taken?" asked Jenny.

"We were married at David's hunting ranch," Madeleine said. "That's a shot from in front of the pond, north of the house."

I remembered that pond well. It was where I tangled with

a Cape Buffalo several months ago … but that's a story for another time. The exotics were gone now, shipped off to wildlife preserves and zoos, but I still had nightmares about that huge animal charging me. I took to a live oak to avoid being trampled.

"Eve, did you hear me?" Madeleine tugged on my sleeve. "I think this is a better picture. It's of the four of us—David, me, you, and Alex."

It was a great shot, me in my slinky red dress, Alex as best man in a dove gray suit. It had been a happy day. All of us were grinning, even Alex, who lately found little to be happy about.

Madeleine looked up at me. "I'm sure it's just temporary, Eve."

Alex's misery mood was clear to everyone around us lately. I was the cause of it. I knew what would made him happy, but I wasn't about to do that.

"Kind of an unusual bridesmaid's dress, isn't it?" asked Jenny.

"I like it," her daughter said, surprising all of us.

"I do, too," said Madeleine. "It's so Eve."

"You don't suppose you could find an outfit 'so Jenny' "? asked Jenny.

"You said you wanted something formal, but tell me about the event," I said.

"It's for my own wedding," she replied.

"Well, that's just great. And the lucky guy?" I asked.

"Some Yankee. I think he's just after Mom's money," Shelley said.

Jenny laughed. "If he is, then he's gonna be surprised, 'cuz I got none."

I was surprised, too. Jenny owned about 500 acres of property east of Sabal Bay. That wasn't a huge ranch for around here, but it put her among the top land owners in this county. She had to be running a large herd of cattle, and beef prices were good.

Jenny must have seen the surprise on my face.

"I'm land poor, Eve. My husband took our life savings and

bought that land, but it's mostly swamp and bog, wetlands. No damn good for beef or cows and calves. Then he up and died on me two years ago. I have no idea what he was planning to do with that useless property. He was a damn fool. Left me with land that only alligators, birds, and snakes have any use for. No money in it."

"That's not true though, is it, Mom? You're gonna make money off it this year." Shelley's tone was disapproving.

I lifted one eyebrow, waiting for an explanation.

"Tell them what you have in mind."

"My daughter doesn't approve. I've been approached by a concern out of West Palm looking for someplace around here to do mud bog races. I underbid everyone for the event this year. Showed all those guys a thing or two about dealing with a woman."

Mud bog races? I'd heard something about them last year but wasn't really familiar with the sport.

Shelley crossed her arms over her chest and tapped her foot on the floor. "All you have to do is let trucks tricked out for mud racing come onto your property and tear the hell out of it, destroying all the plant life and bird and animal habitat."

"But you got to have swampy land, and I sure got a load of that," Jenny said. To her daughter, she added, "You'll be happy enough to see me sign that contract when I get the money that'll send you to the Fashion Institute of New York up north."

Shelley's face turned bright red. Anger or embarrassment? I couldn't tell.

"You've seen those trucks jacked up several feet with giant tires on them?" Madeleine asked.

"Their cabs are usually three feet or more off the ground," Shelley said. "They make normal cars and trucks look like miniatures. You can't miss them 'cuz they're usually covered with mud." Her mother's attention seemed to be elsewhere as she turned and looked out the windows of the rig. That was so like the Jenny I'd come to know. Once she'd had her say, she wasn't interested in hearing out anyone else.

"I remember now," I said. "Last year, one of them drove past me on the Beeline, blew its mud all over my Mustang. It took over ten dollars' worth of quarters in the car wash to get all that goop off."

Jenny waved her hand in a gesture of dismissal. "So, do you think you can find anything in my size? This is a second marriage for me so I think it's appropriate I buy the dress at a secondhand shop, don't you?"

"Is it ever," I said. "I'm going down to West Palm this week. I'm sure to find something for you there. When's the big day?"

"In a month. Unless I change my mind." Jenny chuckled and headed for the door. "Come on, Shelley. Let's leave Eve and Madeleine to their business."

Shelley hung back for a minute. "Eve," she whispered, "Can I come see you one of these days? There's something I need to talk to you about."

"Sure, honey. Anytime."

"Shelley? Let's roll," called her mother from the bottom step of the rig. "Oh hi, Alex," I heard her say.

I watched him step to one side to let Jenny and Shelley pass, then bound up the two steps. My heart did a little pit-pat, which it always did when I caught sight of him. The man was lust worthy, no doubt about it, but I knew we needed more than passion for a long-term relationship. He had more. I wondered if I did. My heart had done that pitter patter thing before my ex Jerry and I married, but we now were divorced. My heartbeat was not a reliable barometer of relationship durability.

"Hi, Madeleine," he said, giving me a half smile followed by his now typical look of unhappiness. "What's happening?"

I tried to send a silent signal to Madeleine to avoid talking about the wedding album, but failed. She was so overwhelmed by her happiness with David that she was immune to the negative "no marriage talk" vibes I was sending out.

"You haven't seen the wedding pictures yet, have you?" She

grabbed Alex by the arm to haul him over to the album, which still lay open on the counter.

Alex shot me a look I couldn't read, but I was certain it held some kind of disapproval.

"Look at this." Madeleine indicated the picture of her and David. "See anything interesting?"

"Sure. It looks like two people who love each other reveling in having said their wedding vows." Alex's azure eyes gazed at me with a penetrating steadiness. "That's what people do who love each other. Right, Madeleine?"

I rolled my eyes.

Alex caught the look. "But some people can't make up their minds about love. Even when it's right in front of them."

Madeleine sighed, closed the album and walked off toward one of the clothes rounds. "I'll let the two of you do whatever it is you seem to be doing lately while I do … something, too."

"Eve, we need to talk." He brushed back the lock of sun-streaked brown hair that flopped over his forehead. He always looked like such an innocent boy. Maybe that's why I felt such anger toward him now. His words were not innocent. They were meant to hurt in a grown-up way. He was being pushy, pushy, pushy. I was not ready to make a commitment. Not yet.

"Why must we talk now, here, at the store? And just what are we going to talk about?" I tried to contain my anger, but lately all we did was fight about our relationship. I thought the wrangling was wearing thin.

"We've been an item for a year longer than Madeleine and David, and they're married. We don't even live together. What's your issue?"

There it was. It was always *my* issue, never Alex's lack of understanding about who I was and what was important to me.

I leaned my elbows back onto the counter, glad that Madeleine was out of earshot and there were no customers in the shop. I didn't want to have anyone hear the prickliness in

Alex's and my discussion. It was bad for business.

Maybe that was my "issue," as Alex called it. I was focused on the business and not on the two of us. How could I not put business first? It had been less than three years since Madeleine and I set up the shop, and those years had some good times and many bad times when I worried we might go under. Now we had a mobile shop—a motor home we drove to flea markets on the coast and to the one here in Sabal Bay. It was a good business, but the rig was a loan from my mob boss friend Nappi Napolitani. I should be moving out of it and taking up full-time residence in our new location, the one being renovated. And although I knew he never wanted any money from us for rent, I felt guilty not paying him for the use of the rig.

And in the middle of all this upheaval, Alex wanted a commitment from me? Was he crazy?

"Yeah, yeah," he said. "I know about your business problems, and I'm not denying you have to put them first, but we can get through these times together. I'll help you like David helps Madeleine. Am I not supportive enough? Do I interfere with your work?"

"No. You never interfere with my work, but you seem to feel I intrude upon yours, especially when it includes people I know and care for. Then you get all bristly about my sticking my nose in and tell me to back off. How can I back off? It's not in my nature to ignore my friends and family when they need help. Just because you've got a license doesn't mean you can push me out of the way. It would be nice just once if you gave me some credit for my ideas." I knew I should keep my mouth shut and let his criticisms go, but I was beginning to feel defensive. When Eve Appel felt attacked, that was when she went in for the kill.

"But, Eve, honey, private investigation is work for a pro." He paused, as if rethinking what he had said. "Look, I know you're one bright cookie, and some of the leads you've developed on cases have been right on. I guess I could try harder to listen to your ideas." He added this with some hesitation.

Damn. He was trying to be nice and accommodating. But was that what I wanted? No. I wanted more than accommodation. I needed a man who celebrated my intrusive nature, who could temper it with his own passion for what was right and share in finding the truth. He didn't get it. I wanted the kind of mate Madeleine had in David, a man whose soul was just as inspired by tearing into trouble and making it yield. I sighed and gave up. I couldn't tell him this. He wouldn't understand, or if he did, he'd try his best to become what I needed and fail. This wasn't a matter of "build the right man for Eve." I pushed off from the counter and put my hands on his arms. "I know, but I think I'm commitment phobic after my marriage to Jerry."

"I'm not Jerry."

"It's just …." I stopped. This casual lie wasn't going to wash. I knew it, and so did he.

"I think you're more than Jerry-phobic. I think you've got some trust issues. I can understand that, Eve. Your parents disappeared, dead in a sailing accident when you were nine. As an adult you chose to marry the most unreliable guy on the planet. Oh, don't get me wrong—I like old Jerry—but I'd never marry him." He paused for a moment. "Okay. Here it is. I'm not certain you love me, Eve."

I wasn't either. Did I have the courage to tell Mr. Perfect that?

CHAPTER 2

———

THE WORD WAS out all over town. Jenny McCleary had indeed signed a contract with a West Palm firm to host the Sabal Bay Annual Mud Bog Races on her property. I knew what holding those races meant for the wildlife, and so did many environmentally concerned citizens in the Sabal Bay area.

Of course, not everyone agreed. There was so much swampy and boggy land in this part of rural Florida that many people wondered how killing off a few birds, snakes, turtles, and even alligators could be a bad thing, especially when the races would bring in money and, temporarily, jobs. Theirs was a short-term view. The long view was more complex: the races might lead to other kinds of development, good for the local economy but very bad for the environment. In the bad old days of Southern Florida, the goal had been to leash nature by rerouting the water, draining swampland, and paving over the wilderness.

Madeleine and I talked about the races and my old "let's do something" side emerged. I hadn't felt this energized around an issue since Madeleine and I had joined a group protesting the building of a shopping mall in Connecticut. That was over ten years ago, but the issue was similar. The developers of the Revolutionary Shopping Mall outside New Haven had gotten past local governing agencies as well as state regulatory groups by filing what many saw as a fraudulent environmental impact statement with the state department of conservation.

Madeleine and I joined the demonstrators when the first backhoe followed by road graters and dump trucks roared across the wetlands. Our effort changed no one's mind about the project; it was the downturn in the economy that rescued the land from becoming all stores and concrete. Vegetation took over once more and all but obscured the rusting machinery that sat silently sinking into the marshy dirt. Birds built their nests among the metal pipes and girders, and turtles crawled through the concrete culverts left abandoned on the site. Nature once again claimed the land. Madeleine and I applauded the decay of human foolishness and the encroachment once more of weed and marshy swamp. But it was clear that, human nature being what is, greed would rear its ugly head in other places. Like here in Sabal Bay.

I hated the thought of Jenny McCleary being behind the mud bog event, but I knew it would do little good to talk with her about it. Jenny needed the money, and once she made up her mind, that was that. When she appeared back in our shop rig the end of the week, I thought it was only fair to tell her that Madeleine and I would be joining the protest scheduled for the opening day races.

"You do what you have to do, honey." Jenny stood in front of the mirror wearing the dress I'd found for her in West Palm—a gently worn, dark green Oscar de la Renta sheath. She turned to look at how the dress hugged her derrière and seemed pleased with what she saw.

"Where's Shelley today?" I asked.

Shelley had called me last week to make a suggestion Madeleine and I had talked about several times—a service for customers who needed their clothing altered. From Shelley's drawings, I knew she would be a perfect candidate for simple and more complex tailoring. I asked her to stop by the shop to discuss the plan in more detail, but she hadn't yet. Since I didn't know if she had mentioned the idea to her mother, I said nothing to Jenny.

"I think she's got a boyfriend. Name's Darrel Hogan, I believe."

Madeleine and I looked at each other and wondered if Jenny had read the paper this week. The name Hogan appeared in the police blotter. Was it a relative or the fellow himself, I wondered.

"I see your looks, and I saw the paper. Darrel has sticky fingers, it appears. He has crappy taste though. He took a Western shirt from the big box store. You'd think he'd target the Western store for a better grade of merchandise. Well, no matter. His daddy bailed him out. Like always. Darrel is a chip off the old Daddy Hogan blockhead. Ask your detective friend Frida. She'll tell you the Hogans have been nothing but a headache for the law around here. Well, I like the dress. Do you think it's too bold for an old lady getting married again?"

"I think it's perfect. It's you."

Jenny laughed. "It was somebody else before it was me, though, wasn't it?"

"Maybe not," I said. "Sometimes it takes a couple of owners before a dress finds the right home."

After we rang up her purchase, she waved goodbye and headed for the door. Before she stepped out, she turned and said, "You gals take care now. The cops have gotten wind of the protest at the races so they'll be on hand. Don't get yourselves arrested. I certainly won't bail you out." She chuckled and waved again.

"She's certainly taking our different opinion of the event well," said Madeleine.

"Yeah," I replied, but I ignored Madeleine's next comment because I was distracted by the possibility of getting arrested at the rally. I'd done that before and wasn't interested in seeing the inside of a jail again. Certainly not the inside of the Sabal Bay facility. It would be especially embarrassing to have Frida, our detective friend, stop by our cell to offer us bread and water.

"Eve, where are you? I asked you if you wanted me to drive to the rally, or will you?"

"Sorry. I will."

"You off in thought worrying about Alex?"

"No. There's nothing I can do about that."

"You could marry him. That's what he wants. Don't you?"

I gave her my flip answer. "I'm not ready to make that kind of commitment yet."

She squinted at me. "Really? Is that what you told him, too? I don't believe it. What's stopping you?"

The words were barely out of Madeleine's mouth when a tall, dark-skinned, startlingly handsome man stepped into the shop. He was followed by an older man, gray hair in braided plaits.

Could that be what was stopping me? Questions about the relationship I had with Sammy Egret, member of the local Miccosukee tribe? Sammy's effect on me when we got together was puzzling. There was something like electricity that hummed between the two of us. We'd spent a night alone lost in the swamps. Nothing had happened out there in the solitude other than an intense awareness of each other. I tried to be a good friend to Sammy, to treat him as I did his grandfather, whom I adored. But somehow when I teased Sammy or touched him in a friendly fashion it was as if the earth stopped spinning and we both couldn't breathe. We'd handled the situation up until now by ignoring it, but the awkwardness persisted. What was the next step, I wondered.

"Hi, Sammy," said Madeleine. "I …." She didn't finish her sentence. "Sorry, I've got to …." She ran off toward the tiny bathroom in the rear of the rig.

"What's with Madeleine?" asked Sammy.

"I think she's caught this flu bug going around. She's been complaining of an upset stomach for over a week." I smiled at both Egret men, then reached out and gave Grandfather Egret a hello hug. The mahogany skin on Sammy's face took on a red tone. A blush? I stepped back and wiggled my fingers at him. "Hey, Sammy. What are the two of you doing here?"

"The blight took its toll on my tomatoes, so we're here to buy some at the market. I've got a lot of cooking to do," said Grandfather Egret. He was a wonderful cook. I'd eaten his dishes many times, and he'd even been generous enough to share some of the traditional tribal recipes with me.

"Making some delicious Miccosukee dish, I'll bet," I said.

He shook his head. "Making spaghetti sauce. You want to come over tonight? Or are you busy?"

"I'm free."

Sammy smiled and shuffled his feet. A roomful of women's designer fashions wasn't a comfortable environment for a guy who loved being out in the swamps or in his airboat, flying down the canals.

"How's the airboat business?" I asked.

"I had to teach my nephews how to operate the boat. We're swamped with all the women from the coast you sent our way. I'm tied up at David's hunting ranch most days although he seems inclined to do more of the work himself out there now." Sammy had stepped in last year when David lost his foreman and ended up staying on.

I was glad to hear David was showing renewed interest in the hunting ranch. He'd inherited it from his father, but hadn't wanted to run the business after one of his clients was killed there. Sammy may have taken on the foreman duties, but his heart was back on the water, taking people out into the swamps. Foreman wasn't a position he wanted to hold for much longer.

"Between the women from the coast and the winter visitors, our business is so busy I think we may want to run a second boat," said Grandfather.

"A second boat?" Sammy blew out a breath. "First we need to think about a reliable first boat. That thing is held together with vines and duct tape. And who's going to run the second boat?" He sounded overwhelmed.

"Me. I could help out," said a voice from behind Sammy.

The voice was oh so familiar. I groaned. It was Jerry, my ex-husband. Why was he here? I thought he would be in West Palm doing whatever he did for my mob boss friend Nappi.

"Did Nappi fire you?" I asked.

Jerry greeted Grandfather and Sammy and then tried to gather me into a hug.

"Hands off, Jerry. Can't you see I'm working? It looks bad if I hug every man who comes in here."

I caught sight of a twinkle in Sammy's eye. "She didn't hug me. Why should she hug you?"

"Because we were once married, so we're kind of related," Jerry said.

I grimaced. "I'd rather hug an alligator than you, Jerry. Didn't it state that in our divorce agreement?"

Jerry looked appropriately hurt. Despite the fact that we had divorced and I found Jerry tiresome, aggravating, and intrusive, I also felt kind of sorry for him. I'd met Nappi through Jerry because Jerry was dating Nappi's daughter and thought he was about to become part of Nappi's family by marrying her, but then she dumped him. Now Jerry was nothing but a gofer for the guy.

I patted him on the shoulder. "Lighten up. I'm just kidding."

Sammy and Grandfather exchanged looks of amusement at our sparring.

"I've got my nephews to help out. They'll be there to cover this Saturday," Grandfather Egret said.

Jerry's face brightened. "I can help out anytime you want. So what's up Saturday?"

"That's why we stopped by. We wondered if Eve and Madeleine were going to the mud bog event."

I was shocked. "You're attending the event? I thought—"
Grandfather didn't let me finish.

"Only in a manner of speaking. I thought we'd join the protest. Many of the tribe will be there. We've had about enough of white folks raping this land." Grandfather's usual pleasant smile was replaced with a frown of anger.

"I thought the event was good for the area. Brings in money, right?" Jerry said.

Three pairs of angry eyes glared at Jerry.

"Right. I get it," he said. "There are better ways. So who's running the boat. Can I? I can handle the whole thing by myself. I did it before."

"And I heard the complaints from my customers in here," I said. "You're not a member of the tribe. Being squired around by a short, pasty-faced Yankee isn't the experience these women or tourists are looking for."

"I'm not that short."

"You are compared to Sammy," I said. "I told them to expect a tall Miccosukee as their airboat pilot."

"I could spend the week in the tanning booths. Might help me look the part."

"Don't be so pushy, Jerry. He doesn't need your help right now," I said.

"But we'll keep you in mind," Sammy said, giving Jerry a pat on the shoulder.

Madeleine emerged from the bathroom, her face greenish compared to her usual rosy-cheeked glow.

"Hi all," she said. "I knew I should have gotten that shot. I think I'm coming down with the flu, Eve."

I felt her forehead. "You're not feverish, but I think you should go home and rest. And you're not attending the rally unless you're better." I pushed her in the direction of the door.

"I'll drive you. No need to call David," Jerry offered.

"I heard this is going to be a bad flu season. Did you get your shots?" I asked Grandfather and Sammy.

They both nodded.

"I hope Madeleine doesn't have something more serious than flu," I said.

"I think she does," said Grandfather.

"What?" I asked.

He shook his head, but said nothing else.

IN A FIT of anger, the woman from whom we'd bought the store had trashed it before we could take possession. We'd once rented at that location, but through a series of unfortunate events, including a fire, she had taken over our store for a short while. Needing money for her lawyer's fees, she was forced to sell the property. She hadn't wanted us to be the buyers, and she made that clear by tearing out all the shelving, writing graffiti on the walls, taking a sledgehammer to the toilet and sink, and in a final fit of rage, using the sledgehammer to penetrate the walls until she could tear at the wiring within. She wasn't a pleasant person, but now she was in prison and no longer a threat to us. Of course we got the shop at a reduced price, but all the destruction meant we had weeks of work to do before the site was fit to open as a consignment shop.

Our carpenters finally arrived on a Monday several weeks ago and then disappeared. I tracked them down and extracted a promise from the head guy to return this Monday. Madeleine and I decided one of us should stop by daily to check on the crew because they had a reputation around town for not working very hard or many hours in a day. We suspected they might take long breaks and lunch hours that ran into the middle of the afternoon. But they were the best we could afford.

There were simply too many tasks and activities for the two of us to handle. Whoever was not supervising at the shop would visit the coast for consignments. There were no flea markets operating nearby during the week, but the one in Stuart on the coast opened for the weekend. We'd miss it this Saturday, so I tried to find a stand-in to run the rig in our place. I called Grandy, my grandmother who lived on a boat in Key Largo, to see if she could come up while Madeleine and I attended the rally against the mud bog races. Grandy called back to say she and Max had several charters on Saturday, so I begrudgingly asked my ex, Jerry, to open the shop. I hated to be in debt to him, but there was no one else to cover for us. I could almost hear Jerry's voice quiver in anticipation. I decided not to consider who would run the shop if Madeleine and I got arrested at the protest.

The week went by without incident, and the carpenters made some progress in the shop. Having either Madeleine or me drop in at odd times might have annoyed them at first, but since whoever showed to check on their work always brought a treat like brownies or sent out for deli sandwiches at noon, the men soon embraced our appearance as a welcome break from fast food. We were celebrated as heroes. Well, at least when we put in an appearance.

THAT WEEK MADELEINE and I talked again and again about the rally. Not only was I concerned about her health, but we knew as business owners we were vulnerable if we took a stand unpopular in the community. I was trying to temper my initial "get 'er done" attitude with one more reasoned.

"I just want to add my voice to those of others in Sabal Bay who are concerned about the impact of the races on our environment," I said. "This is our community now, and I worry about what's being done to the land around here. There are plenty of folks who feel as we do. You saw the letters in the local newspaper."

"I'd feel better if I knew who was writing the letters. I wonder if it's the ranchers and business owners or just us transplants from the North." The worry lines on Madeleine's forehead deepened.

"You think our business may be impacted if we take a stand," I said.

She nodded.

"Can we tiptoe around everything that's a local issue? I don't think so. We'll be respectful at the rally. We'll just yell and wave our signs. We won't throw anything or get too rowdy. That's my perspective, but you have to decide for yourself."

"You're not leaving me out of this, Eve Appel. We'll take our lumps if necessary."

"Okay, but you can change your mind if you want to, especially if you're not feeling better."

THE EMAILS I received from the organizers of the protest rally provided information on where to meet and at what time. Saturday morning around ten, Madeleine and I jumped into my Mustang convertible eager to arrive at Jenny's place early enough to get the lay of the land. Although the event didn't begin until noon, the behemoth mud bog trucks lined up down the sandy road leading to Jenny's land, waiting until the gates opened. The air was thick with exhaust.

"Ugh," I said, sniffing the fumes, "that's enough to chase away all living things even before those giant tires take to the water."

Madeleine nodded. Her face was drained of color.

"Are you sure you're okay to do this?" I asked.

Again she nodded but said nothing and avoided meeting my eyes.

We pulled off the road where it intersected another smaller roadway and soon came upon vehicles parked in a field an environmentally conscious land owner was allowing the protesters to use for parking. We would come out at the entrance and were told not to block the gate, but to line up on either side of the road and call to the trucks and cars entering. The email instructions told us we could shout and wave our signs all we wanted, but we shouldn't prevent anyone from entering or engage in arguments with attendees. This was to be a peaceful, nonviolent demonstration.

"Wow. This is pretty impressive for Sabal Bay. There must be almost fifty demonstrators here already, and it's only eleven." I recognized some of the protesters, but not many. Only a handful of the cowboys or ranchers, bankers, or business folks we saw in our shop were among the crowd. I caught sight of Sammy because he stood taller than anyone else. He saw us and waved. We also bumped into the woman who was my primary care doctor and several of the nurses from the hospital.

Sabal Bay was a pretty conservative community, and this was one of those situations where land-poor folks like Jenny McCleary or workers laid off from local jobs looking for work—the kind they might find at the mud bog event—found themselves on the same side as the land developers looking to make their bucks no matter what the environmental cost. Politics make strange bedfellows, but where minimum-wage jobs met the greed of big business, the sleeping partners were indeed oddly paired.

The workers had opened the gates, and as the crowd increased in size and people began pushing forward, I lost sight of anyone I knew with the exception of Sammy, whose head of long, black hair I could see at the front of the crowd. Grandfather Egret stood next to him holding up a sign, but I couldn't read what it said. I made certain Madeleine and I remained side by side. She was just so tiny I felt I needed to make certain she stayed safe. If anyone threatened to shove her down, they'd have to go through me first, and I was wearing my best four-inch ostrich boots, which made me almost as tall as many of the men.

Trucks revved up their engines and drove through the gate, heading for the area where the competition was to be held. As I understood it, the trucks would enter the bog and attempt to run through the muddy water to the end of the course.

The events would last the whole day and resume the next. Who knew so many folks were obsessed with driving tricked-out, jacked-up trucks through a swamp? The trucks had been customized to do just this. All I could see ahead of me on

Jenny's property were bogs and swamps and … huge trucks. Of course part of the fun was the beer and the scantily clad young women. It was Key West Fantasy Fest with trucks on testosterone.

Chants of "Save the Bog," "Leave our swamps alone," and "There's life in that mud" continued for an hour. The swampers driving the trucks countered with yells of "Back off bitches" and "There's money in that mud." The trucking folks did not have any signs to hold up, but their voices seemed louder and angrier. I waved my sign in the air. It read "Don't harm Mother Earth." One of the truck drivers stuck his head out the window and yelled at me, "Screw Mother Earth."

"That's exactly what you're doing," I screamed. He gave me the finger.

The verbal exchanges continued until the trucks began to line up for their runs. At that point the sound of revving engines drowned out our voices. Mud flew in every direction. Madeleine and I pushed forward toward the fence to get a better view. Several trucks roared into the water, moved aggressively across the bog, and then abruptly stopped, mired in the middle. Neither increasing the RPMs or uttering foul language could coax the trucks from their mucky location. The drivers gave up, their growling trucks finally silenced, machinery defeated by mere water and dirt. A chain was attached to the trucks and a vehicle on land hauled them out. The drivers seemed only momentarily saddened by their failure; then their friends tossed them each a can of beer, and the partying began.

"I think we should step back a bit or we'll be covered in mud," I said to Madeleine. She looked excited to be where she could see what was happening, and her color had improved.

"You feeling better, honey?" I asked just as another truck roared into the water and attempted to cross the bog. As with the other two, it slowed and finally began to spin its wheels midway through the swamp. The driver continued to rev the engine. Muddy water thrown from the wheels catapulted vegetation as well as mud in our direction. The vehicle churned and rocked and continued to throw globs of whatever was buried in the muddy water out of the bog. I dropped my sign and attempted to fend off the gunk by shielding my face with my hands, but to no avail. The mud coated my head, face, and upper torso. I dropped my hands to my sides in disgust and frustration until the truck tried one more time, its spinning wheels sending more mud and a large projectile my way. I had no choice. I caught it like a running back grabbing a football.

What the hell? It was no football, not even a chawed up turtle shell or mangled cattle egret. It was a head, and one I recognized. Two eyes glazed over by slime and death—one brown, one hazel—stared up at me. Madeleine looked over at what was in my hands and threw up all over my ostrich boots.

CHAPTER 3

——

My instinct was to drop the head, but that seemed so insensitive. It had belonged to Jenny McCleary, someone I knew and liked. The horror of the situation almost took my breath away. As bile worked its way up my throat, I swallowed and took air in through my mouth. She wasn't a close friend, but this was shocking. I looked down again at my hands, thinking I had imagined a head there, but no, Jenny's eyes kept looking up at me as if pleading for my help. There was nothing I could do for her—she was beyond my aid—but Madeleine did need me.

Sammy must have noticed something wasn't right because he and Grandfather had changed their positions in the crowd and moved next to us.

"Is that …?" he asked, gesturing to what lay in my hands.

"Yes. Would you take it, please? I need to see to Madeleine. She's sick."

Madeleine was holding herself up by clutching the fence with one hand. "Oh Eve, I need to lie down."

Grandfather Egret and I lowered Madeleine to a sitting position on the ground and let her lean back against the fence.

"Here," I said to a bilious-looking bystander who was staring at the grisly object in Sammy's hands, "Call the police." I held out my cell, but the man refused to touch it.

"I'll do that." Grandfather Egret reached out for the cell. "There's probably an emergency service on site with EMTs. I'll see if I can get anyone at the gate to call them. They could get here quicker."

Sammy stepped forward. "I'm faster. I'll go." He handed the head to his grandfather.

"I don't think medical intervention will do any good. She's dead, Eve. Even I can see that." Madeleine averted her eyes from Grandfather and stared off across the bog.

"The medical help is for you, honey," I said, rubbing her shoulder.

She gave me a shaky smile and turned her head to vomit once more.

WHEN THE POLICE arrived, Frida saw me and immediately came over. When criminal events were afoot and I was in attendance, Frida could expect me to know something useful. She was one of my friends and also the only female detective on the Sabal Bay Police force. She was smart and attractive, with her dark hair and olive complexion. Though not as tall as I was, she exuded authority in her stance and the no-nonsense way she took over a crime scene. She was accompanied by her partner, Linc Tooney.

"So someone told you I caught it, right?" I asked.

She looked confused. "Caught what? The 911 call simply said there had been an accident at the mud bog races. I figured it had to concern you. Trouble seems to seek you out."

Frida knew me too well.

I indicated the head in Grandfather's hands.

Even seasoned detective Frida paled a bit when she saw it. "Uh, could you set it down here?" She pointed to the ground in front of her, then kneeled to get a better look.

"A clean cut, as if someone severed the head from the body using something big—a knife, sword, maybe a machete. Who found it?"

"I caught it." I explained about the truck spitting gunk out of the bog.

"So both of you handled it?" Frida asked Grandfather and me.

"Sammy held it for a while," I said.

Frida looked irritated, an emotion confirmed by her tone of voice. "So how many of you played hot potato with the deceased?"

"I thought it was disrespectful to Jenny to just dump her, uh, here on the ground." I couldn't meet Frida's eyes so I lowered my gaze.

"And where is the rest of the body?" asked Frida.

That was a good question. We all looked around, as if the body might suddenly emerge from behind a palm tree or pop up from the bog of its own volition.

"Never mind," said Frida. "We'll find it." But she sounded less than certain.

"It was murder, wasn't it?" I said. "Heads don't just naturally detach from their bodies, do they now?"

The emergency vehicle carrying the EMTs made its way through the gate. The crowd of protesters parted to allow it through.

"I'll take your statement when you've recovered," said Frida to Madeleine as she was loaded into the vehicle.

"I've seen my share of injuries at these bog events, but never anything like this," one of the EMTs said when they placed Madeleine on a stretcher and loaded her into the ambulance. His attention was directed toward the head, which remained on the ground where Father Egret had placed it on Frida's orders, but Madeleine thought the EMT was referring to her.

"It's not an injury, you jughead," Madeleine said. "I'm pregnant. That's all."

I was shocked, worried, and thrilled all at once, but as usual my feelings spilled out in the form of anger first. "Madeleine Boudreau Wilson, you told me you were fine … that you weren't sick."

"Well, I wasn't sick. Not really. Don't be mad, Eve."

"I'm not mad. I'm furious. Do you know what could have happened to you?"

"That I'd throw up on your precious boots?" she said.

"I'm sorry for yelling at you, sweetie, but I've been so worried you were sick with the flu or something even more serious. I told you you didn't have to come."

"I wanted to, and I felt better for a while this morning. You get to do all the fun stuff, Eve."

I planted a loud kiss on her sweaty face, grabbed her shoulders and squeezed. "Now you get to have some fun. A baby. Oh, honey, you should have told me. Does David know?"

She shook her red curls, now damp with sweat, and sat up on the stretcher to look at me.

"Don't you dare tell him before I do," she said, then lay back again.

As the ambulance door began to close, I heard her say, "I've got to puke again, so move your shoes out of the way."

Frida's officers herded all the protesters and the people attending the event toward the large tent on Jenny's property. It had been set up for event registration and to house several booths offering food and race items for sale. She ordered her partner Linc and the two other officers who had arrived at the scene to move everything out and set up tables and chairs. They then began taking names and contact numbers.

"We don't have the personnel to interview everyone today. There are several hundred people here between the protesters, the participants, and the officials. This is going to take weeks. We'll have to call in people from the county sheriff's department for help. And it's messy. We don't really know what's part of the crime scene and what isn't." Frida shook her head in despair.

Yellow crime tape had already been strung around the bog. The truck that spewed the head out of the mud was encircled by tape and the driver was being questioned by Linc.

"That driver isn't happy, is he?" I asked Frida.

"He's got over fifty thousand dollars of special equipment on that truck, and I won't be releasing it to him until we go over it inch by inch. So nope. No more mudding for days. He is one miserable dude."

The police shut down the mud bog races. According to Frida, they might not continue for several days, perhaps not at all. The authorities had to determine where Jenny was killed, so the entire area was a crime scene. And with Jenny dead, there was some question about whether the races could resume without the land owner's permission. It was likely Shelley would inherit, but first they had to find a will. All that legal stuff took time. So no more races here for the near future. That was fine with the protesters, except that we were the most likely suspects in Jenny's murder. Their motives were obvious, whereas the motives of the others would be less clear. As Frida had indicated, the authorities' work would be long and arduous, and it would be more efficient to focus on the protesters first.

Because we came in contact with Jenny's body, Sammy, Grandfather Egret and I were accorded special attention. Frida wanted to see us in her office. As I walked toward my car, past the protesters waiting to talk with police, I saw a familiar face. I couldn't place the man, but when I turned around to take another look, he'd turned away as if he didn't want me to see him. Who was that? Someone I'd met in the Burnt Biscuit Bar and Grill, my favorite place to eat ribs and do a little country two-step? A cowboy I'd danced with there who didn't want me to know he'd been one of the protesters? No name came to mind, and it didn't seem as if he belonged in the Biscuit. He looked more like a winter visitor—no cowboy hat, and he was wearing sneakers. No self-respecting cowboy ever wore sneakers. I thought it likely they were born with boots on. I shook my head. I never forgot a face, although it might take me some time to remember. Eventually I did.

At police headquarters, Frida took me into her office just as her partner Linc Tooney came back from the event.

"The sheriff sent in some help, so I'm free now," said Linc.

"You take these two," she gestured to Sammy and Grandfather, "and I'll question Eve."

"Hey. What's this 'question' stuff? I thought you were going to take our statements. Why would I kill someone then cradle her detached head in my arms while my friend upchucked all over my best boots?"

"I've stopped trying to figure you out, Eve." She turned to Linc. "Take their statements while I question Eve." I caught her wink at Linc.

"I thought you and Jenny were friends. Why were you protesting the mud bog races?" Frida indicated a chair across from her desk, and I sat.

"I didn't know Jenny well enough for us to be considered close friends. She was a customer, and I found her a wedding dress just this past week. Madeleine and I have strong feelings about what mud bog races do to the environment. We told Jenny that and informed her we would be at the protest."

"Yeah, all you winter visitors have different opinions from those of the locals about how the land around here should be used."

"Don't you? And I'm not a winter visitor. I'm a resident."

Frida sat back in her desk chair. "Okay then, a transplant. Maybe I do have my own opinion, but that's not the issue here. Murder is."

Linc appeared at the door to her office. "Got a call from the guys dragging the bog out there. No sign of other body …." He looked at me. "Uh, no signs of Jenny's … uh … we didn't find any …." Finally he gave up.

"Just say it. I'm over the shock now." Was I? I looked down

at my hands clasped tightly in my lap. If I hadn't entwined my fingers, they'd be shaking.

"Nothing else in there," Linc finally said. "We're searching the edges of the bog to see if she was killed nearby. And oh, I nearly forgot, her daughter is here wanting to talk with you."

"I'll be out in a minute. Get her a cup of coffee and settle her into one of the benches out front."

"Don't I get a coffee?" I asked.

"You want one?" Surprise registered on Frida's face. It was police station coffee, something no one wanted, and the brew here was no better than the typical fare described in cop shows.

"I'd prefer a Scotch, but I'll bet that's not available. I need something to do with my hands or I'll start chewing on my nails and ruin my new manicure."

"I thought you said you were over the shock of catching that head."

"I was lying. No one can ever be over that." I'd never forget those eyes. I knew they couldn't have been pleading with me for help, but that was how it appeared—as if Jenny wanted me to do something. The eyes said so.

Frida reached into one of her desk drawers. "Here." She placed a paper cup and a bottle of golden-colored liquid on the desk.

"Wow. Just like the boys."

"It's bourbon, not Scotch."

I reached for the lifeline but my shaking hands gave away my nerves. Frida poured me a few fingers, and I downed it in one gulp, letting the liquid fire slide down my throat and hit with a satisfying warmth in my stomach.

"So Jenny was engaged?" Frida said. She put the bottle back in the drawer and took a quick look out her office door to make certain no one in the station had observed us. "Do you know to whom?"

"Some Yankee. Ask her daughter. Whoever it is, I didn't see

anyone at the event fitting that description, although word of her death has to have gotten around the county by now. Shouldn't the guy at least be demanding answers from you or the officers at the scene as to who killed her?" Another idea came to mind, so I shared it with Frida. "Or maybe he's the one who did her in."

Frida tapped her pencil on the desktop. "Looking around for other suspects already, Eve? Must I remind you that this is a case for the police, not a consignment shop owner?"

"Please do remind her. She needs to be reminded not to butt into police business every chance she gets." Alex stood in the door of Frida's office. "Do I smell booze?"

Frida's dark face reddened. "Keep it to yourself."

"Only if you don't keep it to yourself," Alex said.

Frida once more took the bottle out and poured Alex a shot, which he put away as quickly as I had. Frida understood how badly a man might need a shot of courage being the boyfriend of a gal like me.

"What are you doing here?" I asked.

"Looking for you. I tried your cell and got no answer, so I called Jerry. He said you were at the protest, but when I went there and saw all the police, I knew where to find you. You're always in the middle of everything criminal around here."

Yes, I am, and so what?

Alex ignored the mulish look I gave him and put his hand on my shoulder, rubbing it gently. "You okay, Eve?"

"Yeah," I said. "I guess. I'm more worried about Madeleine. She's …." I was about to tell him she got sick at the protest and why, but I shut up just in time.

Frida's cell rang. She talked for only a moment, then held it out to me. "It's Madeleine."

"I figured you'd be in Frida's office being questioned. I'm fine and everything's going to be okay."

"Oh, Madeleine, if I'd known, I would never have let you …." I stopped and looked at the two pairs of curious eyes in the room observing me. "I'll pick you up as soon as Frida is finished grilling."

"No, no. I called David. He's on his way. I think he and I need to talk."

I said goodbye and handed the phone back to Frida. "Madeleine is having David pick her up at the hospital. She's fine."

"Madeleine's in the hospital? What's going on?" asked Alex.

I explained to Alex my unlucky catch and Madeleine's reaction to it.

He and Frida exchanged looks.

"I can't help it if these things happen to me. I don't like being at murder scenes. I think it must be bad karma." I glared at them both, then said. "Can I go now? I think I need comfort food and some more booze."

"I'll drive you home then," said Alex.

"My car is in the lot."

"I'll drive you in your car, and we can get mine later," Alex insisted. I gave in.

Outside Frida's office, I encountered Shelley sitting alone on a bench.

"Oh, sweetie, I'm so sorry to hear about your mother. Isn't there anyone you can call to be with you?"

She shook her head and looked up at me with tearful eyes. "No. I have an aunt in Ohio, my dad's sister, but she's really old and can't travel. I can take care of myself, I guess." She swiped at her red nose with a soggy tissue.

"This isn't the time to be alone." I reached out and pulled her off the bench. "You're coming home with me."

Frida stood behind us. "I'm sorry, Shelley, but I need to talk with you first. I know this is hard for you, but there are questions you have to answer."

"Fine. I'll stay here with her until you're through." I steered Shelley toward Frida's office.

"Eve, come back here!" Alex said. "You need to take care of

yourself, not play nursemaid to some young woman you barely know."

"She lost her mother in a horrible way—that's all I need to know. I'll see you later." I led Shelley into Frida's office and pushed her down into the chair I'd just vacated. There were no extra seats. "I'll stand until you're finished." I leaned against the back wall.

"No you don't," Frida said. "You'll wait outside." Frida pointed toward the door.

"But—"

"Now," she said, still pointing.

An hour later, after I had gone to the bathroom and tried none too successfully to remove what Madeleine had deposited on my boots—dried puke was worse than dried-on egg yolk—Shelley emerged, looking much worse than when she entered.

I put my arm around her and said, "What did you do to her, Frida?"

Frida shook her head, looking unhappy and uncomfortable. "I did my job, that's all."

"It's fine, Miss Eve," said Shelley. "She was as kind as she could be, but it's all so awful that I can hardly believe it. How can I live without Mama?"

"You'll live because she would want you to. You'll find the strength, and there are people who will help you," I said.

As tears spilled from her eyes, Shelley asked, "Who?"

"Well, there are plenty of people. Your mother's friends, and ...." And then I had nothing. The poor young woman had no relatives, and her mother had few friends I knew of. I didn't know any of Shelley's friends either. Did she have a best girlfriend? Jenny had mentioned a boyfriend she found unpleasant. I'd forgotten his name, but he didn't sound like the kind of support Shelley needed right now.

"Do you have a best friend you'd like me to call?"

She shook her head. "You could call Darrel Hogan. He's my boyfriend."

Right. That was the guy's name. "We'll do that later. For now let's go to my place and you can rest there."

"Could I just go by the house and get a few things?" Shelley asked.

"I can loan you whatever you need—toothbrush, pajamas, anything."

Shelley looked embarrassed and leaned close to my ear. "I know this makes me sound like a baby, but I have a teddy bear I sleep with."

I gave her a hug. "Sure. No problem. I understand."

"If that's no problem for you, Eve, I think it's a good idea," Frida said. "Shelley gave me permission to search the ranch house, and I think it'll be easier if she's not in it at the time. I'll follow you out to the ranch and accompany Shelley while she gets … whatever." Frida grabbed her jacket off the back of her office chair and joined us on our way out.

I wrapped my arm around Shelley's shoulders, and we walked out the door to my car. Alex was leaning against my convertible. The scowl on his face told me he wasn't happy I'd remained waiting for Shelley and was now escorting her to my car.

"You just can't keep your nose out of police matters, can you?"

I ignored his comment. This was not about "police matters." It was about a young woman having lost her mother. I knew what it was like losing parents. I opened the passenger door for Shelley and then walked to the other side of the car to confront Alex.

"I appreciate your concern for my welfare, but right now it's Shelley we should be concerned for. You need to step back and—"

"And then do what? Step out of your life?" He waited for me to reply, his arms crossed over his chest.

"I need your support, not your interference or your permission to do what I need to do. If you can't let me be my own person, then perhaps it would be better for you to find someone who defines herself in terms of you, because I don't." I got into my car, started the engine, and drove off.

"Did you just break up with your boyfriend?" asked Shelley.

Did I? Maybe so.

CHAPTER 4

―

THERE WAS A black, four-door pickup truck in the driveway of Shelley's house when I pulled in.

"Is that Darrel's truck?"

"No. It looks like my next-door neighbor's." Shelley's shoulders drooped. "He used to drop by a lot to see Mom until …."

"Until what?" I asked.

"Until she got engaged and stuff."

" 'Stuff'? What 'stuff'?" I asked.

"You know, like when grownups disagree about things." She sighed. "I think he said I was too young to date Darrel. Mom told him to mind his own business."

As we got out of the car, Frida's cruiser pulled in behind us. The door of the truck opened and a tall, lean man stepped out.

"The police told me I wasn't to go into the house, but that I could wait out here. I was hoping you'd be home soon, Miss Shelley." The man wore a pair of tight jeans, Western shirt, and a Stetson. He was clean-shaven with the exception of a mustache above his broad lips. "I just wanted to come by and tell you how sorry I am about your mama."

Frida stepped forward. "I can't let you in the house, Mr. Archer. I'm kind of surprised the officers at the drive entrance let you get this far."

"Sorry about that, but I promised them I wouldn't get out of the car." He smiled to reveal his white, even teeth. The smile was dazzling—sexy and friendly.

Frida smiled back. "I don't suppose you know each other. Clay Archer, this is Eve Appel."

He stuck out his huge hand and shook mine. I could feel the calluses on his palm and fingers.

"Mr. Archer owns the next ranch," Shelley said and turned toward the house. "Can I go in now?"

Archer's eyes traveled from my face to my toes with a look that said he appreciated a tall gal. "I heard tell of you in town."

"All good, I hope." I grinned. I found myself attracted to this man. I tried to rein in my flirting. He wasn't here to dally with some gal he just met but to pay his respects to Shelley.

"Depends," he said.

"I'm sorry, but I have to ask you to leave. Shelley needs to get a few things out of the house; then we'll be searching it." Frida opened the driver's side door on the truck and gestured Mr. Archer toward it.

He tipped his hat to Shelley, gave me a look I couldn't decode, and left.

"Okay, Eve, you wait here. Shelley, it's in and out, grab your stuff, then you go home with Eve."

I MADE SHELLEY comfortable in my guest bedroom and brought her a cup of tea. She was too young to drink yet; otherwise I would have offered her some of the Scotch I poured for myself. She held her stuffed bear tightly to her chest.

When I came into the bedroom with her tea, she was talking on her cell with someone. I assumed it was her boyfriend, the guy her mother mentioned in the shop. She ended the conversation and smiled up at me.

"Your fella?" I asked.

"Darrell. He wants to come over. Would that be okay with you?"

I wanted her to feel better, but I wasn't certain I was comfortable with someone Jenny had told me liked to lift items from stores without paying. Still, it wasn't as if Shelley would be here long. What harm could it do if Darrell's presence helped her deal with her mother's death? I gave my consent. She called him back.

"He'll be here in about a half hour. He won't stay long."

"If it makes you feel better, then great." I hesitated. It seemed Shelley had experienced enough difficulty for one day, but I thought I should at least prepare her for what would happen in the days to come. "Do you know where your mother keeps her legal papers? At home or perhaps in a bank box?"

Shelley looked perplexed. "Why is that important?"

"There's the issue of her will and also any contracts she might have signed—especially the contract with the company running the mud bog race."

Shelley's face crumpled with distress and she put her head in her hands. "Oh God! I don't know anything about legal stuff. I don't think I can handle it. Maybe my boyfriend can help. I'll ask him when he gets here."

Well, I'd put my foot in it now. If Jenny was right about the boy, he was the last person who should be looking through Jenny's legal papers.

"Better yet, if you don't know the name of your family's lawyer," I said, and she shook her head, "I'll call mine and she can work with you on this."

I'd covered this problem just in time because the doorbell rang. I expected Darrell was here already, more than eager to help his girlfriend with what might or might not be a considerable estate.

I ran to open it, my best Eve-surrogate-mother-in-residence-look on my face.

Instead of Shelley's young man, it was David, Madeleine's husband, scowling darkly.

"Madeleine just told me about the baby. What were you thinking to drag her off to the rally, Eve?"

"Wait just a minute, buddy. I knew nothing about the baby."

I was dealing with too many men overprotective of their women, men who assumed women weren't capable of running their own lives. First Alex and now David. And it was apparently only the beginning.

I heard a car screech around the corner, then pull up in front of my house. A skinny, stringy-haired guy got out of an old Camaro with battered, black front fenders, the rest of the body a mottled orange. He strode toward the front door where David and I were still conversing.

"Where are you keeping Shelley?" he asked. A cigarette hung out the side of his mouth, and he reeked of something sweet, something I hadn't smelled for a while. Marijuana. He tried to push past me and David, but David—taller and heavier—blocked his path.

"Shelley needs a little rest. She's doing that here," I said.

"She needs me," he said. "Let me in."

Instead of confronting all that youthful testosterone head on, I decided it was best I ignore his surly tone … for now. I gestured him through the door and pointed toward the guest room. "I'm sure she'll be happy to see you."

As he passed by, I reached out, plucked the cigarette from his mouth, and tossed it into the yard. "Didn't you see the 'no smoking' sign?"

He looked confused for a moment, then muttered something that sounded more like a growl than human speech and hurried down the hallway toward the guest room.

Now I needed to calm David somehow.

"I know you're worried, but Madeleine's going to be fine, David. I suspect some morning sickness, common in many pregnancies. That's what they said at the hospital, right?"

David settled back on his heels. His body seemed to relax and he nodded.

"She just overdid it this morning and she knows it, right?"

He nodded again.

"I was so surprised at the news," I said, dropping my defensiveness, and added, "I'm so happy for both of you."

He smiled for a second, then the smile faded.

"I hope you continue to feel that way, because I'm here to tell you that I don't want Madeleine to work at the store any longer. It's just too much for her."

That declaration made me prickly. "She's pregnant, David, not ill. Pregnant women work all the time."

"Maybe so, but not my wife."

Yet another man deciding what a woman could or couldn't do. I stared beyond him toward the street. *God, give me a break and please save me from these guys. At least for today.*

A black SUV pulled up behind the two cars already there. I smiled. Now here was a true macho man, but one who knew what sassy women like me were all about. My kind of guy. Nappi Napolitani, my mob boss friend, must have heard about the murder. Of all of the men in my life, he was the only one I could think of that I did want to see and the only one whose advice about this murder I wanted to hear. My prayers had been answered. Someone up there did like me. Maybe God was a woman after all.

David watched Nappi get out of the car. "Here's someone who knows what's best. He'll tell you Madeleine should be at home and not on her feet all day at the store."

Ever the gentleman, Nappi took my hand, kissed my fingers, and gave me his broadest smile. He always made me feel like I was the most special person in the world. Looking from my face to David's, he asked, "Is this a bad time? I can come back later."

"Nope. I just learned Madeleine's pregnant," David said.

Nappi grabbed David's hand and shook it heartily.

"Congratulations. I am so happy for you both."

"Eve and I would like your input on something. Don't you think Madeleine should stop working during her pregnancy?"

"Oh, is she having a difficult pregnancy?" said Nappi.

"Well, no, but—"

"What does Madeleine say about working? Has she checked with her doctor?"

"She was checked over today at the hospital," I said and filled Nappi in about what had landed in my hands at the rally and Madeleine's reaction to it.

"It wouldn't take morning sickness for me to throw up at that sight," said Nappi.

My mouth dropped open in amazement. He was a "Family" man with a delicate stomach? I found that hard to believe.

"My wife had morning sickness with all our little ones."

"But she stayed at home, right?" David insisted.

"Sure. We had our babies close together. She stayed home to take care of them. She had her hands full. There always seemed to be one in diapers, one a terrible two—running around the house destroying everything he could reach—and one on the way. She had help, however."

David smiled. "Of course. You would have hired a nanny."

"No, when I said she had help, the help was me. At first I was useless, but I soon became quite skilled at the diaper thing. You will be too."

David looked flustered for a moment, then seemed to recover himself. "I've got to get home to Madeleine."

"Tell her I'll call her later tonight to talk." I waved goodbye to David's back. I guess he felt frustrated that his attempt to solicit Nappi's support for Madeleine staying home hadn't quite worked.

"I'm sorry you got in the middle of that, Nappi."

"I told him what he needed to hear, and it's the truth."

I envisioned Nappi wearing an apron over his starched and ironed white shirt with gold cufflinks. The gold twinkled amidst the baby powder he applied to his baby's tender behind. The image made me laugh. "Let's go in, and I'll fix you a drink."

Nappi took a final look at the Camaro and stepped into the house. "You have other company, it seems. Are you certain I'm not intruding?"

I shook my head, explaining how Shelley came to be in the house with her boyfriend. "Darrell is trouble, I'd guess.

"Is it wise to have him here then?"

"Shelley needs someone, and there's no family, no friends. Just Darrell."

"And you, of course," Nappi said.

I handed him a Scotch on the rocks.

"I'll go in and introduce myself, if that's all right with you," he said.

It couldn't hurt for Darrell to understand my house was visited by someone like Nappi, a man whose appearance suggested he was connected and not with the cowboys and guys who fished or owned ranches around here—I mean, in case Darrell's fingers got caught on some of the possessions in my house.

"Go ahead. They're in the guest bedroom." I leaned back into the couch and took a sip of my drink.

Several minutes later Nappi returned to the living room and settled into the chair across from the sofa.

"So you've got yourself into another murder?" His dark eyes sparkled with interest and intelligence.

"I'm just helping out a young woman who has no one else. Well, except for Darrell."

Nappi nodded. "She has only you then. That young man is nothing but trouble. I know." He jiggled the ice cubes in his glass. "How involved are you going to get, trying to find her mother's killer? And what does Alex think of all this?"

"I don't believe Alex will be around here as often as he used to be."

"Does Grandy know what you're doing?"

His inquisition into what my friends and family thought about my helping Shelley was beginning to annoy me.

"I really don't need permission from relatives and past boyfriends to help out this girl."

"Of course not," said Nappi.

I hadn't heard a car drive up, but there was a knock on the door. I hoped it wasn't Alex or Frida or anyone who might want to lecture me about staying out of the murder investigation. So I was relieved to see Grandfather Egret and Sammy. I tried to guess how they might receive the news that Shelley was a guest in my house and concluded they wouldn't like it.

"Okay, you can come in, but not a word from either of you about Shelley being here or my getting involved in finding Jenny's murderer."

Nappi and the Egrets exchanged greetings, and I offered them a seat and a cup of tea.

Neither Sammy nor his grandfather drank much, although Sammy sometimes enjoyed a beer.

"We're just here to find out how Madeleine is doing. Who's Shelley?" asked Sammy. Grandfather Egret sunk into the couch. Sammy remained standing.

When I explained that Jenny was Shelley's mother and that the poor girl had no one else to turn to, Grandfather Egret gave a derisive snort.

"I recognized that car. It belongs to Darrell Hogan. If he's in this house, it's because of Shelley, not you, Eve. He doesn't seem your type. We've had trouble with him and his friends driving through the tribal land of my Seminole relatives, firing weapons from his car at the feral pigs that roam the roads. If that's the gal's taste in men, then she's in for trouble and so are you, Eve."

Guns? That was a whole lot more serious than shoplifting an item of clothing from a store in town.

"He'll be leaving in a few minutes. Don't worry."

"And Madeleine's pregnancy? No problems there?" Grandfather Egret said.

I was about to ask him how he knew about the pregnancy but stopped myself. The man seemed to know things most people did not. At times I thought he learned things from sitting outside on his front porch and talking to the swamp creatures. Her pregnancy? I had no idea. We have wood storks here, but I didn't think they were the kind who either delivered babies or carried news of their arrival.

"Madeleine's fine as nearly as I know, but David's not doing well," I said. I didn't elaborate, and no one pressed me.

"We came to talk to you about a problem to see what you want to do about it, Eve," said Sammy.

"What problem?" What had I overlooked?

"It's clear from the police's interest in the protest that they think one of the protesters is responsible for Jenny's murder."

"That seems likely," I said. I'd already considered that. It meant the three of us and Madeleine were likely suspects in the eyes of the law.

"So the police are looking closely at us," Sammy continued.

"I know that, Sammy. So is there another problem I don't know about?" I stopped talking for a minute. "Unless … we don't have alibis? When was she killed? Do they know? And where?"

"We don't know," said Sammy. "I don't think the police know yet."

"I'd ask Frida, but she probably wouldn't tell me. And she'd say I was interfering with her case." I was stumped. If we had no information other than what we had this morning, what did Sammy think he knew?

"We should line up a lawyer for the next time your friend Detective Frida questions us," said Sammy.

"Don't be silly. She knows none of us would kill anyone," I insisted.

"We're Miccosukee," said Grandfather Egret.

"And you, dear Eve, are their friend—you and Madeleine," said Nappi.

Uh-oh. Now I got it. We were about to run into the racism of some of the folks around here.

Nappi slapped his hand on his knee. "I think I have what you need."

We all looked at him expectantly.

"A lawyer who is familiar with these parts, who knows the system and won't be run off by it. And who is respected by the authorities and the judicial system in the county." Nappi took his cell out of his pocket and held up his finger for quiet.

I, of course, ignored him. "A Yankee?" I asked. "That's worse than being Native American around there."

"Just so," said Nappi. He turned his back to us and spoke for only a few minutes on his cell. When he turned back, there was a smile of deep satisfaction on his face. "He'll be right here. You folks can be the judge of whether he fits your needs or not."

I made a pot of tea for the Egrets, and we all settled in with our beverages. We didn't have long to wait.

I heard a car pull up in front of the house; then someone rang my bell. I opened the door to a short, dark-skinned individual dressed in an expensive cowboy-cut gray suit and black alligator boots.

"Ms. Appel?" he said.

I nodded. Nappi got up from the couch and walked over to us.

"This is Jacob Lightwind, attorney-at-law. He's done some work for me, and he knows more about the rural Florida system of law than any other attorney in this county or the next." Nappi smiled, and this time the smile deepened and spread, revealing his brilliant white teeth. It was Nappi to the rescue. I knew Madeleine wouldn't like using a lawyer Nappi recommended, and David would probably agree with her. They remained skeptical of Nappi's character and morals, but I'd never seen him behave other than in a most upstanding way. That he might have done things in other settings—things I might have found reprehensible—I shoved to the far recesses of my mind.

"Mr. Lightwind," I held out my hand, "I'd like you to meet two friends of mine, Sammy and Grandfather Egret."

"I've never seen you around here, but I know you by reputation," said Grandfather. "I believe you are—"

"I'm half Cherokee, half African-American. I was raised in West Palm and have practiced law here for over thirty years. I'd be pleased to represent you and your friends, should the need arise."

I heard another car pull up. By now the street in front of my house looked like a used car lot.

I opened the door to trouble.

CHAPTER 5

—

Frida stood on my porch, and I could tell from the cop-like look on her face that hers was not a social visit.

"Finished with the house search?" I asked. "And now you're here to tell us what you found."

She ignored me. "This is nice. You've gathered most of the people I need to question again. And a few others." She looked around the room, then her gaze came to rest on Mr. Lightwind. "And you've brought in the big guns to make my job all the more difficult. Why do you hate me, Eve?"

Frida knew I didn't hate her. She knew I liked her. A lot. But she always assumed the worst of me. I wanted to correct her about the lawyer, but Nappi beat me to it.

"Mr. Lightwind came at my suggestion."

"I'll just bet he did." Frida sounded even more annoyed by the news that Nappi had called Mr. Lightwind, not me.

"I have a little announcement to make, then I'd like Mr. Egret and his grandson to follow me down to the station again. No doubt you'd like to bring your legal representative." She directed her comments to the Egrets.

"Not me? Not Madeleine?" I asked.

"Oh, I'm not through with the two of you, but for now, I'd just like to talk with the Egrets."

I waited for Frida's "little announcement," knowing that it could not be good if it meant she'd tracked the Egrets here.

"We found the rest, well, most of the rest of Jenny's body. It was out near your airboat business, Mr. Egret." She looked straight at Grandfather.

"That doesn't mean you found where she was killed," Attorney Lightwind said. "It could have been at the mud bog racing site. Can I correctly assume the ground was so churned up around there that you can't be sure she wasn't killed in the same place Eve found her head? That's not evidence of who did it."

"We'll talk about that at the station. Now, if the Misters Egret would like to come along in their truck …." Frida directed her next suggestion to the Egrets. "Or you could ride with me. My partner is waiting in the car."

"We can drive ourselves," Sammy said and started guiding his grandfather to the door. At that moment Darrell and Shelley emerged from the guest room.

"Lotta people," observed Darrel, then gave a nervous laugh when he saw Frida. "Cops too. Is this some kind of a party I don't know about?"

Frida fastened her gaze on Shelley, then Darrell, and finally on me. "You had to offer her a place to stay, didn't you? You just couldn't stay out of this."

"She don't need no place to stay. She's coming with me." Darrel draped his arm over Shelley's shoulders in what might have been seen as a protective gesture. To me it looked more possessive than caring.

"Is that what you want, Shelley?" I asked.

She hesitated a minute then nodded.

Damn. With all the people visiting and Darrell taking up her time in the guest room, I hadn't had the chance to ask her questions I needed answers to, such as when had she last seen her mother. I knew Frida had asked, but Frida wasn't about to share the answers with me.

"Well, okay, honey. Maybe we can have lunch tomorrow."

"She'll be busy," Darrell said.

Shelley gave me a sideways glance as Darrel shoved the Egrets to one side and hustled her out the door. I signaled her to call me. She nodded understanding and smiled.

Frida, the Egrets, and Attorney Lightwind left also.

Nappi and I stared at each other.

"I should call Madeleine and fill her in," I said.

"You do that, and I'll make us another drink." Nappi got off the couch and came over to me. "It's going to be fine, Eve. You know how the cops are, even your friend Frida. They have to look at the most likely suspects first, those with obvious motives. They'll probably be doing background checks on the protesters. I know most of them are good people, but some probably have a long history of participating in these kinds of rallies, and I'll bet there's been violence associated with some."

I nodded. "I know."

I did know. I'd seen violence erupt before. Madeleine had too. Frida would soon find out how familiar we were with protesting against environmental destruction and how that knowledge was obtained. Until then, I'd try to prepare Madeleine for the possibility that the past wouldn't stay hidden. I wondered what Madeleine had told David about her "green" side.

"Hi, David," I said when I connected. "I know I'm the last person you want to hear from, but I am Madeleine's best friend and partner. I think you know I'd never put her in harm's way."

There was silence for a minute on the other end; then I heard Madeleine's voice.

"Eve, did you hear the good news? The doctor at the hospital confirmed it: I'm pregnant."

"I heard. That's wonderful. The two of you must be thrilled, but I wish you had told me before."

"Are you still mad at me?"

I sighed. "I'm not mad at you, but like David, I'm worried about you. And the baby."

"I didn't know he stopped by your place to blame you for my participation in the protest. I just chewed him out good for that. He wants me to quit working. I told him we can't do that. We have possibly two shops to run."

"Don't worry about that. We can work it out." I assured her everything would be fine, then told her about Shelley, Darrell, and our legal representative, Mr. Lightwind.

There was a long silence.

"I know you don't like Nappi to get involved in our affairs, but we might just need this lawyer, if you get my drift," I said.

"I do."

"I'll bet David doesn't know anything about what happened, uh, before, does he?"

"It's history, Eve. Long ago. Of course I didn't tell him."

"I think you should. Frida will find out, and then we're in trouble. Besides, I saw someone at the rally I recognized, and I think he recognized me too."

"Who?'

"I can't remember his name, but I'm sure he's from up North."

We talked for a few minutes longer, then agreed we'd meet tomorrow at our RV shop.

I ended the call. This hadn't been a good day, not for anyone. I felt defeated and more than a little guilty that I hadn't been able to figure out why Madeleine had been so sick the week before the protest. *Dumb me.* I thought it was the flu. She knew and didn't share. It still rankled some.

Nappi walked over and put his hand on my shoulder. "I'm assuming you'll tell me about whatever 'trouble' you and Madeleine are hiding if necessary. And you'll certainly be honest with your attorney." He handed me my drink. "It's a short one. We need to get some food in our stomachs. How about the Burnt Biscuit for ribs? Unless you already have a date …."

Nope. No date. I hadn't heard from Alex since we'd argued at the police station earlier today.

Things in my life certainly had gotten jumbled—good with bad with who knows what the future might bring. A rack of ribs might make it better. I slugged down my drink and pasted an uncertain smile on my face. The smile didn't remain there long. My cell rang and I heard Shelley on the other end of the call.

"Eve? I wanted to talk to you, but Darrell, well, he's just so concerned about me, you know?"

No, I did not know that. What I saw in my house was not concern—more like possession and control.

"He was certainly clear that you were leaving with him."

"See, that's Darrell. Always so protective."

"How long have you known Darrell?'

She ignored my question. "I need to talk with you."

"Darrell seemed against that idea."

"I know. He thinks no one else can take care of me like he can."

I wasn't certain how much longer I could listen to her delusional view of the guy before I said something negative about him. I held my tongue because, for now, Darrel appeared to be her lifeline.

"I'd like to come to the store tomorrow. In the morning."

"Are you bringing Darrell?"

She giggled. "Don't be silly. I told him I needed to go shopping for something appropriate to wear to the," she stopped talking and the giggles turned into sobs, *"funeral."*

"We open at ten. I'll see you then."

"The young woman you took under your wing?" asked Nappi after I put down the phone.

I remembered what Jenny had said about Darrel. Then there was Grandfather Egret's story about the guy coupled with what I had observed here tonight.

"She needs someone's wing to shelter her, and I think Darrell Hogan is poor mother-hen material."

"What does she think?"

"I don't get the feeling she's doing much thinking when it comes to Darrell. Her grief over her mother's murder and a big dose of adolescent hormones are getting in the way of intelligent reasoning."

TONIGHT WAS ONE of the karaoke nights at the Biscuit. The music coming from the bar area was sometimes pleasant, but most of the singers sounded like me in my shower. I ignored the music when it was bad and tried to forget about the day's events by tapping my foot to the tunes I recognized and liked.

Nappi ordered the whole rack of ribs.

"Ribs sound good," I said.

"I'd recommend the smaller portion for the lady," said the waitress.

I looked up and realized I hadn't seen her at the Biscuit before.

"You're new here?" I asked.

She nodded, her smile firmly in place.

"I thought so. I never order anything but the whole rack of ribs. I may be skinny, but I've got quite an appetite, wouldn't you say, Nappi?"

"I would," he agreed. "So I think we should go with double orders of coleslaw."

The waitress hurried away with a strange look on her face.

"Southern ladies try never to look as if they eat much, so I guess that makes me other than a lady."

"Never, my dear," Nappi said. "You are the ultimate in lady-ness."

We both broke into laughter, knowing that was not true. I might have been the ultimate in mouthiness or impulsivity, but no one would ever call me ladylike.

"I think they eat in secret so as not to ruin their ladylike images," I said.

I spied a rancher I knew coming out of the bar area. "Jay, Jay

Cassidy!" I called to him. He was accompanied by several men, one whom I'd met earlier at the McCleary ranch. I couldn't remember his name, but I remembered his face. Where earlier there had been a flirtatious smile on it, now there was none. I assumed the others in the group were ranch owners like Jay. Jay hesitated and looked uncomfortable, as if he didn't want to acknowledge my greeting. Funny that, for a guy who had helped me out in a number of tight spots. I considered him a friend, and if Alex hadn't been in the picture, he might have considered me more than a friend. What was going on with him tonight?

He walked over to our table with a grim look on his face.

"I guess you heard about Jenny McCleary," I said, thinking her death might be on his mind and responsible for his demeanor.

He nodded.

"Can you sit for a bit?" I gestured at the empty chair across from me.

He shuffled his feet around and his look of discomfort deepened.

"What's up?" I asked.

"I really like you, Eve—you know that—and I don't even care that you're a Yankee, but when y'all begin to interfere with what we folks down here do with our land, well …. Those mud bog races would have brought a lot of money into this town, but then one of you protesters decided to stop it by killing Jenny. Well, you've stopped the races for now. I know you weren't responsible for her death, but I hope to God you don't know the person who was."

He tipped his hat to me, spun on his boot heels, and left.

The rancher I'd met at McCleary's stepped up to the table, and I remembered his name.

"Mr. Archer, I assume you feel the same as Jay."

"I told you earlier I'd heard about you around town, and

when you asked me whether it was good, I said it depends." He paused.

"And the protest is what it depends on, right?"

"Right. It would be smart if you didn't stick your nose into what's not your business." He nodded and followed Jay out the door. He didn't seem quite as attractive as he had earlier. The other men didn't bother to acknowledge our presence as they left.

Nappi said nothing, but put down the rib he was eating and took a sip of beer.

"Not everyone can feel this way," I said, "but I'm shocked that Jay does. I thought he was my friend."

"I suspect some people here will find it difficult being your friend now."

It was what Madeleine and I had talked about before taking part in the protest. Our stance on mud bog racing *would* matter, and it might impact our business. I hoped Jay and his friends didn't hold the majority opinion around here. After all, Jenny had known I was against her using the land for the races, and she hadn't held it against me.

"Can't friends have different views on religion or politics or land use?" I asked Nappi.

"Some friends can. Like you and me. But this is about money, Eve. And money is a strong persuader that can lead people to take steps you might not understand or like." Nappi patted his lips with his napkin. How could the guy be so neat eating ribs? I looked at my wrists, covered in sauce.

"But we—" I started to say.

"You and I are unusual. And we never talk about how I make my living."

I nodded.

"You and Madeleine are about to find out how much your protesting will cost you in this community. In dollars, Eve."

I nodded. He was right. "In that case, you may have to wait on our repaying you for the motor home."

"I know that." He reached out and patted my hand.

I picked up my last rib and looked at it, then tossed it back onto my plate. Somehow I'd lost my appetite. "By the way," I said, "what do you think of our joining the protesters this morning?"

Before Nappi could answer, a shadow crossed my plate. I looked up and into the eyes of Alex.

"Oh, hi there."

"We need to talk, Eve," Alex said.

That seemed to be Alex's favorite line. Well, maybe it was time we did talk about us.

Nappi pushed his chair back from the table. "I just caught sight of one of my business associates. I think now would be a good time to buy him a drink." Nappi gave me a knowing smile and left.

"I don't trust that guy, even though you do," said Alex, dropping into the chair beside mine.

"If you are sincere about us talking, that's not the way to begin the conversation. Nappi's proven his worth as a friend over and over again."

I observed a look of anger briefly cross Alex's face, but then he seemed to think better of getting his hackles up.

"Sorry Eve. Look, here's the thing .... I know I've been pushing you too hard about our relationship, and I understand why you're so gun-shy about involvement. Jerry, much as I consider him a real great guy, isn't commitment material, as you well know. He hurt you pretty bad with all his philandering. I get that. But you know I'm not Jerry. I'm your true blue guy, even though I can't be there for you every time you need me. Like when someone dumps you into the swamps and leaves you for dead or when someone drives your car off the road, but ..." he continued to talk, but my mind wandered off to those horrible events and all I could picture was the way Sammy Egret came to my rescue those times, getting us out of the swamp and calling the ambulance when my car was run off the road. Good old Sammy. Tall, sexy, dark, understanding Sammy ….

"Eve! Hey, what the hell are you smiling about?" Alex's voice interrupted my dreams of dark eyes and smoky gazes penetrating my soul. I sighed and turned my attention to what Alex was saying. I was being unkind, and I knew it.

"I'm sorry, Alex. I guess this day has been too much for me." I reached out and put my hand on his arm. That seemed to placate him for a moment. But weren't we going down a road we'd traveled so many times before? What was different now?

"So here's what I'm thinking, Eve. I think we need to make a real commitment to each other, so you'll know I'm serious about my feelings for you." At this point Alex got out of his chair and dropped to one knee.

Oh, God, no. He wasn't going to ask me …. Was he?

He pulled out a small box from his jacket pocket, popped it open with one finger and presented it to me. "So how about it, Eve. Will you marry me?"

At the same moment another shadow crossed my plate. Sammy.

"I thought I saw you over here. I wanted to stop by and tell you about Frida's …." Sammy must have noticed Alex on one knee and the glitter of the ring in his hand.

"Oh, gosh. I'm interrupting, aren't I? I'm sorry."

We both looked up at Sammy. Alex got to his feet and slipped the box back into his pocket. "No, I guess you won't," he said, turned, and left.

I reflected for a brief moment on what I was feeling. Shouldn't I have wanted to yell at Sammy, then run after Alex? But that wasn't what I wanted at all. Instead I was profoundly relieved to have avoided the need to reply to Alex's question. I also realized I was unsettled by Alex's proposal and what it would mean to be married again. I was at the edge of uncertainty, an comfortable spot for someone like me. I had not handled Alex's proposal well. I owed him more than I gave him.

CHAPTER 6

___

"WAIT HERE, SAMMY," I said and ran after Alex. I caught him just as he slammed his car door.

"Alex." I put my arm through the driver's side window and touched his cheek.

He stiffened at the contact.

"You didn't answer my question, Eve."

"And I'm not going to, not under these conditions. You can't really believe that I had Sammy show up to ruin a marriage proposal I never saw coming, can you?"

He laughed—an unhappy sound—and in the light from the streetlamp, I saw the bitterness on his face.

"But that's just it, isn't it, Eve? How could you be so surprised at my proposal? You know how I feel about you."

"And you know I care for you, too. But I'm not ready to make a commitment, and it's not your fault. Nothing you do will change my fear of marrying again. This is something I need to work out. Can you understand that?"

His shoulders slumped, and his eyed bored into the steering wheel as if the answer to our problems would be found hiding there.

"I guess. I'm just so crazy about you that I don't want to lose you. Not to Sammy, not to anyone. You're right. I should have known better. Jerry told me—"

"Jerry? You talked to Jerry about this proposal?"

"Well, kind of. He was married to you. I thought he might have some insight. He told me not to do this."

"You should have listened. For once, he was right on the money." I slapped the side of his car and turned back toward the building. How could he have run this proposal by Jerry, the husband who betrayed me? Really, how could he run something like this past anyone besides me?

"Eve," I heard him say.

I faced him again. "Look, Alex, my day has been devastating. You don't seem to get it, do you? We'll talk, but not now. I need to decompress."

That was what it felt like, as if the pressure was building inside me to the point where I'd blow like an overinflated tire. *Bang!*

Back in the bar, I headed for the ladies' room and threw water on my face. When I looked in the mirror, my skin was bright red and my mouth was set in a tight white line. My teeth were beginning to hurt from all the grinding.

I walked back to our table to find Nappi sitting there, his smile tremulous.

"Don't worry," I said. "I won't hurt you. I feel fine now. Really." I sunk into a chair.

I looked at my place setting. My plate was gone.

"I wasn't sure you would be coming back so I sent Sammy away and had the waitress remove your ribs. They were cold anyway."

"Right. I think I need to go home."

After Nappi dropped me off, I hurried into the house without saying good night and headed for the bathroom, where I threw up all my dinner. Some of the tension dissipated, and I felt better. At least this horrible day was over.

*

I AWOKE LATER that night with a taste in my mouth as foul as if I'd licked one of those highly toxic toads we have down here, and with a feeling someone was watching me. I opened one eye, certain I was gripped by a nightmare that would go away as soon as I awoke. It didn't. There was someone standing over my bed and blinking didn't make the figure go away.

"Uh, Eve, don't be frightened. It's Sammy. Your front door was unlocked. I tried calling from the gas station up the road, but you didn't pick up, so I came on in."

"Go away, Sammy. I've haven't had a chance to brush my teeth." I rolled over to face the wall. My hand hit the bedside stand, and I knocked the phone onto the floor with a crash.

"I think your phone was out of the cradle. Didn't you hear that insistent buzzing sound? It's really unpleasant."

"Not as unpleasant as the sound of the buzzing coming from inside my skull." I sat up in bed and switched on the light.

Sammy jumped backward. "Whoa!"

"Do I look that bad?" I got out of bed and walked toward the mirror over my dresser. If I thought I'd set a new standard for ugliness in the ladies' room mirror last night at the Biscuit, this was much worse. Mascara had migrated from my lashes southward in a long stream, dried now on my cheeks, and my face looked as if I'd buttered it with margarine.

"Are you sick?" Sammy asked.

"Sort of."

"Maybe I can take care of this myself then."

"Take care of what? Something important must be up for you to break into my house and invade my bedroom."

"There was no breaking or invading. Like I said, the door was open. I yelled your name, but got no answer. I thought something bad happened to you. I was worried."

Oh, crap. I must have been in such a state last night that I forgot to lock the door. I was lucky it was Sammy who came in.

I leaned into the mirror to get a better look at the wreckage that was my face. "What's going on that can't wait until morning?" *Until I'm once more my sassy self*, I didn't add.

"I was heading out to the hunting ranch early and drove by your new shop. Or your old shop—I mean, the shop you and Madeleine will be moving into—and I saw lights on."

Oh, no. Not the shop. Just when I thought we'd be back in permanent, non-mobile digs soon.

"So you called the cops, right?"

Sammy said nothing.

"No cops. And why not?"

In vain I looked around the room for my cell.

"I know you don't like the police right now after spending so much time with them yesterday, but that would have been the wise thing to do. And where the hell is my cell? Does that land line work?"

Sammy handed me the phone I had knocked to the floor. In two pieces.

"Let me wash my face, and we'll go." I looked down at my body. The body had to be in better shape than the face, right? I was still wearing my clothes. Even my shoes.

Something was happening to Sammy's lips. "Don't you dare laugh at me, Sammy Egret! My night was hell."

Shaking his head, he assumed a more serious expression, turned away, and headed toward the kitchen to make coffee.

I detoured into the bathroom and washed up. Then I heard some kind of gurgling, choking noise coming from him.

"You're laughing at me, aren't you?"

He shook his head. "Better lock up."

"You think some other Miccosukee might come snooping in here?"

I grabbed my purse off the couch to get my keys. My cell fell out on the carpet, and when I picked it up, I noticed it needed recharging.

I PULLED UP a block away from the store, Sammy in his

truck behind me. We approached from the alleyway that ran alongside the building. Like my house tonight, the door to the shop also stood open, but there were no lights on inside.

"I don't know what those lights could have been, but someone would have had to pull the breaker to get juice," I said.

"Someone with a flashlight, maybe," said Sammy.

"We could use one of those things right now. Did you think to bring one?"

"In my truck. I'll be back." Sammy turned around and soundlessly ran down the alleyway.

"Don't leave me here," I whispered, but he was out of earshot.

Scared, Eve? a voice chided me from inside my head. *Nope,* I replied silently and swung the half-open door wide. I heard a sound from within, a kind of rustling that stopped suddenly.

"Hello?" I called. "I called the police, and they're on their way." *But I hadn't called the cops, had I? Oh, stupid me.*

I listened for a moment, then stepped inside the door. "I think I hear the sirens now."

Nothing.

I took a tentative step forward, then another. The rustling sound again. "They're in the next block. Here they come around the corner."

Another step, then another and finally my feet hit some impediment. I nudged whatever it was and heard a rustling again.

Sammy came up behind me and clicked on the flashlight.

"Better move your foot, Eve, before that alligator takes a bite out of your favorite boots."

The alligator's eyes peered up at us for a moment, and then the animal hissed and dashed for the far corner of the shop where it stood its ground, tail swishing back and forth, hissing sounds emanating from its open mouth.

"Looks like he could use some orthodontia," I said. The joke fell flat, my voice quavering with fear.

"Let's just back up slowly and leave. I'll pull the door behind us." Sammy grabbed my hand and led me toward the exit.

"What? And leave an alligator in my store?"

"What damage can he do?"

"Do alligators poop? I'll bet they do. I'll never get the smell out."

"It'll only be for a few more minutes … or hours at most. Let's drive to the police station and tell them what we found."

I hesitated, but what could I do?

At the police station, we got the sad news that someone, and not the officers on duty, would have to remove the animal before they would enter the scene.

"We're police, lady. We don't do wildlife rescue."

"I don't want the thing 'rescued.' I want it removed. It's in my store."

"Well, we can't get anyone out there until morning. What can the thing do trapped in the store? Are you afraid it won't like the décor?" The officer, a guy I'd never met before, looked as if he could run for Southern good ol' boy sheriff. He was almost bald and had—you guessed it—combed several strands of hair that grew a few inches above his right ear over to the left side of his head. His protruding stomach almost hid his belt and holster.

"Can I borrow your phone?" I asked.

"Help self." He turned away, still chuckling at his own joke.

"Hi, Frida. Sorry to wake you, but I've got a problem here." Before she could hang up on me, I explained what was happening.

"Unless there was a murder in your store tonight, I can't help you. I'm a homicide detective. Even if the alligator is guilty, it's still not my department. Call game and wildlife in the morning." She hung up on me.

So Sammy and I went back to my place. We stopped by the store to check on the alligator. Still there. Still kind of pissed. This time we noticed the lock was broken and the door couldn't be secured, but who cared? I had an alligator guarding the place.

NAPPI CALLED EARLY the next morning to see how I was doing. When I told him about the events of the night before, he wanted to take the blame for everything and jumped in his car to be on my doorstep with coffee and pastries in ten minutes.

"I thought you were staying in West Palm," I said, opening the door to him.

"I stayed here last night."

"As in Sabal Bay," I said, knowing better than to question him further.

I grabbed a coffee and stuffed a pastry into my mouth, savoring the simple carbs with all the relief of a drowning person being tugged to shore by a lifeguard.

"Can this be fixed?" I asked, holding up my broken bedroom phone for Nappi. He shook his head.

After I'd arrived home earlier I'd been awake enough to remember to put my cell phone on charge, so I got the county's wildlife and game number to contact them about the alligator. As I waited for someone to answer, I filled Nappi in on the details.

At the connect, I reported the reptile, and the person on the other end chuckled and said, "Maybe it's a female looking for something classy to wear."

Everybody had a joke.

"Just get it out of there before it poops all over the place."

"How big was it?"

"I don't know. Big, really big."

"About a size sixteen then?"

And another one.

"Ha, Ha. How soon before you get here? The cops need to take a look at the place."

"I'll send Gator Gus right on over. Can you meet him there?"

"Can't he do this by himself? I'm not going to help him, am I?'

There was the sound of an impatient sigh from the woman talking to me. "No, ma'am, but we do need permission from you to enter the premises."

"And does the alligator have to sign off on his capture, too?" I asked.

The lady hung up on me.

The front door was flung open, and Grandy stood in the doorway. For those who haven't met her, she is the woman who raised me from the time I was nine years old when my parents were killed in a boating accident on Long Island Sound. She was as short and round as I was tall and skinny, but that's where the differences ended. We were both sassy, in-your-face, never-back-down women. She was better at attitude than I was. She'd had more practice.

"It seems I arrived just in time. What is going on, Eve? You look as unappetizing as yesterday's oatmeal." She dumped her suitcase on the living room floor and hugged me. Then, sniffing the air, she made a beeline for the pastries.

"Nappi," she said on her way to sugar heaven. She blew him a kiss and perused the donuts.

"I thought you and Max were too busy with charters this weekend for you to come up."

"Yesterday we were slammed, but today we had two cancellations. Besides," she said, puffing powdered sugar out her mouth, "it would seem there's more than just your business that could use my help."

"I think I've got everything under control for now," I said. That was Eve bravado speaking. I was secretly glad to see her. Whatever I couldn't get on top of, I knew she could.

"Really, Eve? Let's see now …. Someone you knew and disagreed with was killed and you and Madeleine were protesting how she was using her land and then you found an alligator in your shop. The only good news is that Madeleine is pregnant. Somehow you'll get yourself up to your bangle bracelets in this murder investigation, won't you? Thank goodness Nappi found you and the Egrets a good lawyer." She paused for another bite of a chocolate-covered donut.

"That's about it, although I wonder how you found out so much in such a short period of time," I said. "Even Nappi didn't know all that until just now."

"I have friends in high and low places, Eve. Just like you, although I suspect with your background and your participation in that protest yesterday, some of your local friends might be rethinking their connection to you and Madeleine."

I waved my hand back and forth to silence her. Nappi looked puzzled by her reference to my "background."

"I get it. Haven't told everybody everything yet, huh? Not Nappi, not your lawyer, not Alex, not Frida—in fact, not anyone around here. Okay, it's your story. I'll keep my mouth shut."

There was a knock on the door. I opened it to Frida.

"Uh-oh. Did the alligator kill someone and now I'm being arrested for harboring a criminal?" I asked. "Come on in. I think there are some donuts left. Or is that an insult to your profession?"

Frida gave me a snarky little smile, nodded at Nappi and crossed the room to envelop Grandy in a big hug. She then reached into the box and extracted a pastry.

"It's my day off. I hoped to catch you before you left for the store. I'm just dying to see this alligator roaming around the place."

I held up my finger to signal silence. "Don't you dare make a joke about whether it's shopping in there."

"Of course not," she replied. "I'm just worried about your reputation."

"My what?"

"You know. You sell used items, including alligator shoes

and boots, but this looks as if you're intending to skin him and sell new. Not your line of merchandise, Eve."

She bit down on the donut and grinned, showing sprinkle-covered teeth.

CHAPTER 7

—

THERE WAS ONE little task I'd neglected, an important one. I hadn't let Madeleine know about our late-night visitor to the shop. So I let Grandy drive my car while I called Madeleine on my cellphone.

"Did I wake you, honey?" I asked when I heard her voice.

"Nope, I was up already, busily tossing my cookies as usual. God, Eve, I hope I don't grow to hate this baby before it's even born. Morning sickness is the pits. Hold a minute, would you?" I heard a door close, a sound like someone being sick, a toilet flush, and then Madeleine came back on the line.

"I hope that's it for a while."

"There's some news about the shop you should know."

"I'm guessing it's not good or you wouldn't be calling me at this early hour. You're not a morning gal. Is it about the contractors? Are they going to delay another week or so?"

"There may be a delay of sorts, depending upon the outcome."

"Eve, get to the punch line before I'm sick again."

"There's an alligator in the shop."

There was a long pause on the line. Finally she said, "Not

some alligator shoes or an alligator bag, but an actual reptile, living and breathing?"

"And hissing and probably pooping all over. I'm meeting an alligator guy there now, and the cops."

Grandy made the turn into the shop parking lot. I quickly filled Madeleine in on what Sammy and I had found last night, then disconnected to let her take another bathroom break.

A beat-up truck, painted camouflage, was parked in front of the building. Leaning against it was a guy, age and facial features indeterminate because of the shaggy salt and pepper hair and the beard that covered his face. He wore baggy camouflage trousers, an oversized T-shirt, and scuffed-up leather boots.

"You the lady with the alligator?" he asked me as I got out of my car and walked over to him.

"Yes. I'd like you to remove him, if you would."

"Miss Sally took the call. She said it was a secondhand store. So is this alligator a hand-me-down too? You get it from a friend maybe?" He smiled and laughed, a sound like a snorting pig. The sight of him tee-heeing at my expense was not pleasant. His teeth were stained brown, some broken off. He let go with a huge glob of tobacco juice, which he spat to one side. "Watch yer feet. Sorry 'bout that."

"Hi, Gus," called Frida as she jumped out of her car.

"Miss Frida, how you doing?" He took off the Aussie-style hat—brim pulled up on one side, camouflage also—and dipped his head to Frida.

"Howdy, Gus. Never too early to grab critters, I guess," Frida said.

Two officers arrived in a blue and gold patrol car, greeted Gus and Frida, and threw the rest of us a curt greeting.

Sammy pulled up in his truck and said a cheery hello. He and Gus did a man hug and slapped each other on the back.

Any more arrivals and we'd have to park the cars in overflow.

"Ah, Mister …. What is your name, anyway? I'm Eve Appel, owner of this shop."

"Just call me Gus. Let's go see about this gator of yours."

"He's not my gator."

"What's he doing in your shop then?"

I groaned. "Do I look like the kind of person who keeps an alligator as a pet?"

Gus stared at me for a minute or more. "I can't rightly say about that, but you do look kinda different, like you might have some funny ideas about selling stuff around here. You can't sell alligators, you know."

I gave up. "Just follow me, Gus." I led the way to the shop's side door, pushed it open with my foot, and stood back while Gus preceded me into the shop.

The morning light was weak, but strong enough to reveal our resident reptile, up against the far wall, looking displeased with the man approaching him.

"Well, that's just a bitty one, only about four feet or less. No problem." Gus dangled a rope with a noose over the creature and when it looked up, pulled the noose over the head and tightened it around the jaws to prevent them from opening. "Hold this," he said, handing me the rope, "and don't let that noose slip off."

"Hey, I'm not …." I grabbed the rope and held it taut. The alligator started toward me.

Gus leaped toward his prey and onto its back. Throwing a towel over its eyes, he clasped his hands around the jaws and extracted duct tape from his pocket. He wrapped the tape around the mouth to keep it closed, then picked up the animal, removed the noose, and carried the gator to his truck. I followed him, the rope dangling from my hand.

Without another word, he placed the gator in the back, jumped into the cab, and drove off. I stood with my mouth open and continued to hold the rope. The truck belched black smoke as it pulled onto the road. Suddenly the brake lights came on, and it backed up into the parking lot, turned, and reversed across the lot.

"I'll take that," he said, rolling down his window and grabbing the rope out of my hands. The gears ground as he shifted again into forward and the truck sped off once more with a backfire of smoke and sparks.

"Best gator trapper in the county," said Frida. "You're lucky he was available. You can close your mouth now, Eve."

I took a gulp of air and kind of shook myself back to the present.

The officers examined the door and said the lock was broken by someone slamming something heavy into it.

"That's how they got in," one of them said.

Duh. Sammy and I already had determined that last night.

David and Madeleine arrived in time to see Gus drive off with his catch.

"Was that our animal rescuer?" Madeleine pointed to the cloud of black smoke that rose from the street behind the departing vehicle.

"It seems more likely he rescued the shop rather than the animal," observed Nappi.

The whole crowd from the parking lot and a few others curious about the police car pushed into the shop behind Madeleine and me.

"Anything missing?" asked the officer who'd so cleverly determined the manner of ingress.

"There was nothing here. Yet," I said.

"Lucky," said Frida.

"Oops, watch that," said Sammy. "Looks like the gator left you a present."

He'd spoken too late. I had planted my almost new emu-skin boots into the alligator's gift.

I lifted my boot. "Ugh. Now I'll have to throw these out."

"You can clean them," said Frida.

"Never," I replied.

MADELEINE AND I needed to talk about our business, but first I called some commercial cleaners to come in and use industrial strength detergents on the floor and giant fans to blow out the smell of the chemicals and what was left of the gator's scent. I'd believe they'd done the job only after the air passed my sniff test. David insisted we go back to the house at the hunting reserve to have our discussion. He and Madeleine were still living in her house in town, but planned to move to the ranch soon.

"The fridge is still stocked with food. We can have breakfast out there," he said.

"It's nearly time to open the motor-home shop," said Madeleine. "I know you don't want me working, but someone has to be there."

"I'll do that," said Grandy.

"And I'll drive her there," offered Frida. "I could do a little shopping. I haven't been in the shop to browse for weeks."

Since Sammy was working part-time at the ranch as foreman, I followed his truck back to the David's ranch.

"Gangway!" cried Madeleine. "I've got dibs on the bathroom." She rushed into the house before anyone else could get a foot out of their vehicle.

Before Madeleine came out of the bathroom, I wanted to say a few words to David.

"I realize you want the best for her and your baby. I know she looks like a little, helpless gal, but she's a grown woman with almost as much pluck as Grandy. Don't treat her like a kid. Let her make her own mind up about how she's going to handle this pregnancy."

David's face reddened. *Uh-oh.* I was about to be banned from the house.

He approached me and reached out with both hands. No, I was wrong. He was going to toss me out bodily. To my surprise, he enveloped me in a hug.

"You're right, Eve. She is a grown woman who knows her own mind. Thanks for reminding me."

"Reminding you of what?" Madeleine closed the bathroom door and turned toward the kitchen.

"Reminding me that I need to buy some more crackers for you to settle your stomach."

Madeleine gave David a look filled with suspicion, then shrugged. "Later. Right now I'm starving. I want bacon, eggs, and pancakes. What do you say? Who wants to join me?"

As it turned out, David, Sammy, and I watched in awe as Madeleine tore through two eggs, four slices of bacon, and a stack of pancakes. Sammy did the cooking while Madeleine and I talked business. She and I decided, with David's support, that nothing would change in our shops unless Madeleine said she couldn't work. If and when that happened, we'd figure out something. We put off deciding whether to return the motor home to Nappi, since we didn't know when the other shop could open. I called the foreman of the crew we'd hired to renovate the shop. He said the renovations would be delayed. Again. When I tried to pin them down on a restart time, he was vague.

"Soon. Maybe next week," he said. "We'll get there when we get there."

Driving back to the motor home to see how Grandy was faring, I thought about Jenny's murder. I trusted Frida's skill as a homicide detective, but not as much as I trusted my own nosiness and ability to annoy people enough that they'd tell me stuff just to get rid of me. I wanted to find out the name of Jenny's fiancé, since Jenny and Shelley both said he was against Jenny's signing that contract for the mud bog races on her property. That hardly seemed like a strong motive for murder for a man who was going to marry the victim, but who could say how a killer's mind worked? *Who benefits from Jenny's death?* I wondered. Probably Shelley. Or perhaps the fiancé. Love could make people incautious. Frida probably knew the answers to all these questions, but she wasn't going to share her knowledge with me. Still, Frida said she had the day off. That didn't mean the case simply shut down. Her junior partner Linc Tooney would be working the leads. If Linc hadn't left home for work yet this morning, maybe I could cruise on by his place. I'd park around the corner, wait for him to go to work, then follow him wherever he went.

"Grandy," I said, connecting on my cell, "can you manage the shop by yourself today? I've got some business to attend to. What? No, I'm not interfering in Frida's case." After I ended the call, I uncrossed my fingers and headed for the trailer park where Linc lived. *Darn.* I'd almost forgotten Shelley said she would stop by the shop this morning when we opened. I checked my watch. I had just enough time to check on what Linc was doing and then drop by the shop. I'd ask Shelley who the fiancé was. Simple. We'd see how the day rolled out. I turned up the local country station and pressed on the accelerator in anticipation of an adventure to come.

LINC'S OLD BLUE Buick sat in front of his trailer. I pulled my Mustang in around the corner from the road running past his house and waited. I'd only taken one sip of the coffee bought at the drive-thru when I spied Linc in my rearview mirror. He locked his front door, got into the car, and drove down the road, pulling into the street that ran past the trailer park. My heart did a flip-flop of joy when he pointed his vehicle in the opposite direction of the police station. I followed, careful to keep a few cars between his and mine. At the stoplight in the center of town, he turned left onto Highway 441 and increased his speed as we left Sabal Bay. Few cars were on the road, and I worried he'd make my distinctive Mustang in his mirror, but he continued at speed limit until he got to the country route that was the shortcut leading to Fort Pierce on the coast. This was the way to David's hunting ranch, where I'd already been earlier. What the heck? Sure enough, he turned into the ranch. Curious, I followed. He'd parked his car in front of the house and was heading to the door when I pulled in behind him.

"Not following me, are you, Eve?" He gave me a smile that did not quite reach his eyes. Was he onto me?

"Nope, just visiting my friends." I walked with him up the steps. He knocked.

David came to the door and looked surprised at my presence.

"What are you doing here? Not that we don't love seeing you, Eve."

I signaled him with a twirling motion of my eyes followed by a twist of my neck and shoulders, which I hoped translated into "Don't say a thing."

Though puzzled, David invited us both in.

Madeleine was lying on the couch eating something in a box that looked as if it housed chocolates.

"Hi again, Eve." She waved from the couch. "Want a piece?" She held the box out to me.

"Thanks, no. I had a big breakfast."

"So you did. Me, too, but I'm eating for two, so I need the calories and the energy." Suddenly her face turned green and she held up a finger. " 'Scuse me." She dashed into the bathroom.

"So, Detective Tooney. What can we do for you?" asked David.

"I'm here to talk to Madeleine, but since Eve followed me, I assume she's eager to be a part of the discussion."

I was busted.

Our 'discussion,' as it turned out, was simply going over the events of yesterday: at what time we arrived at the protest, who was near us, did we see anything suspicious—ground we'd covered before. Halfway through his questions, I yawned and reached for one of Madeleine's chocolates. Maybe I needed at little energy. I hadn't slept well last night with everything on my mind—the murder, the protest, Alex, Sammy, the alligator. Linc's next question woke me up.

"Ever taken part in protests like this before?"

Madeleine and I exchanged glances.

"You mean against mud bog racing?" I said.

David seemed to be looking at me intently.

"No, this was our first," Madeleine said.

After several more routine questions, Linc put his notebook back in his shirt pocket and stood to leave.

"Want to follow me, Eve? Or do you think you can find your way home by yourself?"

I made a face at him and watched him walk out the door.

"Okay, you two. What's going on?" asked David.

Madeleine and I mollified David by telling him about some of the protests we'd joined while in college up North.

"You know," said Madeleine, "demonstrations against increases in tuition, changes in the grading system, college stuff. When we were students. Years ago." She omitted the demonstration against the new mall, the one where we got arrested.

He seemed convinced that we were not eco-terrorists, just a couple of students trying out our social consciousness wings.

I looked at my watch. "Oops, I've got to go. I should be meeting Shelley. Maybe I can talk some sense into her about hanging around with that creep she's taken on as her love interest." I explained to them my concerns about his manipulative and criminal nature.

"He's giving her a short leash like he thinks she might say or do something … that would betray him."

"Like what?" asked David.

"I don't know. He's needy and controlling, and that's a bad combination."

Madeleine nodded in agreement. "She needs to find someone who trusts her and will let her be independent." She looked up at David from her place on the couch and gave him one of her thousand-watt smiles.

There. That should remove any doubt he had about her past experiences exercising her social conscience.

*

I STOPPED BY the store just after Grandy opened and waited for Shelley. By eleven, it looked as if she wasn't going to show, so I called the McCleary house. There was no answer. I left a message for her to meet me at the Biscuit for an early lunch if she could. At the Biscuit, I waited for her inside. By twelve thirty, I knew she wasn't going to show, and I was worried, so again I called the house.

A male voice answered. "Who's this?"

"Not even 'hi, who's this?' " I said.

"I can hang up, you know."

"This is one of Shelley's friends. We were supposed to get together today."

"Oh, yeah. Eve somebody from last night. Forget it. She doesn't want to meet you."

The line went dead.

As if that would stop me.

CHAPTER 8

—

WHEN I PULLED into the McCleary's driveway, I saw only one car. Maybe I got lucky. The car looked like Jenny's and not the infamous Darrel's beater. As soon as I opened my door, Shelley came out onto the porch.

"You didn't show for lunch. Is everything okay, or didn't you get my message?" I said.

"No, I …."

Someone pushed the door open and stepped out behind her. Not my lucky day, after all. No lunch and a lotta Darrel.

"She don't wanna talk with you. Buying lunch won't change that, so you just skedaddle out of here."

"I need to hear that from Shelley."

Shelley twisted her head around to look back at Darrel. "I really do want to talk with her, honey."

" 'Bout what?"

"About a dress for Mom's funeral."

"You inherit. Seems you're rich enough to afford somethin' new, not some old used rag." Darrel had rested his hand on her shoulder. Now his fingers splayed out and dug into the soft flesh near her neck.

"Darrel, honey, that hurts."

"Huh?" He seemed unaware he was grabbing her too tightly and let go.

"So talk. I'm watching a game on television." He backed into the house and slammed the door behind him. I could hear noise from inside. It got louder, as if he had turned up the volume to drown out our conversation. Maybe I was wrong about him. Maybe he wasn't a bad guy, just a dumb buffoon. Regardless of what he was, I was certain Jenny would be horrified to see him settled in her house.

I gestured toward the car. "Why don't you come into the shop now? I'll drive, and we can look at what I have in for you."

She hesitated, looked back at the closed door, then smiled. "Gosh, I hate to leave Darrel alone, but … I'll grab my purse."

When she returned, Darrel accompanied her. "Maybe it would be a good idea for him to come along so I can get his opinion."

No, that would be a bad idea.

"What do guys know about appropriate attire for a funeral?" I asked. "Besides, I wouldn't want to interrupt the game."

He looked relieved and kissed her goodbye with a warning. "You git back here before supper 'cuz I am already getting hungry."

I refined my opinion of him. He was a demanding, stupid buffoon.

"HOW ARE YOU doing, Shelley?" I asked as I pulled out of the drive.

"Okay, I guess. Sorry about not showing up earlier for lunch, but I couldn't get away. I guess I should have called."

"No problem. I was kind of tied up with business things anyway."

"It's nice having Darrel to look after me. And about lunch … Darrel said you really didn't mean it when you invited me. That you were just trying to be nice because of Mom."

I laughed. "I guess you don't know me well enough to understand that when I say something, I mean it."

She gave me a sad smile.

"How's your mother's fiancé—I can't remember his name—taking her death? When were they getting married?"

"They weren't."

"Really? I thought it was soon. What happened?"

"She broke it off with him. He was so pushy about the mud bog thing that she couldn't stand him anymore."

"But you agreed with him, right?"

"Sure, but I wasn't all in your face every minute. That can get pretty tiring."

"Was he okay with the breakup?"

Shelley looked at me, puzzled. "You think he might have killed Mom because they disagreed about the event?"

"What do you think?"

She shrugged. "I don't know." She hesitated, then added, "Yesterday, early morning, I heard Mom downstairs arguing with someone."

"You told the police this, right?"

"Yep. I couldn't tell who it was."

"A man or a woman?" I asked.

"Man, I think."

"Do you think it was her ex-fiancé?

"I don't know."

This conversation was netting me little information, so I took a stab in the dark. "They were living together, weren't they?"

"How did you find out? No one was supposed to know."

Now it was my turn to shrug. "Your mom alluded to it once."

"That's not the kind of thing a woman wants to admit down here, surrounded by devout Christians."

"I hear tell that in some places even devout Christians live together before they're married."

"Not around here." She looked worried, then said, "So would you keep it hush-hush that Darrel sometimes spends the night at the house?"

"Sure, honey."

"This morning Darrel made it clear to George that he needed to move his stuff out of the house."

"George?"

"You know, Mom's fiancé."

"So the breakup was recent."

She nodded.

"George came back this morning to get his clothes and other stuff he'd left in the house when he and Mom parted. Darrel took Mom's shotgun and pointed it at him. He got moving darn fast. Left half his clothes in the bedroom. I don't know what to do with them."

"Well, they're his, so you need to give them back or the cops will accuse you of stealing them." I hated making up stuff, but I needed to move this conversation ahead to get any important information.

"Really? I didn't know that. Darrel said he was going to burn them."

"Here." I handed her my cell. "You call Darrel and tell him to leave those clothes where they are."

"But we don't want them. I know Darrel doesn't want me to call George to come get them, and he certainly wouldn't be happy if I took them to George's house."

"No problem. Give me his address, and I'll take them to him."

"Would you? Gosh, Eve. That would be great." She took the cell and connected with Darrel.

I made a U-turn and headed back to Jenny's ranch to get George's clothes before Darrel decided in a fit of pique that he'd burn them anyway. When we pulled into the driveway, we saw Darrel stick his head out the front door, then clothes began flying out onto the porch, followed by other items, including shampoo and conditioner bottles and a can of shaving cream.

After Shelley and I picked out a dress for the funeral, she told me the funeral home had called earlier to inform her that the body would be released after the autopsy.

"They told me I needed to figure out what Mom would wear in the casket. I was wondering what you thought of her wearing the dress she bought here, the one she was going to wear at her wedding. She really loved it."

"I think that would be lovely. How thoughtful of you to choose something you know she felt good about wearing."

"Putting it on her for the funeral isn't creepy, is it?"

I thought about it. "Did anyone but you know it was for the wedding?"

"No."

"Then we'll keep it our secret."

A car horn blaring outside the motor home caught our attention. It was Darrel. "Get out here," he shouted through his car window. "Shopping is over. We're going to the coast for a little fun."

I stepped down from the rig and approached Darrel's car. "I hope you don't intend to drag Shelley into some bars and get her drunk. She's underage, and she's just experienced her mother's murder. She's pretty vulnerable right now." Didn't he understand that knowing the head of one's mother had been removed from her body was awful?

"It'll be good for her. Cheer her up."

Shelley followed me, holding tight her purchase.

Before she got into the car, she gave me a warm hug. It felt as if she didn't want to let go.

"It's as if you like her better'n you do me. Who was holding your hand all night and wiping your nose while you bawled?" I heard Darrel say as he shifted into gear and they took off. I saw Shelley lean toward him and say something, then kiss his cheek. There was just no accounting for the power of young hormones. The woman was as deluded about Darrel as I once had been about Jerry. *Not quite true*, I told myself. Jerry had manners, money and style, and a wandering eye. Darrel had friends with questionable morals and relatives who would bail him out of jail—useful qualities if you were a criminal, which I was certain Shelley was not.

I called Madeleine to see how she was feeling.

"I'm fine as long as I eat my saltines in the morning. And maybe avoid pancakes, eggs, bacon, and sausage. And chocolates. I'll be in the shop tomorrow, I promise."

"No need. Grandy is here, and she looks as if she's willing to stay a while."

"What about you, Eve? You'll be there, won't you?"

"Sure. Most of the time."

"What's that mean?" Madeleine's voice held that note of suspicion which told me she thought I was up to something. "You're going to keep your nose out of this murder, aren't you?"

"Uh, sure. There are just a few things I need to look into."

Grandy grabbed the phone out of my hand. "How you doing, little mama?"

Saved by Grandy.

They talked for a few minutes, then Grandy disconnected. "What trouble are you going to get yourself into this time, Eve?" she asked.

I took a quick peek at my face in the shop mirror. Was there a sign on my forehead that said, "I'm planning to interfere in this case?" Was I that transparent?

"Because, if you're following up on some lead, then I want to go along. Let's get Grandfather Egret to help out Madeleine tomorrow, and we'll sleuth together." Grandy winked and gave me a conspiratorial smile.

"Is the position of shop girl too boring for you, Grandy?"

"I haven't had my hands in a good murder investigation since our first one, and that was a couple of years ago."

"Are you certain you want in on this? You got yourself beat up on that case. It could happen again." I knew Grandy to be a tough gal and as intrepid about going after the bad guys as I was, but she also was in her seventies—not frail, but a bit chubby and not an über-athlete. Was I wrong to judge her as unfit for crime fighting?

"Eve, dear, I'm as buff and strong as you are. How many pounds can you bench-press? How many sit-ups and push-ups can you do?'

I had no idea if I could do one or any of those activities. The last time I'd seen the inside of a gym was when I was in high school wearing one of those silly and degrading gym suits better suited to girls with waists, hips, and boobs—girls who managed to look cute in them. Me? I looked like a totem pole with diapers on. Anyway, I was savvy enough to feel a bit ashamed for trying to humiliate my Grandy. I had a comeback, though.

"I keep in shape by chasing killers around the swamps," I said.

"Sure you do, honey. I'd believe you if you said you kept in shape by chasing Alex out of your life and Sammy around the swamps."

"I do not chase after Sammy. We're friends, and that's all."

"Whatever you say. So, do I get in on this case or not? If I do, I'm going to need some sleuthing clothes. Something fashionable in case we get arrested, but comfortable and warm enough to keep me cozy in one of the county's jail cells. Also dark enough to be invisible on a stakeout."

"We are not doing breaking and entering, but if you see something here you like, try it on. It's on me."

"I liked that little black velvet warm-up suit I wore when we did that breaking and entering bit down in West Palm."

I remembered it well. Nappi helped us enter the place, and Grandy scoped out the kitchen for clues. The cops didn't arrive until after we left, thank goodness.

I searched my selection of petite but round and comfy togs and found Grandy another warm-up suit, this one in midnight blue with silver trim.

I held it up to show her. "How about this?"

"Great for day wear and dark enough to hide my butt if we get into a tight spot at night. Yowza." Grandy grabbed it from my hand and left for the changing room.

While she was in there, I connected on my cell with Max, Grandy's husband. It wasn't that I didn't trust Grandy as a fellow sleuth; I just wasn't certain I could keep her and me both out of trouble. I was a go-it-alone kind of gal.

"Hiya, Max. How are things going?"

"Slow. Now I got a repair that could take forever." I knew then that Grandy was going to share in my reconnaissance of Jenny's former fiancé.

Grandy and I had our feet up on my coffee table that night, slices of pepperoni pizza in our hands and a gallon of Diet Coke sweating on the kitchen counter. I was reaching for my third piece when Grandy's words stopped me in mid-seize.

"Things are not going well with Alex, I presume," she said, wrapping a string of cheese around her finger to prevent it from decorating her chin.

"He asked me to marry him. I'm not ready for that just yet."

"You may never be."

"Are you saying that because I couldn't make a go of it with Jerry, I'm not marrying material?"

"Not at all. I'm saying Alex may not be the material you should marry."

"Uhm," I said, licking my greasy fingers.

"But I'm not suggesting you pursue that yummy Sammy guy."

"Stay away from him, you're saying?"

"No, no. Get to know him better. Just keep in mind he's not a replacement part for where your heart has a hole in it."

"I don't think Jerry left that big a hole."

"No, but your parents' deaths did. I did my best to help you deal with that, but it had to have left a scar."

It had. Was that what all my uncertainty about love was about?

Perhaps Grandy was giving me sage advice. I'd store it for consideration later. For now, filled with fat and carbs, Grandy and I were ready to hit the sleuthing trail.

"I don't have his full name, but I do know where he lives," I said to Grandy as we buckled ourselves into my car.

"What if he's home when we get there?"

"I hope he's home. I told you. We're not doing illegal entry. Not this time."

I heard grumbling from her side of the car.

"Maybe soon," I added to placate her.

Jenny's former fiancé lived on the road skirting the edge of the rim canal where a number of fish camps were located. Some of these had recently gone out of business because of hard economic times. One had been sold to a buyer who had taken the former owner's shingle, Bud's Place, off the camp sign and substituted one with a more picturesque name—Hee Haw Home Habitat.

The sun was going down over the lake, and the clouds sitting on the horizon provided us a view of soft colors—mauve, misty purple, and pale pink. It was lovely, but when we took our eyes off the horizon and looked around the camp, the beauty was marred by the seedy condition of the place. What must have once been a quaint piece of old Florida now looked like a rural ghetto. The fish-cleaning station was lopsided, one leg broken off and propped up by a metal clothesline pole. The waste water treatment facility seemed to be failing. The odor of sewage permeated the place. A scrawny pelican sat on the fish-station railing, a look of hopeful desperation on his beaky face.

The small streets wide enough for only one car needed gravel. My tires threw up dust as we pulled into the camp, looking for number 225. Few houses had street numbers or outdoor lights.

"Let's ask someone. I saw an arrow back there that pointed this way to the office." I pulled around a curve and saw another office sign. This one lay on its side, the arrow pointing downward.

"You think that's some kind of sign?" Grandy asked. "You know, I mean a 'woo woo' sign. This place is giving me the creeps. Let's get out of here."

"Don't be silly. That's just a broken-down sign. No 'woo woo.' "

I pulled up in front of the only trailer in the area that had a porch light on.

"I'll wait in the car. Leave the keys," said Grandy.

I knocked on the screen door, careful to keep my touch light. The pitted aluminum frame looked as if it might vibrate off its hinges with little jarring.

"Yup," said the man who answered the door. He wore baggy jeans, no shirt, and suspenders that stretched over a huge, hairy stomach and chest. The hair—so black it might have gone through a Miss Clairol processing—didn't stop at his neck but continued up onto his chin and covered his face. He was bald on top with a fringe of white hair over his ears.

I jumped back a bit at the sight. He reacted the same way when he saw me.

"Whoa. I never seen a gal with such spiky hair. That's real scary."

Scary? Me? I considered saying something about the kettle and the pot, but thought better of it.

"It's a fashion statement. You get that, right?"

He looked puzzled, then smiled to let me get a look at his two remaining teeth.

"I'm looking for number 225."

"You ain't more cops, are you?"

"No. We're, uh, friends of his fiancée."

"She's dead."

"We're here to pay our respects."

He leaned forward. I leaned back.

"Just wanted to get a better look at ya. How do you get your hair to do that?"

"How do you …" I began, but stopped. "Gel."

"You mean like Vaseline?"

"Kinda."

"Something I should try."

I wondered where he might try it, but decided not to pursue that line of thought.

"Number 225," I repeated.

He pointed, and I stepped off his porch with a thankful wave of my hand and made for my car.

"You were smart to stay in the car," I said to Grandy.

"I saw. These doors automatically lock when you drive, right?"

We pulled up to the trailer pointed out by my hairy office informant. There was a light on inside.

"You staying in the car?" I asked Grandy.

"I can't figure out what's safer. We can't come back later, when no one's home?"

I shook my head.

She hesitated for a moment, then opened the car door. "This is no fun at all."

We walked up to the door. This trailer, although it had no outside light, seemed newer than its neighbors, and there was even some attempt to tidy up the yard with plantings, a bougainvillea in bloom, and a small palm tree that looked as if it were making a valiant attempt to stay alive, although its fronds were yellowing.

I knocked and waited. We heard footsteps, and the door opened. The man who stood there was over six feet tall and had longish brown hair that curled against the collar of his polo shirt.

He looked familiar. This was the man I'd seen at the protest rally yesterday morning.

"Well, well. Eve Appel. Long time no see. Come on in. I wondered when you'd try to look me up."

He was also the man who held the secret of Madeleine and my "green" history.

CHAPTER 9

—

I HOPED MY surprise didn't show on my face because I wanted the upper hand in dealing with this guy. He held too many of the cards in play: he was Jenny's former fiancé, and he had spotted me at the rally and recognized me and Madeleine. And he could be the killer.

"Well, well, George Bennet. I certainly wasn't surprised to see you at the protest—it's still your kind of thing, I see—but I'm a bit taken aback to discover you were Jenny's fiancé."

" 'Was' is the operative word. She broke it off." He waved us into the trailer.

"Oh, by the way, this is my grandmother. I don't think the two of you ever met."

He shook Grandy's hand and stepped back, his gaze taking us in. "The two of you don't look alike, but I heard about Grandy enough in the past to know that Eve has come by her spunk honestly."

Though Grandy produced one of her magnetic smiles, I knew she wasn't taken in by George's we're-just-old-friends gambit. There was no accompanying sparkle in her eyes.

I decided to let him do his welcoming act and see what he had to say.

"Coffee? Tea?" He gestured to a sofa. "Have a seat."

Grandy, still smiling, pulled me down onto the sofa next to her.

"Thanks, but we're not staying long. We …." I could hardly admit to the real reason we were here—to snoop. Returning his clothes had been my pretext, but I'd been so thrown by the trailer park and its sleazy manager, I'd left them in the trunk.

He filled in where I left off, "… wanted to offer your condolences on my fiancée's death?" His tone was no longer welcoming or friendly, but sarcastic.

So he wasn't really happy to see me nor did he think we were simply paying a social call. I never was real good at playing sociable. That was Madeleine's forte.

I shrugged away his cynicism. "I knew Jenny. She was a customer of mine. I'm curious about your relationship and why it ended."

"Let's be honest here, Eve. You mean you want to pry into that relationship now that Jenny is dead. Did I kill her? No, I did not. I loved her. With reservations."

"Those reservations got in the way of enduring love, I gather."

Grandy put her hand on my knee and pinched me to let me know I was being too pushy. I ignored her. We were here now, so I wanted answers.

"The cops questioned me earlier. Now you show up. Does your friend Detective What's-her-name think I'd be willing to tell you more than I told her? Is that the plan?"

Years ago and back up North, George and I had shared similar values when it came to land development. That was all. We had never been close friends. There was always a hostile edge to the man. And it was certainly emerging again. Yet I couldn't blame him for being offended by my visit. If he did love Jenny, and if I could believe he didn't kill her, then I was interfering with his grieving in a most intrusive way.

I decided to play nice. "I'm sorry about Jenny, but I do think it's kind of odd that the two of you got together. You seemed to be on different pages when it comes to protecting the environment."

"When the company approached her about the races, I thought I could talk her out of it. But then I couldn't, so I decided we'd simply agreed to disagree on that matter. She may have felt differently."

" 'May have'? Isn't that the reason the wedding was called off?"

He ran his fingers through his graying hair, most of it tied back into a ponytail. "I really don't know why she called it off. She just said there would be no wedding. She would give me no reason other than she just changed her mind about things."

"What things? Did she say?"

"Nope. She wouldn't talk about it. She told me to get out and said not to call her or try to see her again. That was that."

"Sorry about that."

"Are you?" There was that hostile edge to his voice again.

Grandy rose from the couch and walked over to where George stood on the other side of the room. "Listen, buster, if she says she's sorry, then she's sorry. Eve doesn't lie."

George looked down at his feet and muttered his own "Sorry," to which Grandy replied, "You damn well better be. Let's go, Eve."

I had some other questions I wanted to ask him, especially about his discussions with Jenny concerning the mud bog event, but Grandy's hand was firm on my sleeve, and she pulled me out of the trailer and over to the car before I could object.

"We were just getting warmed up, Grandy."

"You think so? I think he was winding down. We wouldn't have gotten anything else out of him tonight, not with that other woman there."

What other woman? I guess Grandy's eagle eye or keen hearing had detected something I missed because I was too busy focusing on George. Why was I not surprised that he had so quickly replaced Jenny with someone else?

"You saw or heard something that tipped you off to her presence?"

"Nope. I smelled something. The strong fragrance of the perfume, Poison."

"You've got the nose of a bloodhound."

"Did you sleep with that man when the two of you were back up North and taking part in those protests?" asked Grandy.

"Good God, no. He asked, but I refused. There's something about him I never liked." I started the car and spun the wheels on the dusty road leading out of the fish camp.

"Well, that was fun," said Grandy as we bumped along. "And we know so much more now than we did."

"Really?"

"Yep. George has a new woman, but I wonder if she's all that new. Maybe she's the real reason he and Jenny broke up. I'll bet you have some opinions on that." She fixed me with her probing eyes.

"When I knew him, he thought he had to bed every woman he met. I get the feeling that hasn't changed."

"So Jenny breaks up with him and his ego can't take the blow? He kills her?"

"I don't think George feels deeply enough to want to take that kind of radical action." I yawned. I hadn't had much sleep since the protest and the discovery of Jenny's head. I shuddered at the memory, then yawned again.

"Protests aren't taking action of a radical nature?" asked Grandy.

"They're part of his persona. I'm not certain down deep inside what he believes. In fact, I'm not sure there is a deep down inside."

MADELEINE CALLED AND offered to take the early shift the next day, saying her morning sickness was progressing into an afternoon condition. When I suggested she stay home the entire day, she insisted she needed to get out of the house because David followed her around as if he expected her to expire at any moment.

"He went through the pregnancy with his first wife, so you'd think he'd know better. He's driving me crazy. I told him I was pregnant, not terminal, but he still hovers."

I heard something in the background of the call, then Madeleine's voice again. "Go away, honey. I'm talking to Eve. It's girl stuff and nothing you need to know."

She came back on the line. "Is there some kind of sickness called 'pregnant husband'?"

"Hang in there. Grandy and I will pop over to the coast while you mind the store and visit some of our clients to see if they have any consignments for us. We'll be back around noon."

"Could you take David with you?" she asked.

"I hope you're kidding."

MADELEINE MUST HAVE heard us pull up because she started down the steps from the motor-home shop and waved at us as we got out of the car. The look on her face was troubled.

"We had a really bad morning. No sales. I think most of the community found out about our taking part in the protest and are boycotting us. Our business may be down the tubes."

A car drove in and parked behind mine. Darrel's beater. Shelley got out, carrying a cardboard box and some clothes slung over her arm.

Shelley toted everything up the stairs to the rig and dropped the items on the counter. She smiled a hello to Madeleine, then said in a whisper, "Eve, I need to talk to you. Alone."

Madeleine gave me a hug. "I'm off, and I'll give Grandy a ride to your place. We can all have dinner together tonight. How's that sound?"

I nodded, and the two of them left.

"So what have you got there?" I pointed to the box and clothes in Shelley's arms.

"Consignment items. Mom's stuff. I thought you could sell them. I've got more things in the car. I'll get them." Shelley ran back to the car and opened the trunk to extract another box and more hangers with clothes on them.

She certainly had been busy cleaning out her mother's house. And in such a short time. Only two days ago Jenny had been alive. I never knew Shelley was so cold-blooded.

"Darrel says there's no sense in keeping this stuff around the house when we can make some money off it."

So, the idea for closet cleaning was Darrel's, not Shelley's. That made sense. I wished I could shake some sense into Shelley when it came to Darrel. The guy was an insensitive lout. I knew I should keep my opinions about her boyfriend to myself.

"Darrel's being an insensitive lout."

She flopped down on one of the chairs inside the door. "I know, but that's Darrel. I kind of admire his honesty."

Oh, so that was what we were calling crude behavior these days.

"Anyway, I want you to do something for me. I'll have some money soon, and I want to hire you as a private detective to find out who killed my mother."

"That's up to Frida."

"I know, but I don't think the police will do a good job. I know you will, Eve. You've solved murders before and you have lots of friends who help you like your mob-boss guy and your boyfriend, Alex."

"I don't think we can count on Alex. He's real busy right now. Besides, I'm not an investigator. You can't really hire me." I hesitated before I continued, "I don't want to be nosey, but you mentioned money. What money? I thought your mother was having trouble making ends meet."

"Oh." She looked disappointed. "Well, I guess I can tell you, but don't tell Darrel I let you in on this. I re-upped the contract for the mud bog event to be held later this summer on the ranch."

"What? I thought you didn't approve of using the land that way."

"Well, I didn't, not until I talked to Darrel. He pointed out that the land would just sit there. This way it'll be used."

"You mean abused, don't you? Think of destroying all that habitat for birds and other animals. Alligators even."

"I don't like alligators. I wouldn't mind if they all disappeared from Florida. They're ugly, ugly animals."

Well, yes they are, but they are part of the ecosystem. I opened my mouth to say just that, but she stopped me.

"Look, Eve, I'm not going to change my mind. Mom was right. I don't like it, but I need the money. Think about what I asked and get back to me. Please don't tell Darrel I asked for your help. He'd think it was a waste of our money."

So now it was "our" money. Darrel was moving right in. Could he also have been responsible for the murder, knowing that with Jenny out of the way, he could make a grab for the money, little as it was, through Shelley? Maybe he thought there was more money than there actually was.

I watched her drive off and wondered if Frida considered Darrel as much of a suspect in Jenny's murder as I now did.

SEVERAL DAYS LATER, Grandfather Egret called, divining in his Miccosukee way or through some mechanism unknown to me that Grandy was still in town. He invited us all out to his and Sammy's place for swamp cabbage, collard greens, beans, home fries, and frog legs. Madeleine's evening stomach seemed to be adjusting to housing a new life. She thought the idea of fried food sounded just fine. Nappi was also in town with Jerry, so we all gathered at the small, rustic house near the Egrets' airboat business. Since the number of chairs in the house was limited, I brought in a few of my lawn chairs for extra seating. It was elbow to elbow for the eight of us, but the food made up for lack of space. The only person missing was Alex. I don't know what anyone else thought, but it felt odd without him there. I hadn't heard from him since our blowup. I'd tried to call him, but his cell went to voicemail, and I didn't leave a message.

I sat next to Sammy, and he and I chatted in our usual friendly way. He seemed particularly upbeat during the evening, as if something important was on his mind. Finally he leaned over and whispered, "My mother is coming for a visit. I want you to meet her."

I almost swallowed my frog leg whole.

"That would be lovely, Sammy."

He seemed relieved at my answer. "Good." He patted my knee.

I was aware of the stares of several people across the table, including Grandy and Nappi, who had both kept close tabs on me throughout the evening.

"Let's go outside and sit on the porch with our coffees," said Sammy.

I knew that would only stir the fires of curiosity in our watchers, but I didn't care. Sammy and I were adults, and Alex, well, I told him we would talk, but neither of us had reached out since his proposal at the biscuit. I knew I didn't want to leave it this way; however, for now I was confused and didn't think my confusion would help us.

We settled into the two old porch rockers and put our feet up on the railing. A limpkin screeched from across the canal behind us.

"Beautiful birds, but their call is so penetrating," I said.

"Some say they sound like a woman screaming," Sammy replied.

The night was silent for a minute, then a chorus of frogs took up their croaking, calling to one another in tandem. The sound of something moving through the water drifted up to us.

"Alligator," said Sammy.

A loud splash followed. Sammy smiled at me. "I guess that was the frog or fish that got away."

Laughter from inside the cabin drifted out to the porch, and I turned my head to look through the open door. Everyone was spellbound by one of Nappi's stories. No one seemed to notice we were gone.

"Are you feeling as uncomfortable as I am?" I asked Sammy.

"Sure."

"Why is that? We've been friends for a while now, and we've never had trouble talking to each other, but suddenly …."

"Suddenly there is no Alex."

I said nothing in reply.

Silence yawned huge between us once more.

"So tell me about your mother."

"You remind me of her."

Uh-oh.

"I mean you're both such bold women. And you're tall like her, only her hair is dark, and it was long the last time I saw her."

"Of course."

"She's not Miccosukee. She's white."

"Grandfather Egret raised you?"

He nodded.

"No siblings, but you have nephews, right?"

"Yep. My father was married before he met my mother. He had several children by his first wife. She died of cancer when she was young."

"Sorry to hear that. So you only have two half-brothers here. And your father and mother, are they still together?"

He chose to ignore my question about his father, but spoke eagerly about his mother.

"Mother couldn't stay here. She felt she didn't belong with the tribe, but she wanted me to connect with my Miccosukee heritage. Once I became an adult I chose to stay with

Grandfather Egret instead of adjusting to the white world. She accepts that choice, and we see each other as often as we can."

"Where does she live?"

"Las Vegas."

The silence settled in once more. I broke it by saying, "Well, I'm out of coffee, and it's getting late. Time to go, I guess."

I stood up and began to walk toward the door. Sammy also got out of his chair and reached out his hand. It rested lightly on my shoulder for a moment, then tightened. He turned me around to face him, then pulled me close. I may have hesitated for a moment, but no longer. I stepped into his embrace. His lips touched mine, at first softly, then with more insistence. Finally our tongues found an ancient language as they caressed. We broke away and looked into each other's eyes; then we came together once more. This time our hands reached out and tried to bring us closer as if each of us was trying to crawl into the other's body.

"Sammy," I whispered.

His hands gripped my waist, then worked their way down over my hips. I felt as if I were being molded into another being, a woman more passionate and primitive. I'd never experienced anything like it. What was this man doing to me? I shuddered and thought to draw back, but instead I leaned in. I never wanted to leave his arms.

"Hi, guys. What's up?" said a voice next to my ear.

"Jerry, go back inside," I said.

"Sorry. I didn't mean to interrupt." Jerry turned back and entered the house.

"Yes, you did, you twit!" I yelled at him as he retreated.

"That's a bit of a mood killer." Sammy stepped back and ran his fingers through his long hair.

I couldn't see the expression on his face or discern in his voice what he was feeling.

"Jerry has a way of ruining things."

"I didn't mean Jerry only. I meant your yelling at him."

This time I could see his mouth twitch and then a smile spread over his lips.

"Well, maybe we should think about what we're doing anyway."

"You're right. It wouldn't be appropriate to make love to you on Grandfather's porch and certainly not in one of his rockers."

"No, but it might be an interesting challenge."

We both laughed.

"There should be a full moon tomorrow night. How would you like to take a ride in my canoe?"

"Sounds great. You won't get us lost in the swamps, will you?"

"Maybe. Would that bother you?" Sammy stepped forward and looked down at me with eyes as black as the heart of the swamp.

"I've been lost in the swamp with you before, Sammy Egret. I trust you to get me home."

"I'll see what I can do."

I thought I knew what he could do, and I was eager to be proven right.

CHAPTER 10

———

Today was the day the inspector was coming to the new shop site to examine our wiring and plumbing. Since the previous owner had built the store only a little over a year before on the site of our original business, I wasn't worried about getting a passing grade.

I stopped at the store early, around seven in the morning, to see how the drywall installation and painting was proceeding. Madeleine and I had taken turns checking the work to make certain the crew continued to make progress for several days in a row, but neither of us had had time in the past few days to drop by. With all the donuts and pizza we'd fed the crew to keep them on the job and happy, I was certain the walls would be up by now and perhaps even painted. Or maybe the project was finished. Wouldn't that be wonderful? New walls and no alligator.

I unlocked the door and reached around to flip the switch that turned on the lights. I flipped, but nothing happened. *Uh-oh*. Maybe the workers had pulled the circuit breaker. I fumbled my way through the store to the side door where the breaker box was located. Sure enough, the breaker had been pulled.

I flipped it back and reached for the wall switch by that exit to turn on the overhead lights. The light glared off an empty space—no walls or studs up to begin the room divisions. Not a sign of any work done beyond the flooring and the installation of larger windows in the store front, which had been complete when I'd inspected the space after our gator visitor. I extracted the cell from my purse and hit the number for the owner of the company. My call went to voicemail.

"This is Eve Appel. Where are you? And where have you been? The work should be almost done by now. Call me."

"Anyone here?" called a voice from the front door.

"Back here. Come on in."

Just my luck. Not my construction guys, but someone carrying a clipboard.

"Ms. Appel?"

I nodded and waved him in.

"I'm Mark Stevens, here to inspect your wiring and plumbing."

"Right." Thank goodness I'd found the breaker and got the lights on. Before I could count myself lucky, the lights flickered and went out.

"There must be a short somewhere." My cell chirped a tune. "Hello." I listened to the voice at the other end. Thank goodness. It was the construction company owner. What he told me was anything but good.

"You've got some major electrical issues. The lights kept going on and off, so we shut off the electricity at the breaker."

Yeah, so I'd discovered.

"And there's more. Have you checked the bathroom?"

Now what? I walked over to the bathroom door and pulled it open. A dirty puddle of water stood on the floor.

"There's water all over the floor," I said.

"Yeah, we caught that leak before it took over the entire building. Shut off the water at the main pipe coming into the store."

"Why didn't you call me?"

""Because I knew you'd do what you're doing right now. Yell at me. Besides, it's not my problem anymore. We're off the job."

"This can all be fixed. I'm sure it's minor stuff, isn't it?"

"Minor or not," the company owner said, "I'm just not interested in doing any more work for you and your partner. I'll send you the bill for what we've done so far." He disconnected.

I looked around the space. A bill for what they'd accomplished since last I'd checked? Turned off the electricity and located a puddle of water?

Mr. Stevens tapped me on the shoulder. "I heard you say the problems were minor. And considering how new this place is, I'd expect that too. But the work is all inferior. The wiring is not up to code. In fact, I'm surprised the place didn't catch on fire."

I sighed and clenched my teeth in frustration. The woman from whom we'd purchased the place had left us with a real lemon, and knowing the kind of person she was, I was certain she was aware what she was selling us. I wanted to get her on the phone and give her what's what, but I expected she didn't have her own cellphone in the prison cell she now occupied.

"I'll send you a list of what you'll need to do before I can pass on this place." Mr. Stevens nodded to me and left.

I backed up against the wall and slid down to the floor. That's where Nappi found me.

"Ready to go, Eve?" he asked.

I'd almost forgotten that he and I were on our way to West Palm to visit the company that arranged mud bog events in the area. Our plan was to act as if we were land owners interested in having an event on our property. We hoped to find out who else in the area was in contention for these events. Maybe Jenny had beaten someone out for the honor of holding the event, and they'd been angry enough to want her dead.

"Have a seat," I gestured to the dirty floor next to me.

"I'll pass. So. Bad news?" Nappi asked.

I told him about the construction crew and the wiring and plumbing problems.

"I guess you didn't do an inspection before you bought the property?"

I shook my head. "It was new construction, so neither the bank nor I felt it was necessary. I should have known better. How can I tell Madeleine?"

"Leave it for now. Let's do a little snooping in West Palm. After that, I'll buy you lunch."

"Nope."

Nappi looked surprised. "I thought poking your nose where it's not wanted and food would be an unbeatable combination for you."

"I haven't had breakfast yet."

"Okay then, let's go to the Sabal Bay Diner for some of their waffles."

I thought about that. It was enough to make me want to get out of here.

I reached out my hand. "Help up?" I asked. Nappi smiled and lifted me to my feet, then continued to hold my hand. From the compassion in his eyes, I knew what he was about to say.

"Oh, no. You are not loaning us the money to fix those problems and do the renovations here. Forget it. You've already done enough for us. Besides, even if I okayed it, Madeleine would throw a fit. As would David. She loves you in her own way, but she's opposed to borrowing money from you. You know that."

"Don't tell her."

"What do I say then? 'We needed extra money, and I just happened to find a sack of it on the sidewalk, so we're covered.' "

He shrugged.

"Besides, I'm sure I'll come up with something."

"You always do." He put his arm around my shoulder, and we headed for the door.

"Oops. Back in a jiff." I ran toward the side exit and flipped the breaker. "We don't need a fire."

"We don't?" Nappi lifted one eyebrow and flashed me a wry grin.

I gave him a playful punch on the shoulder. "I guess the old mob-thinking creeps back in now and then."

He continued to grin at me.

The diner was crowded with the early morning breakfast crowd—store owners who stopped in before they opened their businesses and the usual complement of cowboys and a few winter visitors who had discovered from the locals how good the cooking was. When we walked in, the buzz of conversation stopped, all eyes on us. I knew they weren't staring because of my appearance. Everyone in this town was used to my stilettos, punk hairdo, and designer jeans and shirt. Even Nappi's smooth looks weren't drawing their attention. The hostility in their gazes said I had crossed a line, the line between what they tolerated in Yankee behavior and what they considered unforgiveable and insensitive.

"C'mon, Nappi. I don't think I'm as hungry as I thought."

But Nappi had other ideas. He pushed me toward the only open booth and shoved me into it. On our way past everyone, he nodded and smiled, then turned around when we were seated and said, "Best darn place this side of the Georgia line for waffles, wouldn't you say?"

He'd spoken to the individual in the booth behind us. She nodded and replied, "Oh, yeah."

"Howdy, Miss Eve," said the waitress. "Who's the good-looking fella?"

I introduced Nappi as another Yankee who had converted from hash browns to grits and who adored red eye gravy. She took that as a hint and headed back toward the kitchen.

Nappi leaned over the table and spoke in my ear. "I know what grits are, but I never heard of red eye gravy."

"You're going to love it." I hoped he did or we would be thrown out on our ears.

My singing cowboy friend, Jay Cassidy's foreman Antoine, got up from his table and headed my way.

"Okay, Antoine, I know what you're going to say. Jay already told me where he thought I went wrong."

"Scootch over." Antoine slid into the seat beside me.

"I work for Jay and I like it, so I'm going to keep my mouth shut on that demonstration thing. I know you'd never hurt Jenny regardless of the two of you not seeing eye to eye. Jay and I have our differences. I think Jay knows he was a little rough on you the other night. Just let it go. He'll come around."

"Will the other folks come around too?" Nappi asked.

"Some … probably not most of them. Times are tough around here. People are land poor. Many of them can't afford to graze cattle and supplement with hay from out of state. Then some of you come in here and accuse us of mishandling our own land." Antoine got up, tipped his hat to me and left.

"People here are in the same bind as small farmers in upstate New York and Pennsylvania," Nappi said. "There was no money in milking a small herd so they sold off and now they're sitting on land they can't farm. Then the gas companies come in and pay them to lease their land for fracking. Now they've got polluted ground water, cancer, and even earthquakes."

"So what do those poor farmers do for money?" I asked.

"That's the point, isn't it? Just like the ranchers around here, just like Jenny."

"So you're saying Madeleine and I were wrong?"

"Not at all. We have to find a way for people to live on land we don't destroy."

I looked at him expectantly.

"I don't have the answer, but maybe part of it is that we talk to one another."

"Do more than simply protest, you mean."

"Especially if someone is murdered."

I tapped my spoon on the tabletop. "I don't think the protest caused Jenny's murder."

"No, but the strong feelings on both sides aren't going to make it any easier to find the killer."

NAPPI AND I were silent on the drive to West Palm. He'd given me a lot to think about—not that I didn't already know that protests could only raise awareness of an issue, not lead to its resolution. That was one of the reasons Madeleine and I got out of the demonstration business up North. There never seemed to be any follow-up after the banners and signs were stowed back in the garages and people dispersed to take up their everyday lives. The protest itself was a high, a great feeling of shared commitment, but after that, most protesters left others to search out avenues for change.

I broke the silence as we turned off the turnpike onto Okeechobee Boulevard and headed into the city. "I wonder what happens to the land where the mud bog race is held once the event is over."

Nappi glanced at me, then turned his attention back to the busy road. "I don't know. Maybe that's something to look into."

"Maybe that's something we should ask the company that runs these venues."

THE ANSWER TO what happened after the mud bog trucks left and the company collected their rather large share of the profits was simple, according to Mr. Johnson, president of Mudder Events, Ltd.

"It's their land. They can do what they want with it, can't they?" The man across the desk from us yawned, showing yellowed teeth. I got the impression that yellow was the color of his personality too. He seemed to care for nothing other than the bottom line. "We tell the ranchers what we want and inspect the property before we sign with them and just before the event to make sure it's the way we want it. Then we collect our share of the take and leave. What did you expect us to do?"

I shifted forward in my chair. "Well, maybe help clean up

the place and turn it back into wetlands for plant and animal habitat. Put it back the way it was."

Nappi placed a restraining hand on my knee, but I was fired up.

"Don't you feel at all responsible for mucking up all that vegetation and running off the animals that depend upon it for their food and breeding area?"

"If you mean am I worried that we destroyed an alligator's nest, then no. They're ugly creatures, don't you think? Better to get rid of as many as we can. The other animals, like birds and turtles, can move somewhere else."

"There will soon be no 'somewhere else' for them to move to. Except maybe the area where you live, Mr. Johnson. How would you like that, huh? A big ol' alligator swimming around in your pool, building a nest on your patio." I'd stood up and begun gesturing with my arms. Johnson moved his chair back and away from me.

"Are you threatening me, Ms. Appel? I thought you were here to make a deal?"

Nappi pulled me back down into my chair. "We're here to see if it might be possible to use our property for the races."

Johnson calmed down a bit. "You've got some competition in your area. We only run one or two mud bog events each year in any region. It doesn't pay us or the land owner to saturate a county with mud bog races." He began to shuffle through the papers on his desk. "Let's see here. We've vetted all these places near yours to make certain they're appropriate for our needs. It looks like there are three you'd be in competition with." He read off the names. "You know any of these ranchers?"

I recognized two of the names. One was Shelley's neighbor, Clay Archer. No surprise there, since swampy land stretched across both the McCleary and Archer properties. The other familiar name was my old friend Jay Cassidy. No wonder he was so steamed at my taking part in the protest. If things had turned out differently, Madeleine and I might have been protesting on his land. I was disappointed in Jay. He was a big rancher with many head of cattle, and he was breeding ponies for polo. The man was rolling in money. What did he need a mud bog racing event for? I needed to talk with Jay. And the others.

"Like our neighbors, we want to make money, Mr. Johnson," I said, "though not at the cost of our land. We understand we have to ready the property for the event, but we want a company who's willing to work with us after the event."

"Well, it seems damn stupid to set up a mud bog race then put the property back the way it was. What if you want to rent it out again in a few months?"

"Crop rotation," I said.

"Huh?" Johnson said.

"Never mind. I think we have what we need." I got up and moved toward the door. Nappi followed.

In the elevator, Nappi said, "I don't think he liked you. The chances of his doing business with us is nil."

"Well, we really don't want to do business with him anyway, do we? And don't be so sure about that. If we put in a low bid to host the event, I bet he would jump at it."

Nappi shrugged. "Well, we know now that his company is the only one doing mud bog racing in our area, and we got the names of potential competitors for hosting the event. I guess the visit was worth it." He paid the fee to the garage attendant, and we pulled back out onto the street.

"Oh, I think we got more than that. That slimy jerk gave me an idea for how to hold the events *and* honor the land."

Out of the corner of my eye, I watched a knowing smile light up his face. "Crop rotation," he said.

I nodded.

"That didn't take long. What did you bring back?" Madeleine hung several new consignment shirts on a round in the motor home, rolled her eyes at me, and gestured with her head toward the dressing room at the back of the rig.

I was so wrapped up in what we'd found that I missed the significance of her signal.

"Nothing, but we found out who else was interested in hosting the mud bog races other than Jenny."

The door to the dressing room opened, and Frida walked out. "So you found out those names, did you? I guess you figured I wouldn't tell you, and you were right. You just can't stay out of my murder investigations, can you, Eve? And I guess you've pulled everyone around you into this one too."

Well, not everyone. Not Alex.

There was no point in pleading innocent. Frida was right. Grandy, Nappi, Madeleine, and I had formed an unofficial posse in this case and formed a plan of action. Anyway, why not? After all, Madeleine and I were suspects in Jenny's murder.

"Jenny's ex-fiancé called the station and told my boss that I sent you out there to pump him for information because the two of you were "old friends." I didn't know that, did I, Eve? And I certainly didn't send you out there to interrogate him. We're only days into this case and already you're making trouble for me." Frida walked up to the counter with several dresses in her hand.

"Find something you like, Detective?" Madeleine said in her sweetest voice.

"I did. I shouldn't do this, but I'm buying this dress. Fits like it was made for me. How can I turn it down? But I'm not fooled for a minute by you, missy. You're as bad as your partner here. And please don't offer me a ten percent discount on merchandise because I'm an officer of the law. Under the circumstances, it'll sound like a bribe."

"It does look nice on you, Frida," said Grandy.

"Don't you bounce your silver curls at me, lady. You're the one who taught them all this snoopy-snoop stuff."

Frida paid her money, grabbed the bag with her dress in it, and exited the shop. I could hear the tires of her cruiser spit gravel as she sped out of the market parking lot.

"She's hot," said Grandy.

"You could have warned me, Madeleine," I said.

"I did. I nodded toward the dressing room."

"Oh, big signal."

"Girls, girls," interrupted Nappi, "let's not fight among ourselves."

"What's going on here?" Madeleine's husband David stepped into the shop.

"Oh, nothing," Madeleine said.

David's gaze traveled from Nappi, to Madeleine, to Grandy, and finally settled on me. I do not do innocent looks well, not even when I have nothing to be guilty about.

"What the hell. You might as well know too. Everyone else does," I said.

Madeleine shook her head in warning.

I ignored this one too and told David what Nappi and I had been up to.

He said nothing for a minute; then a red flush began to work its way up his face.

He pinned Madeleine with his look. "Okay, that's it. From now on, you'll stay at home, out of the line of fire, out of Eve's interference in this case."

Madeleine stepped up to David and stood toe to toe with him. "David Wilson, as much as I love you, you are truly an idiot. You should know better than to think Eve is the only one who likes a bit of snooping and who has ideas about how to do it. Do not order me around."

Her blue eyes were snapping with displeasure. I knew from experience it was better not to cross little Eve Boudreau when she went for something.

"But you're pregnant," he said.

"Right, but being pregnant doesn't mean I'm giving up my life. I still have some say in what I do."

He was smart enough to keep any comeback to himself. I was certain this argument would be continued at home.

"Well, look at the time!" I pointed at my watch. "I'll take over the shop this afternoon. You go on home, Madeleine, and, uh, do whatever."

"First I want to stop by the other shop and see how the renovations are coming. I want to reconsider the paint color we picked for the walls. And wasn't the inspector supposed to be here today?"

"About that, "I said, and told her the story.

CHAPTER 11

—

MADELEINE TOOK THE news about the shop quite well. Or maybe she was just speechless with shock. Anyway, she asked David to take her straight home. If she weren't pregnant, I think she might have imbibed a strong gin and tonic.

It was up to me to find someone, *anyone* in the area who was willing to do electrical and plumbing work for two Yankee women—murder suspects as well as demonstrators against individual property use. That wouldn't be easy. And there was wall construction and painting and sanding the floors and …. And I had to find the money to pay them to boot. I felt a headache coming on, and after I'd called all the firms in the phone book with no luck, it bloomed into a doozie.

"I can help," offered Nappi. "I can call in someone from West Palm."

"I can do that, but there isn't a chance in hell I could afford them."

"I …" Nappi began.

I held up my finger for him to stop talking. "I know what you're going to say. We've had this conversation before. Forget it. Anyway, it's time to shut down for the day. I need a break.

And a Scotch." I gazed out of the windows of the rig toward the sun, now low in the afternoon sky.

"I can give Grandy a ride home if you have something else to do," Nappi offered.

"I'm cooking tonight, chicken piccata. What do you say to that, Nappi?" Grandy collected her purse and started down the steps of the rig.

"Great, but I promised Jerry I would have dinner with him."

Grandy sighed. "Invite him. If he's stuffing his face, we won't have to listen to him say something ridiculous or moan about his lack of a love life."

I thought about the chicken piccata, my favorite. The mental image of tender chicken cutlets and flavorful lemon sauce made me drool. But then so did the thought of a canoe ride in the swamps with Sammy.

I would have preferred a quiet dinner with only Grandy and me. I was already anticipating moonlight reflecting off the water's surface with just Sammy and me, some frogs, a gator or two, and no one else to bother our solitude. Surely my dreamy expression would give me away to everyone at the table. And I wasn't ready to share my plans for the evening yet.

Nappi said he'd take Grandy food shopping while I snugged up the rig for the night.

My cell rang minutes after they left.

It was Sammy. "You haven't changed your mind about spending time under the moon with me, have you?"

"I can hardly wait."

"How was your day?"

I told him about the problems in the shop and my visit with Nappi to the mud bog racing firm in West Palm.

"I think I may be able to help you with the shop."

"You're not going to offer me money too, are you?"

I heard laughter on the other end. "I have no money, you know that, but I do have connections."

"I don't think you're in any better position to convince the construction firms around here to work for me than I am."

"Not most of the firms, but I do have pull with one of them. It's a Miccosukee company run by a relative of mine."

"Bonded and licensed?" I asked.

"Of course. And he's very reasonable. If I asked, he might be willing to work on the weekend and charge you the usual rate, not overtime."

"Oh, Sammy. You are a real peach."

There was silence for a moment.

"You think I'm sweet and juicy?" He sounded puzzled.

"Yes, you are."

"Well, you seem to think I should view that as a positive, so I will. I'll pick you up around eight at your house."

"Why don't I meet you at the airboat landing?"

Again there was a pause.

"Okay. Fine. At the landing."

Did Sammy think I didn't want anyone to know we were getting together? He was correct, of course. I wasn't ready to talk about him to anyone. Not just yet.

We disconnected. I hummed a happy little tune and leaned against the passenger side window of the rig. A flash of something in the late afternoon sunlight caught my eye, and I leaned to my right to get a better look.

The window exploded and glass flew into the rig.

I slid to the floor. What was happening? My cell was still in my hand, a very bloody hand as it turned out.

FRIDA SHOWED UP minutes after I called her.

"You're covered in blood. I called the EMTs, and they'll be here soon. Meantime let's make sure you didn't sever an artery or something."

I could hear the sirens of the emergency vehicles on the road. I looked down at my arms and saw tiny shards of glass twinkling on my bloody skin. Then I caught my reflection in the full-length mirror. Every place my skin was exposed, blood bloomed and tiny pieces of glass stuck out. My fingers reached out to extract one of the splinters and suddenly the room turned green. The next thing I knew, someone was leaning over me, telling me to breathe into a mask he held over my nose.

I struggled to sit up. Frida and the EMT lifted me into a sitting position on the rig's couch.

"I called Grandy and got her while she was in the store. She'll be right here and follow the ambulance to the hospital. Meantime I'm going to take a look around to see if I can determine where that shot came from." Frida patted me on the shoulder. "I'll be right back. Lonnie here will take good care of you."

I looked up at Lonnie, the EMT tending me. He gave me a wink of encouragement. "I think these are all superficial cuts. No arteries involved. You may need a few stitches, that's all."

I looked at my arms and hands again, but this time, the world around me didn't spin, and it retained its normal non-green color.

"Maybe I don't need to go to the hospital."

Lonnie and another EMT shifted me from the couch to a stretcher.

"Trust me, Eve honey, it's better to get everything checked out." Grandy's face came into view.

"Naw, I'm fine. Just a few scratches. See?" I raised up off the stretcher and tried to show her my arm. My world clouded over again—tinged with yellowish green and viewed through tunnel vision.

Lonnie nodded. "Told ya. Lie back. We'll even turn on the siren for you."

"DO YOU KNOW I've spent more time in the emergency room here in the few years I've been in Sabal Bay than the rest of my life put together?" I said to the emergency room doctor stitching up a cut on my cheek.

"I, for one, am not surprised by that," said Grandy. "You have a way of attracting trouble in these parts."

"What time is it?" I asked.

"Around seven thirty," said Grandy. "Why? You got a date or something?"

From the look on her face, I could tell she wasn't kidding. She did think I had a date. Now how could she know that? She was as psychic as Grandfather Egret. The mere thought of the man must have caused a ripple in Sabal Bay's energy field because Grandfather floated into my line of sight. Behind him stood Sammy. I knew I hadn't taken a blow to the head, so why was I hallucinating?

"Eve, my dear, I hope this is nothing serious." Grandfather Egret reached out and took my hand, massaging it with a tender touch. No, I was not imagining his presence. He was here and very real. And Sammy stood beside him with a look of concern on his face.

I signaled to Grandfather Egret and whispered in his ear, "I'm wearing the talisman you gave me. I'm never without it." I showed him the tiny rawhide bag on a leather thong around my neck. My good luck charm from Grandfather had gotten me through some difficult times, including a run-in with the Russian mob.

To everyone else I said, "I'm just fine. Nothing serious at all."

"You would be wrong. It is serious," said Frida. "Someone took a shot at you. I found a thirty-thirty cartridge on the ground over by the produce stand."

"The most common rifle used around here," added Sammy. "Almost every cowboy carries a thirty-thirty. Good for feral hogs, rattlers, and—"

"People," Frida broke in.

"Couldn't it have been a mistake? Someone firing a rifle at something else?" I asked.

Frida wrinkled her nose. "What? Like the booth selling used books or the rug shop in the market? I don't think so. There's nothing but your rig on that trajectory. I'm just guessing here, but knowing you, Eve, I've got to think that your snooping around in Jenny's death has made someone very uncomfortable. Why can't you just leave things to the professionals?" She sounded both aggravated and worried.

The aggravation I got. I had been snooping, but I just couldn't help myself, especially since both Madeleine and I had caught the attention of the authorities looking into Jenny's murder, thanks to our presence at the demonstration. I was confident Frida didn't suspect us—she knew better—but she had to do her job, and her boss, as well as others in the police department, weren't so convinced of our innocence. I was just itching to get us off the hook and find the bastard who killed Jenny. I was touched by Frida's concern for my safety. If I were any kind of a friend, I would back off out of respect for her work and to reassure her of my well-being.

Tell that to my impulsive and nosy nature.

The doctor working on my face cleared his throat. "Uh, could all of you step back while I finish up here?" He signaled to a nurse, who moved my visitors out of the area and drew a curtain around the doctor and me.

"There we go," he said, cutting off the suture thread. "That shouldn't leave a scar, or maybe only a small one."

For a moment I envisioned myself with a slash across my cheek and wondered if it would lend my face character or simply scare the bejesus out of anyone who met me. No scar? Maybe that was just as well. I kind of thought my face had enough character already.

Several minutes later, carrying a paper with instructions on post-emergency care and several prescriptions for drugs to aid in the healing process, I walked out of my snug little cubicle to find my support group hovering near the entrance of the emergency room. They greeted me with a collective gasp.

"What's wrong?" I asked.

"Don't worry, folks," said my doctor. "That's mostly

disinfectant. But she's going to be a mess of cuts, purple, black and yellow bruises, and stitches for a while. Then she'll be back to her old self."

"Great. Back to her old, interfering self," muttered Frida as she headed for her SUV.

Grandy put her arms around me. "Let's get you home to bed."

I shook my head. "I was promised a ride in a canoe in the moonlight, and I want my ride." My voice grew louder and shriller at the end of my sentence, and I felt close to tears. I was far from back to my old self.

"A ride on the water? Now? She must be in shock," said Nappi. "Let's get her home."

"No way!" I didn't so much say this as shout it. Everyone in the emergency room turned their heads toward my group.

Sammy stepped forward. "Let me handle this for now." He took my arm and led me out of the hospital toward his truck. "I'll get her back home in good shape. Don't worry," he called back to Grandy and Nappi.

Grandfather Egret slid into the backseat of their truck while Sammy helped me into the passenger seat.

As we drove toward the lake, Grandfather leaned forward and said into my ear, "I'm glad you put trust in your talisman, but beware, Eve. It cannot ward off all harm, and I feel there are particularly strong forces of destruction around you now."

"I heard you, Grandfather," said Sammy, "and I think you're wasting your breath. She doesn't do 'beware Eve' at all. Haven't you noticed?" Sammy wasn't smiling.

At Grandfather's house, Sammy helped me out of the truck, while Grandfather headed down the path to his place. Sammy and I walked to the canal, where the canoe was pulled up on the bank. He settled me into the craft and pushed off, then dipped his paddle into the canal. The boat cut through the water soundlessly.

I trailed my fingers through the ripples and watched the shore go by. Silhouetted by the moon, a silver wading bird, probably a snowy egret, trod with careful steps at the edge of the reeds. It was bright enough for me to see the head of a turtle poke through the surface, then submerge as we slid past.

I broke the silence. "Thank you. This was what I needed."

"Grandfather knew it would be. He said it would heal you better than all those medicines."

I looked down and was surprised to see I still held my release papers and prescriptions. "Maybe I should just toss these all away then."

Sammy laughed. "Grandfather did not say this was a replacement for white medicine. He just said it was better."

"Do you think Grandfather knows that we … well, you know."

"Grandfather says we remind him of my mother and father."

A chill moved through me. "I'm really bad at commitment stuff, Sammy. I can't promise you anything."

Sammy stopped paddling for a minute and used the paddle like a rudder to direct us toward the shore. We slid onto the soft bank. "Do you feel like a short walk?"

I nodded. He took my hand and led me into the dense vegetation, along a path that felt somewhat familiar.

My heart did a quick skip. "Sammy … it's the place where we spent our night in the swamp, when those two brothers dumped us here, hoping we'd get lost. You told me you didn't know where we were, but that we weren't really lost."

"I don't want you to promise me anything, Eve. I'll take my chances. We'll find our way from here just like we did when we first came to this place."

Sammy didn't want a promise now, but I knew someday he would. What would I say to him then?

We continued to walk along the path, our way lit by the shimmering moonlight. Soon the vegetation gave way to a clearing in which sat an old shack. One side of the structure stood, its roof supported by a palm tree that had grown up through the floor. The corner post had long since fallen and decayed on the floor. The other side of the roof had fallen in. It was just as I remembered it that night we used it for our temporary housing. This night, however, instead of offering me rainwater from an old metal pan, Sammy led me to the center of the shack where a cloth lay on the floor, and on it, a picnic basket. Sammy opened the basket to reveal two slices of pound cake. He took out a thermos and poured us each cups of a hot, steaming liquid. From the chocolaty smell, I knew it was cocoa.

"I wanted this to be dessert, but I guess given your earlier adventure, it will have to serve as your dinner." Sammy handed me a cup and offered me a piece of the cake.

Saliva collected in my mouth. "Oh, yummy, just what I need." I hadn't realized how hungry I was.

I stuffed the cake into my mouth and took a sip of cocoa, burning my lips on the hot liquid.

"Slow down, Eve. We have plenty of time here. All night if you want."

"Are you going to eat the rest of your cake?" I asked.

"I tell you we can stay here all night and all you want to know is if you can eat my cake too? You are a true romantic."

"I'm sorry, but I'm starved."

Sammy split the remainder of his slice with me, and we leaned back on the blanket and looked up into the stars.

"Tell me about your parents," I said. "I know your mother is coming to visit soon. You talk about her a little, but you never say anything about your father."

"My father left us when I was a kid."

"And where is he now?" I asked.

Again Sammy dodged the question by acting as if he hadn't heard it. Instead he began to talk about his mother.

"She was a white woman who moved here from the North just like you did, Eve. She was young, and as Grandfather tells it, kind of wild. When she met my father, I guess she thought it would be an adventure to be married to a Native American.

She found it hard to fit in with our people. Once I was born, she tried for my sake. She could see how I loved the life among my cousins and the other tribe members, and she could see how I loved this place, this land of the Big Lake. Grandfather knew she was unhappy here, so he told her she should go find a place for herself, that he would raise me. I missed her. I still miss her. She is truly an unusual woman. Where I am calm water, she is fire. You are like her, Eve."

He took my hand, brought it to his lips and breathed on it, so gently I thought at first it was the wind fluttering across my hand. Soon I knew it was the breath of his soul weaving into my fingertips.

"And because you are like her, you are the fire that burns me, that can warm me. You can also sear me and wound me."

"Sammy, I don't know what to say."

He leaned away from me and looked into my face. A smile slowly curved his lips. "I can hardly believe it. I thought for certain you'd have something sassy to say to make this moment light. I didn't intend for this night to be a torment for us."

"Then if I am fire and you water, perhaps you can bank these fires into harmless but toasty embers."

"That's better."

I wanted to reward the revealing of his most precious thoughts with a smile, but it turned into a yawn.

"I'm so sorry. I guess the day has caught up with me."

"And I'm being insensitive. This was meant to heal you, not to aggravate your injuries." He gathered up our picnic items, took my hand, and pulled me up. "Let's go, gal."

"I guess this wasn't the night you had planned." I leaned on his arm as we walked the path back to the canoe. Each step was like lifting a concrete block.

"Not exactly as I'd planned, but any night alone with you is fine with me. There will be other times for us to mix fire and water."

I must have drifted off in the canoe on the ride back to

Grandfather Egret's. I only remember being lifted out of the canoe and into Sammy's truck, then carried into my house and put to bed.

Later that night I woke up, the cuts and abrasions from the glass nagging me out of sleep. The night with Sammy was not what I'd anticipated, but perhaps it was even more than I could have imagined.

What did my feelings for Sammy mean? He had reached deeper into my soul than any other man. He complemented me with his understanding and acceptance of the person I was. That was something I'd never had in a relationship with a man. It was a new aspect of loving. And I was betting it wasn't the only surprise I'd find with Sammy.

I didn't want to hurt Alex, but I now understood better why I couldn't commit to him. As much as we had chemistry together, it wasn't enduring, and his love for me wasn't enough to sustain me. Alex loved his vision of me, not the me Sammy knew me to be—the me Sammy loved. I hoped Alex would come to understand that my caring for him wasn't what he needed either.

I smiled to myself and fell back asleep, wondering why Sammy had ducked all my questions about his father.

CHAPTER 12

——

I AWOKE AND rolled over to check the time on my bedside clock, which read six a.m. Out my bedroom window, the sun was coming up over the eastern horizon. It cast light on the clouds sitting low on the coast and turned the sky indigo and coral. Too early to get up. I rolled over for another hour of sleep, but my eyes popped open, and I stared at the ceiling.

Frida told me the medical examiner was working on Jenny's body—or her head and what they'd found of her body near the Egret's airboat business—so the funeral couldn't be scheduled for several more days. I was convinced that Darrel had put pressure on Shelley to re-up the contract for the mud bog races. Darrel and I seemed to be in a tug of war for Shelley's allegiance. What other of her decisions would he influence? What right did I have to try to convince her my opinion should count more?

A voice sounding very much like my friend Frida's whispered in my ear, "It's not your problem, Eve. Stay out of it."

I couldn't do that.

What the hell. Maybe it wasn't too early to get up. I threw off my covers, intending to make a run for the bathroom. I put one foot on the floor, followed by the other, the usual way I got out of bed. This time I fell onto the floor. My body wasn't interested in obeying my brain. *Someone took a shot at you yesterday and you spent part of last night in the hospital and then went for a canoe ride with Sammy.*

Mmmm. I could still taste chocolate on my lips.

I slowly got my feet under me and grabbed the side of the mattress to steady myself. Pulling my body back onto the bed, I sat for a moment, then eased myself to a standing position. There.

When I glanced into the mirror over the dresser, I was horrified to see a skinny, wounded animal looking back at me. What the …? Some swamp creature had crawled into my room. Nope. Not true. That thing reflected in the glass was covered with cuts, bruises turning all the colors I'd never considered wearing, and was sporting a set of eyes that used to be blue, I was sure, but now were so bloodshot they looked like sunset on the lake when a storm was brewing—deep carmine with streaks so dark they looked black. That wounded creature was me.

There was a soft tap on my bedroom door.

Grandy entered, carrying a tray of food. "Are you up for a little breakfast, Eve?"

"Food? No, I couldn't eat a bite." Or could I? The smell of bacon and eggs infiltrated my nostrils and journeyed into my stomach, triggering a growl of welcome. Of course I was hungry. I'd only had a slice and a half of cake last night—not enough food to keep this gal moving. Besides, I had wounds to heal.

As if she had read my mind, Grandy said, "Don't forget to take your meds. I got them filled for you late last night."

Between her and Grandfather Egret, my thoughts were not my own.

"Did you enjoy your evening with Sammy?"

"It was a canoe ride. And dessert. That's all." I wondered if I sounded defensive.

"Sure it was." She winked at me as she closed the door.

I ate everything on the plate and considered going for more but decided against it. Instead I tried out my legs again. They worked well enough to get me into the bathroom and under a hot shower. The water made my cuts sting in places, but I didn't care. It made me feel human once more.

Grandy poked her head into the bathroom as I was toweling off.

"There's a call from Sammy. I think you'd better take it."

Grandy was usually so protective of me that I was surprised she'd let anyone intrude, even Sammy.

"Here." She handed me the phone.

"The police arrived several minutes ago with a search warrant. It's very specific. They want to search Grandfather's shed out back."

"What's in there?" I asked.

"Well, you know how he's always making items peculiar to tribal customs?"

I thought of the talisman he'd made me.

"Yes."

"So it's filled with leather, feathers, animal skeletons, animal teeth—material he uses to create items we use in our rituals and celebrations, dances, festivals."

"Call Attorney Lightwind. I'll be right there. Is Frida with them?"

"Yes, but why do we need a lawyer? Do we have to let them search?"

"You know, Sammy, one of your most sterling qualities is that you avoid watching too much television. However, I've learned some things from all those cop shows you avoid, and one of them is that you do need to let them search if it's a legal warrant."

"But—"

"And that's about all I know about the law in this case. So call Attorney Lightwind, and do it now."

I disconnected and tossed the phone to Grandy. As I threw on some clothes, I told her what Sammy said.

"You need to take it easy, Eve. You shouldn't be running out to the Egrets' place."

"Are you coming along or what?"

"You're in no condition to drive," said Grandy.

I dashed into the kitchen, grabbed my keys off the counter and tossed them to Grandy. She burned rubber out of the drive and passed every truck hauling oranges and horse trailers. A motor home about to turn onto the highway from a secondary road in front of us reconsidered when Grandy blew the horn and shook her fist. She fishtailed into the airboat business drive and raced down the dirt driveway to Grandfather's house.

"Where did you learn to drive like that?" I asked.

"I watched you."

As I jumped out of the car, I saw two officers leading Grandfather down the front steps of his porch. He was handcuffed. Attorney Lightwind pulled up behind me.

"Do something!" I grabbed Mr. Lightwind by his arm and tugged him toward the house.

"Everything will be fine, Ms. Appel. Let me talk with my client before they put him in the patrol car."

The two officers allowed the attorney to speak with Grandfather, but they pushed Grandy and me out of the way.

"Why am I not surprised to see you here?" Frida stood behind me, a look of disgust on her face.

"Why am I surprised to see you party to this … this *stupidity*?" I knew the arrest was not Frida's responsibility but I was so distraught and angry I needed someone to blame. Who better than my good friend who had the misfortune at this moment to be part of the police department?

"She doesn't mean that." Grandy put her arm around my waist. Her touch had the intended effect. My anger was still there, but I felt awful about what I'd said to Frida.

"Sorry. I'm just so …." I dropped my arms to my sides and held out my hands to her.

Frida's stern look softened. "I know. But trust me, will you? We're doing this by the book, and he has his attorney to guide him through."

I watched as a familiar figure approached. Where Frida might have been able to appeal to me, I knew she'd have little luck with Sammy.

"The tribe will hear of this. It's nothing more than harassment. You're going to have a dandy lawsuit on your hands."

I'd never seen Sammy so furious. Standing next to him, I felt as if he were a lit rocket about to go off.

"You were right there when we found it. You know how incriminating that is." Frida stood her ground, standing toe to toe with Sammy.

"Found what?" I asked.

"You tell her. I've got work to do." Frida turned her back on Sammy and strode toward several officers who were carrying what looked like evidence bags.

"What did they find?" I asked, this time of Sammy.

"A hand. They claim it's Jenny McCleary's. They also confiscated Grandfather's rifle from the shed."

I gulped down the bile that rose in my throat. "Why were they looking in Grandfather's shed, not the house or the business?" *Why so specific a place?*

Grandy had pushed her way toward the officers when we first arrived. Now she retreated from the authorities and approached Sammy and me. "I overheard someone say the police got a tip early this morning to look in the shed."

"And how would they know it was Jenny's hand? It could be anybody's." As the words exited my mouth, I realized what I was saying. It didn't have to be the hand of anyone we knew. It was a hand that only could have come from a person who was now probably deceased. That meant Grandfather would be considered a killer no matter whom it belonged to.

"I've got to go, Eve. I need to be at the police station with Grandfather." Sammy ran toward his truck.

"They probably won't let you see him!" I yelled as he retreated. He didn't hear me.

"Sammy's pretty steamed at me." Frida stood beside me once more. "I can understand his concern and his anger." She looked at me. "And yours too."

"Thanks. It must be difficult being a cop in a town this small. Everyone is either a friend or the friend of a friend."

"You want to be helpful, Eve?"

I nodded.

"Did Jenny wear any rings on her fingers?"

I thought back to the last day I saw Jenny. She was a kind of no-nonsense gal, but I did recall seeing an engraved gold band she wore on the pinky finger of her right hand. You couldn't miss it; it was so large that it would have looked odd on anyone except Jenny, who had large hands and long, thick fingers. I shared this detail with Frida.

"That's exactly what the person making the phone call said to us this morning."

My mouth dropped open. "You can't possibly think I called you."

"I know better, but my boss wonders if the call was from someone who knew something … something that would get him or her off our suspect list."

I felt relieved that Frida knew I'd never make such a call.

"So it was a woman who called?"

"I can't tell you that."

"But surely everyone can see it was a ploy to falsely implicate Grandfather Egret. Your boss must know that. And what's with the rifle?"

"We've determined the cause of death wasn't because she was decapitated."

I shuddered, remembering Jenny's head in my hands. "What was it then?" I asked.

"Gunshot wound to the back. I think the decapitation was simply to slow the police down in the investigation. The killer must have thought an alligator would be interested in the body. As it turns out, one was." Frida's glance traveled to the canal behind Grandfather Egret's house.

"All my boss will want to believe once he knows what we've found is that the ring was our murder victim's, and it was in the possession of Mr. Egret. The rifle would be additional evidence. You do the math."

"You know that rifle didn't kill Jenny. Won't anyone try to track down who made the call?"

Frida's shoulders slumped, and she shook her head. "That's not the way things work from our point of view. We've got our suspect in custody."

It looked to me as if proving Grandfather Egret's innocence might depend on finding out who made that call.

I CONTACTED MADELEINE to make certain she could handle the store today.

"I'll be in later," I told her and gave her no other explanation. I didn't want to load additional worry on her.

My thinking that tracing the phone call was the key to proving Grandfather's innocence was correct, according to Attorney Lightwind, but it took me an hour to track him down so I could confirm my suspicions.

First Grandy and I had gone to the police department, only to be told we couldn't see Grandfather. We waited around for Frida in hopes of extracting more information, but she was, according to the desk officer, "busy in her office." *Well, you can't hide from me forever*, I thought. You'll have to come out to use the bathroom. After an hour of stewing and getting nothing out of anyone in the department, I collapsed on a bench in disgust.

Then Grandy had a revelation. "They probably moved him out the back and transported him to the county jail. That's why we haven't seen anybody here—not Frida, not Sammy, not Mr. Lightwind."

I shot an angry look at the desk sergeant. "You could have at least been honest and told us he wasn't here."

"You didn't ask." He grinned and turned his attention once more to the papers in front of him.

At the county jail, Mr. Lightwind was just stepping out of the building as I drove up.

I rushed over to him. "Frida told me earlier that the police aren't interested in who made that call."

"No, they aren't. They were delighted when they called in Shelley McCleary and she ID'd the ring as her mother's. I've never seen the authorities complete paperwork and shuffle a man off to jail as quickly as they did Mr. Egret. Tracking down that caller will be our business. We'll need a good PI to handle the job."

I knew just the man. Maybe Alex wasn't so keen on me just now, but he liked Grandfather Egret and he would be offended if I didn't at least tell him we needed help.

"I know someone who's a pretty good PI, and—"

Mr. Lightwind interrupted me. "Alex Montgomery. Yes, Mr. Napolitani told me the two of you were friends. I know his work. I've hired him a time or two to do investigations for me."

I called Alex on my cell.

He answered immediately. "Eve? What's up?" His voice sounded friendly, filled with expectation.

"Grandfather Egret is in trouble, and we could use your help. I mean, Attorney Lightwind who's representing Grandfather said you'd done some work for him in the past. Could you free yourself from your other cases?"

I heard silence on the other end of the call. "Alex. Are you there?"

"Of course I'll help in any way I can. I'm between jobs now, and I'm returning to Sabal Bay as we speak. What's up?"

"Let me put Mr. Lightwind on."

The last time Alex and I had been in touch was that night he proposed at the Biscuit. Our status was unclear. We should have talked about it, but neither of us had made contact. It already felt as if our relationship had shifted—and not in the direction of permanence. His involvement in Grandfather Egret's case meant we were back in touch, only not in the way I might have predicted. Now it was certain we'd be running into each other.

Mr. Lightwind ended his conversation with Alex and handed my cell back to me.

"Uh, I'm just curious. What else did Nappi tell you about Alex and me?"

Mr. Lightwind's deep-black eyes twinkled for a moment, and I thought I saw the corners of his mouth twitch as if he was suppressing a smile.

"Mr. Napolitani only said that you two are better friends at some times than at others."

True, that.

"He also said that you occasionally join Mr. Montgomery in his investigations and that Mr. Montgomery finds that very annoying."

I feigned surprise. "Alex has never told me that. In fact, on more than one occasion I saved his ass as well as uncovered significant information in a case."

"Well, then. This should be interesting." Mr. Lightwind tipped his cowboy hat to me and walked toward his car.

"Can I get in to see Mr. Egret now?" I yelled after him.

"Tomorrow." He slammed the car door and drove off.

I shuddered to think of what a night in jail might do to my dear friend.

WHEN GRANDY AND I arrived at the jail the next morning, we learned that Grandfather Egret was being arraigned and we would have to wait to see him. Sammy entered the jail only minutes after we did. In no time cars and trucks filled with tribal members entered the parking lot. Soon there were no slots left. The tribe gathered at the door but were refused entry. I could feel the mood of the crowd begin to shift from anxious to angry.

Attorney Lightwind stepped out the door and held up his hand.

"Mr. Egret has been arraigned and charged. He asked me to convey a message to you that he is eagerly awaiting justice and that he is certain it will come quickly. He wants you all to return to your homes and prepare to welcome him back soon."

Sammy took his place next to Attorney Lightwind. He added, "I know we want justice and we want it *now*, but we must learn to be patient like Grandfather. He counts on us for his support, and we must not fail him."

There were mutterings among the people, but then the crowd began to disperse. Soon the parking lot was empty.

Sammy turned to Mr. Lightwind. "Don't let that speech fool you. I do not have the patience of Grandfather. I want to see him. Now."

"I understand, but I must abide by my client's wishes. He asked that Ms. Appel come in to see him first."

Sammy's gaze left Mr. Lightwind's face, and he fixed his eyes on me. They were as cold as black ice.

"Sammy," I said, "I'm quite certain he has a good reason."

Sammy seemed about to speak, but then he turned on his heel and strode toward his truck. "Maybe he'll want to see me tomorrow," he shot back at us, "after he's spoken to all the *important* people in his life." He started up his truck and spewed gravel as he drove from the lot.

"Mr. Egret said his grandson wouldn't like his speaking to you before he talked with Sammy," Mr. Lightwind said.

"I don't understand why he wants to see me first."

"He indicated there was something evil he needed to warn you about."

I needn't have worried about Grandfather. He appeared quite relaxed as I entered the visitors' room. He was sitting cross-legged on a chair, humming quietly a tune I recognized as a Miccosukee song he chose when he was at peace.

He reached for my hand and looked into my eyes. "Something came to me last night, and I knew I had to warn you about it right away."

I stopped him from speaking further. "Grandfather, you must know how angry, how hurt Sammy is because you asked to see me first. What could be so important that you would ask to see me before Sammy?"

"Sammy is safe, but you are not. I should have talked with you about this before, but I wasn't sure then. Now I am. The new shop you're having worked on has been invaded by bad spirits. I could help get rid of them, but I'm trapped here and I don't know for how long. You must not enter that shop until I can chase out the bad."

"Don't be silly, Grandfather. It's only the plumbing and the electrical. I'm sure Sammy's relative's company will fix it. No problem."

I was so wrong about that, and all because I dismissed his warnings, like I always did when people who cared about me gave me good advice.

I don't listen well, if at all. Maybe I should work on that.

CHAPTER 13

—

GRANDY AND I got to our rig late in the morning. When we drove up, I noticed that the side window had been replaced by plywood. I assumed that was Nappi's doing.

Last night I'd called Madeleine to tell her I might be late, so she'd offered to open in the morning. She greeted me by asking how my wounds were healing, and after I told her "Well," she proceeded to chew me out for not letting her know about Grandfather Egret's arrest.

"I'm sorry, Madeleine. I didn't want to worry you more."

"I worry when I don't hear from you hourly," she said in a snippy tone. "Sorry. I don't mean to be so, you know, so—"

"Bitchy?" I suggested, then wished I hadn't said anything.

Madeleine took my comment better than I expected. "Right."

I felt a twinge of guilt. Madeleine had been minding the shop too often while I ran around tracking down clues and getting myself shot at. To placate my guilty conscience, I reflected that her color was once more peaches and cream, and that she looked better than she had for days. That was only partially true. Her brow was furrowed, a sign of her concern for Grandfather. As it turned out she was worried about more than that.

"How is Grandfather?" she asked.

"Better than all of us, I expect. Mr. Lightwind has hired Alex to find out who made that phone call to the police."

"That should add some drama to this case," she observed.

Grandy nodded.

"Look, you two, Alex understands this is purely professional. I'm certain we can both behave as friends for the time being."

I got skeptical looks in return.

"How is Sammy reacting to all this?" asked Madeleine.

I chose to ignore the part of her question I knew she really wanted answered and addressed Sammy's response to Grandfather's arrest.

"Sammy is furious, as are many of the tribe members. They see his arrest as blatant racism on the part of the police department. You can't blame them for feeling that way. They're afraid that arresting a Miccosukee will end the murder investigation. Mr. Lightwind agrees. He told me he knew the police weren't interested in determining who made that damning call." I didn't share with them Grandfather's insistence on talking with me rather than Sammy this morning.

The arrival of Sammy meant I didn't have to.

He pulled up in his truck, jumped out, and bounded up the steps of the rig. "What the hell was that all about, Eve? My own grandfather prefers his first visit after being arrested to be with you."

Though I understood Sammy's anger, it was misplaced, and I felt my own grow as he continued to blame me for what happened.

Before I could lash out, Grandy stepped in. "Sammy, my boy, calm down. Your grandfather had a reason for what he did. It was his decision to talk with Eve and not her fault. Get your butt back to that jail and do it now or you'll regret not coming through for him."

Sammy stopped talking and looked at Grandy in astonishment. His size and demeanor usually cowed people, including me at times, but Grandy had not backed down. She knew there was more hurt than anger in his outburst.

My cell rang. I answered and listened to the caller.

"It's for you, Sammy." I held out the phone.

He talked for only a short while, then ended the call. "I have to go." He started to leave, then turned back to me. "Sorry, Eve."

"What was that all about?" asked Madeleine.

"Grandfather Egret sent a message to Sammy through Mr. Lightwind. I think he told Sammy the same thing you did, Grandy: 'Get your butt back here.' "

"I like that man. Nappi couldn't have recommended a better lawyer for this case," Grandy said.

Madeleine nodded enthusiastically. I was about to make a comment to her about how wrong she had been about Nappi, but Grandy placed a restraining hand on my arm. This ability to read my mind on the part of both Grandy and Grandfather Egret was robbing me of my privacy. How did they do that? What kind of special receivers did the two of them possess to be able to tune into the frequency of my brain waves?

"We need to talk, Eve," said Madeleine. She rolled her eyes toward the back of the rig, indicating that the conversation should be private.

We walked back to the dressing room.

"When I got here this morning, there was a crowd of people at the entrance. Several of them held up placards reading, 'Yankees keep your hands off our land.' "

How ironic. Now we protesters were the target of other protesters.

"Several of them told me they were going to boycott our shop."

"So how was business this morning after that?" I asked. I knew what the answer would be, but I had to hear it from Madeleine.

"The same as since the protest. No one showed up." Madeleine looked sad and droopy. Her entire demeanor expressed defeat.

"Don't worry about it. We'll take the rig to the coast to Stuart. We always sell well there on the weekends. We'll pick up the snowbird trade and some of our patrons from West Palm will drive over to see us. This will all blow over."

I sounded confident, but was I correct? How long would it take the people in Sabal Bay to forget? Maybe the best we could hope for was for them to forgive us our Yankee intrusion into what they saw as their business.

Alex drove up shortly after the lunch hour. He didn't stay long, only long enough to tell me he had taken the case and that he'd assured Mr. Lightwind I would not be interfering.

"Thanks a lot," I yelled at him as he strode back to his car.

To round out the day's unpleasantness, Sammy returned after visiting Grandfather and conferring with Mr. Lightwind.

"I understand you recommended Alex to Mr. Lightwind. So should I assume it's back on with you two?" He towered over me in a confrontational stance, his voice cold and clipped.

I sighed. Much as I adored Sammy and Alex, these men wanted to intrude into my life in ways I didn't like. Both of them were trying to make me feel responsible for things I had no control over. I was a curious gal. That was my nature, a special compound in my DNA. I was proud of it. I had been helpful on numerous occasions. Grandfather could verify how useful I'd been in trapping those Russian mobsters. I knew the difference between friendship and something more. I'd made that very clear to Alex. Well no, not really. We never got around to discussing exactly what our relationship was now. Maybe it only felt different to me. Maybe we did need to talk about it. As for Sammy's comments about Alex, I could only say that Alex was a damn good detective, especially when he had me to help him.

Grandy sunk her fingers into my shoulder and squeezed, a signal I should keep my cool.

I hated having Sammy angry at me, so I decided to play nice or at least as nice as I knew how.

"What we need to focus on here is getting Grandfather out of jail. Alex is the best person to help with that, don't you think? You've seen him work. Can you think of anyone better?" I reached out and touched Sammy on the arm, while looking up into his face as beseechingly as I knew how.

Sammy's eyes softened from the black of obsidian to the warm brown of milk chocolate. So compelling was his gaze that I almost forgot what we were discussing.

"You're right," he conceded. "Grandfather told me I shouldn't come here with anger in my heart. He said I'd only be using you as a scapegoat for the authorities—how wrong they were to arrest him." His eyes welled up with tears. "I love that old man. He's my life."

I pulled Sammy toward me and put my arms around his waist. "I love him, too. He has the best team working on this. He'll be out of there before you know it."

Grandy and Madeleine joined me in hugging Sammy. When we stepped back, I knew all of us felt better because we'd been able to reach out to one another. It was more than a hug of comfort. It was as if we were transferring some kind of healing energy. Looking into the eyes of the others, I knew they felt it too.

"Well," I said, clearing my throat, "I guess we'd better close up for the day."

My call to shutter the rig must have brought Madeleine's thoughts back to our business issues. The light in her eyes dimmed and her face drained of color.

"Oh, honey," I said, "I know you're worried about the business, but everything will be fine."

"Do you really think so? I think we've lost a significant portion of our clientele, and I don't know how to win them back. No one will work for us to fix up our new shop, and we can't do it ourselves. Not that it matters. Nobody will trade there either." Madeleine's earlier healthy color seemed to drain from her face.

"I told Eve I'd get her a Miccosukee company I know to do the work on the shop," Sammy said. "I just haven't had time to contact them yet."

"It doesn't matter." Madeleine looked as if she might burst into tears.

"Well, this might," said Sammy. "Grandfather told me why he wanted to speak with you, Eve."

"He warned me I was in danger."

"Yes, because he believes there is evil in that shop. He told me not to let either of you enter it until it had been cleansed of the bad spirits."

Madeleine snorted in disbelief. "Oh, please. You can't mean the place is haunted? And that's why our business is off? Don't be silly. Ghosts or evil spirits have nothing to do with it. It's our stance on the mud bog thing."

"Maybe it's related to what's happening to your business and maybe it's not. Grandfather is convinced you need someone to help you cleanse the place." Sammy looked desperate to help us, despite his own troubles. I felt grateful he was trying to cheer up Madeleine with Grandfather's theory about what was going on. The rig wasn't possessed but no one wanted to buy here either. But what the heck; it was worth a try. It was taking action instead of just feeling helpless while waiting for the business to fail. I touched the amulet around my neck. Who was to say Grandfather might not be correct? The store had been owned by a malevolent woman. Maybe her bad energy had contaminated the place.

"Come on, Madeleine. Let's give it a go," I said.

She perked up a bit. "Okay. Why not? We have nothing to lose. Now don't forget that all of you are coming by my house tonight for dinner."

"Are you sure? You've had one heck of a day. Maybe we should postpone. Grandy and I can graze in the leftovers in my fridge."

Grandy looked skeptical. "There are no leftovers in your fridge, Eve. There's pretty much nothing in there. As usual."

"So ribs at the Biscuit?" I asked.

"Absolutely not," said Madeleine, her tone insistent. "I've already made a huge pot of beef stew in my slow cooker, and I told you I planned on having you all over to help me finish up the food in my fridge before David and I move out to the house on the game ranch. If you don't come, I'll have all this food to cart over to the ranch and David and I will be eating stew for days."

"But Madeleine—" I interrupted.

She stamped her foot. "It's more than just dinner. Since I'm packing up my kitchen tomorrow, I thought you could help me tonight. If anyone spies anything in the kitchen they'd like, let me know. If I don't need it for the kitchen out at David's house, you can have it. Anything you don't take, I'll donate to the church charity shop."

No one dared refuse Madeleine's invitation, which sounded more like a command performance from an elf with attitude.

As we shuttered the rig for the night, I reviewed what I needed to do over the next few days: cleanse the shop and—since Alex insisted he didn't need my help on the case—follow the leads I had and perhaps he didn't.

Nappi came by just as we were leaving and was included in the dinner invitation.

"You heard what happened?" I asked.

He nodded.

I wiggled my finger at him to signal him outside, away from Madeleine and Grandy.

Once we were outside, I said, "I think I need to visit some of those folks Jenny beat out for the mud bog event."

Nappi shook his head. "You don't listen, do you, Eve?"

"What do you mean?"

"Alex must have told Mr. Lightwind he would keep you out of this investigation."

"Alex is not the boss of me and certainly not now that we're only friends with no benefits." To be honest, Alex had never been my boss, lust or no lust.

"If you insist upon visiting these men, then I'm coming along. If one of them is Jenny's killer, you're putting yourself in harm's way, as you so often do."

Nappi might be right, and to be honest, I hoped by telling him my plans that he would volunteer to accompany me. As for his comment about my not listening, I'd heard that just yesterday from Grandfather. So maybe it was true.

My first stop on the list of the three ranchers in competition for the races would be Jay Cassidy. I didn't consider him a suspect in Jenny's murder, but he had always been a good source of information about the ranching community in Sabal Bay. Perhaps I could mend a few fences with Jay, while coaxing him to talk about rumors on the range.

Madeleine was in fine form as she hustled around, putting the finishing touches on dinner. We all offered to help, but she shooed us onto the large porch that spanned the front of the house. We all settled in on the chairs and rockers there, sipping our drinks.

The phone rang several times; Madeleine took the calls before David could get up out of his chair.

"I think you'd better cede control to her or you'll find yourself in trouble," I told David. Looking contrite, he nodded and sat back in his chair.

Madeleine stepped out onto the porch with a wooden spoon in her hand and a frilly white apron tied around her waist. "Dinner will be a bit delayed for the sake of some guests arriving late."

"God, you look like something out of a 1950s cookbook," I observed.

Madeleine shot me a sharp look, then signaled me to come into the kitchen.

"What can I help with?"

"You can serve as referee between Alex and Sammy at dinner."

"What? Are you crazy? You invited them both? Tonight?"

"I want this whole thing settled between your two men, Eve. It's too disruptive when Grandfather Egret needs our support. So make them work it out." She shook her wooden spoon at me. I wanted to laugh at the sight, but the tenacity with which she wielded the spoon and her tone of voice forced me to comply. Best not to cross Madeleine when she's mad.

"Okay, but I'm warning you … I may not be able to control them. And why is this my problem anyway? Why can't they behave like adults?"

"I ask myself that question daily about you every time you go off chasing some clue in this case, like I'm sure you're planning to do tomorrow. Using either Grandy or Nappi or even Jerry as your accomplice."

"You're just jealous I didn't ask you to come along."

"I'm busy tending the shop and incubating right now," she spit back at me.

True, but I could see I'd hit home with my remark about her being jealous at being excluded from our snooping trips. She spun on her heel and lifted the lid to the crock pot, hiding her expression.

I came up behind her and sniffed at the food.

"Do it or no food," she said and slammed the lid back on the pot.

She knew I'd do anything for food.

"Before or after we eat?" I asked.

"Before, or you don't eat." She gave me a brilliant smile and stirred the contents of the pot.

Sammy arrived the same time as Nappi, followed five minutes later by Alex. He nodded at me from across the room, hugged Madeleine, and said hello to everyone else, including Sammy. They shook hands and exchanged some words I could not hear. Everyone was behaving, so maybe I didn't need to intervene.

Madeleine prodded me in the back. "Do it. Now."

When everyone had settled back on the porch with their drinks, I worked my way over to Alex and asked if I could have a few private words with him out in the yard. He nodded reluctantly, as if I were ruining his evening. When I approached Sammy with the same request, he smiled. "Sure."

I'd humiliated Alex in public by refusing his marriage proposal, and that was something he'd find it hard to get over. So my problem was Alex. Or was it? Sammy understood why Grandfather wanted to speak to me today before he talked with Sammy, but I knew Sammy was suspicious of Alex being around even though he'd been told Alex was working the case.

I needed Madeleine's diplomatic skills for this one, but all I had was Eve's in-your-face-whether-you-like-it-or-not approach. Honesty was worth a try.

"Look, you two. I know there's been some, um, miscommunication with respect to my, um, friendship with each of you, but I don't want my feelings for you and yours for me to create difficulties in this case. Grandfather needs us, all of us, to support him and to work any leads we have—"

"You have leads you're not telling me about, Eve? I hope you're not holding anything back, because it could have an impact on Grandfather's fate. The authorities don't have much on him, but they're happy with what they have, and they're not going to work this case beyond the evidence they've already gathered." Alex tapped his foot impatiently.

"Even Frida? I know she doesn't think Grandfather killed Jenny."

Alex swept his hand to one side and shook his head, dismissing the idea that Frida shared the assumption of Grandfather's guilt. "No, of course not. She's a savvy detective, and she knows there's more to this story. She also knows the prosecutor can't make a case with the evidence they have.

Soon her boss will see that too and have her reexamining all the evidence. In the process she may run down something important, but if her findings don't agree with the authorities' belief in Grandfather's guilt, they may be shoved to one side. So even if Frida doesn't believe Grandfather had anything to do with the murder, she's going to be of no help."

"And you can use all the help you can get," I added eagerly.

For a moment a red flush passed over Alex's face, and I thought he was about to deliver his usual stay-out-of-this-Eve lecture, but the flush quickly disappeared and was replaced by a smile—a sly smile.

"You're right. I do need help. I need someone who knows all the players in the case."

I didn't like that clever-as-a-fox look on his face. "You can't mean Jerry, can you?"

Alex snorted out a laugh. "God, no."

"So, me? You want me to help?" I practically bounced on my toes in eagerness.

The short burst of laughter now became a drawn-out roar. I thought he might drop to his knees.

"It's not that funny," I said, feeling hurt and angry.

He stopped laughing and turned to Sammy, who had been watching the two of us with an amused look on his face.

"Should we tell her?" Alex said, his voice filled with what I could only identify as satisfaction.

Sammy glanced at me, the amusement gone, a soupçon of fear marking his dark features.

What was he worried about?

"Sammy," Alex said.

"Huh?" I said.

"Sammy will be assisting me on the case."

"What!"

CHAPTER 14

—

"**Y**OU'RE NOT EATING, Eve. I thought you were starved," said Madeleine.

I picked at my stew, chased the pieces of carrot around the plate and then stabbed them with ferocity, pretending they were Alex and Sammy. So far the score was Eve 7 and the carrots mush.

While we were in the backyard, Alex told me that he had talked with Sammy shortly before they came to dinner. He knew he'd need assistance and thought Sammy, motivated as he was to free Grandfather, might be the perfect person to help in tracking down leads. Sammy correctly guessed that I wouldn't be happy with this unusual alliance. Alex had to know also. My first thought was that Alex did it to get my goat, but I knew he was professional enough to choose only the best man for the job. And he thought the best man was not a best woman—not me.

I caught Nappi staring at me across the dinner table as if he knew what I was thinking. I scowled back, and he winked. Grandy saw the exchange and smiled. Did everyone here know about the partnership between Alex and Sammy? Were they all as amused as Alex seemed to be? I wondered what Sammy thought. He never raised his eyes from his dinner to spare me a glance.

I had my work to do. At least Shelley believed I was the right person to find out who killed her mother. This thought raised my spirits so that by the time Madeleine offered lemon meringue pie for dessert, I asked for a large piece.

After we all pitched in to clear the table, I yawned and said I was ready to leave. "How about you, Grandy? You can stay if you like. I'm sure someone here will drop you off at the house. I'd stay longer but it's going to be a busy day tomorrow. I'm off to the coast to make some money."

Tomorrow I was taking Grandy with me to the Stuart Flea Market.

Grandy shook her head. "I need my beauty sleep, too." She picked up her purse, hugged everyone and stifled a yawn.

Grandy and I said our good nights. Everyone but Nappi seemed content to remain for a while to let their dinners digest.

I grabbed Nappi before he could get into his car.

"Are you busy tomorrow night?"

He shook his head.

"How about we attend to some unfinished business, like we discussed?"

He agreed.

Grandy said nothing at the time, but she didn't remain silent for the entire ride home.

"What are the two of you up to?" she asked.

She'd keep bothering me until I told her what we were going to do.

"I have the names of three ranchers who were in competition with Jenny for the mud bog event. Maybe one of them didn't like being beaten out of a lot of money."

"Frida probably already questioned them, don't you think?" she said.

"Probably, but I can be very persuasive. One of them is a

friend—well, he *was* a friend until Madeleine and I took part in that protest rally. You met Jay Cassidy."

"Jay couldn't have had anything to do with Jenny's death. You know that."

"I do, but I want to mend fences if I can because—"

Grandy finished for me, "because you want to pump him for anything he might know."

"Um-hm."

"Well, don't think you and Nappi are going to leave me home alone to watch television while the two of you are out having fun."

"But—"

"There are nothing but reruns on. It'll give me the opportunity to wear my midnight-blue warm-up suit. It makes me nearly invisible at night."

"We're not going to be doing any breaking and entering, just talking with people."

"You never know. Then I can go?"

I looked at Grandy's round, sweet face and knew I couldn't refuse her a caper with Nappi and me.

WHEN GRANDY AND I got to the motor home the next morning, I found the glass in the side window had been replaced. I assumed my old pal Nappi had come through for me again. The drive to the coast down the canopy road beneath the sabal palms and the overhanging live oaks with their veils of Spanish moss was the perfect beginning to the day. The tunnel created by the trees offered a shady retreat from the brilliant sunlight, a serene and comforting journey away from the worries over Grandfather's arrest, Jenny's murder, and Madeleine and my business woes. I wished the drive would never end, that I could remain enveloped in the shadowy embrace of this leafy paradise forever.

"I wonder if they've released Jenny's body yet so that Shelley can set a date for the funeral," I mused aloud to Grandy. I had broken the tranquility of the drive for both of us by my intrusive question.

Grandy sighed and shrugged. "Give her a call after we've set up."

The shade of the canopy was broken by a stretch of sunlit road ahead. I pushed harder on the accelerator. We needed an infusion of money into our business, the sooner the better.

After parking in our assigned spot next to other vendors in temporary locations at the rear of the rows of buildings that housed merchants who rented permanent shop space, I set up my folding chair and punched Shelley's number into my cell. A man answered after the first ring.

Oh, no.

"Darrel?" I asked.

"Who's this?"

I didn't want to tell him. He hadn't been very receptive to my friendship with Shelley.

"A friend of hers. Is she around?"

"What friend?"

Oh, crap.

"Uh, Amy from high school."

"Just a minute."

I heard voices and noise in the background, then Shelley's voice came on the line.

"Amy, I can't believe you called. I haven't heard from you in months."

Now that was a real shot in the dark. Shelley actually had a friend named Amy.

"No, really. It's Eve. I was just making a joke."

"Oh." Shelley sounded disappointed.

"How are you doing?"

"I don't know if I should talk to you. You're friends with that Miccosukee who killed my mother."

"You must know that's not true."

I heard Darrel say, "Who is that? Really. Tell me."

I couldn't quite hear Shelley's reply. She whispered into the phone, "I gotta talk to you." She sounded confused and anxious.

"Sure. What about?"

"Hang up. Now," Darrel said in the background, then there was silence on the line.

"Hello, hello. Anyone there?" I said.

"That damn idiot," I said to Grandy after I disconnected.

"What's going on?'

"Darrel's intruding again. He wouldn't let Shelley talk to me. And she seemed almost desperate to tell me something."

I called her number again, but the call went to voicemail. I left her a message to call me, then called again to let her know I'd be back in town this evening. I wasn't able to leave the second message because the system indicated that the phone had been turned off. What the hell was going on? I was worried enough about Shelley that I decided I'd have to put off my visit with Jay Cassidy and the other land owners interested in mud bog racing until later this evening or even tomorrow. I was about to let Nappi know our night sleuthing was postponed when I decided it wouldn't be a bad idea to show up at Shelley's with reinforcements: Nappi and Grandy, the dynamic duo of threat and mothering. They might appeal to Darrel's better nature, assuming he had one.

I hurriedly parked the rig in its usual slot in our flea market and then made a quick call to Madeleine.

"We sold well today," I said. "I told you we would."

"That's wonderful, but our original plan for this consignment shop was to locate in Sabal Bay and sell used designer clothes to the women of rural Florida. Now we're just selling those clothes to tourists on the coast. What happens when the season is over and the snowbirds go back north?"

Madeleine was right. We had to find a way to get back our local clientele.

"I'm working on that tonight." I still planned to visit Jay Cassidy to try to smooth things over using him as my contact with the residents of Sabal Bay. But first I had to see what was going on with Shelley. Darrel wouldn't hurt her. Or would he?

Nappi, Grandy, and I grabbed burgers for dinner at a local fast food place and ate in the car as I drove to the McCleary ranch.

Jenny's car sat in the drive, but there was no sign of Darrel's beater. Maybe Shelley was alone.

The three of us approached the house, and I rapped on the front door. I waited a minute and pounded louder. No noise from inside, although I had noticed a light burning in the kitchen window when we pulled up.

"Shelley? It's Eve! Are you in there?" By now I was worried something might happened to her. Grandy must have shared my concern.

"So now do we break down the door?" she asked.

At that moment I heard footsteps from inside the house. The door opened a crack and Shelley peeked out.

"Oh, good. It *is* you. I thought maybe it was the cops again. I don't want to talk to them anymore."

"Can we come in? You've met my grandmother and my friend Nappi, haven't you?"

As Shelley opened the door to let us in, Nappi stepped in front of me, and in his usual gentlemanly manner, took Shelley's hand. "I hope you don't mind our intrusion, but Eve was concerned about you. I trust you are well." He made a tiny bow over her hand, then flashed her one of his winning toothy smiles.

"Oh, I, um, oh, thank you." Shelley returned his smile.

"Darrel here?" I looked around the room expecting his weaselly face to appear.

"No, he's off with his friends tonight. Come in. There's not much in the house, but I could make us some instant coffee."

"We just had dinner," said Grandy. "We're fine. Is it okay if we sit for a while?'

"Of course. Where are my manners?" She gestured to the

sofa and chair in the living room, but she remained standing near the door as if intending to bolt if the conversation went the wrong way.

"I dropped by because you sounded upset on the phone today. You said you needed to talk with me?"

Shelley's gaze traveled from me to Grandy to Nappi. Maybe I shouldn't have brought them. She seemed uncomfortable in their presence.

"I guess I just wanted to touch bases with you now that the police have found my mother's murderer."

"I don't think that's it at all. And I don't think you believe Mr. Egret was the killer."

"Oh yes, I do. Darrel said—"

I stopped her by holding up my hand. "I don't give a pile of 'possum poop what Darrel said. And if the police really have arrested your mother's killer, why don't you want to talk to them? You should be feeling grateful and relieved."

Shelley's eyes widened in fear, and I knew it wasn't my harsh words that had frightened her. She had grown up with a strong, opinionated mother, a no-nonsense woman she could count on. She might not always have liked her mother's way or shared her beliefs, but she trusted Jenny to tell her the truth, at least the truth as she saw it. Shelley knew I was the same kind of woman. I hoped she also knew I was on her side. I wouldn't desert her.

"This is awful." She dropped her head into her hands and began to sob.

Moving from her seat on the couch, Grandy went over to Shelley, put her arms around the young woman, and patted her back as you would a baby needing to be burped. "There, there," Grandy crooned.

The comforting worked. Shelley stopped sobbing. Grandy rummaged around in her purse and handed her a tissue. Shelley wiped her eyes.

"Darrel would kill me if he knew I was telling you this."

"He can go kiss a toad for all I care," I said, waving away Darrel's concern.

"Darrel's the only friend I have," said Shelley. She began to cry again.

Grandy reached out to hug her once more.

Enough of this coddling. "Buck up, woman. Darrel is not your only friend. Why do you think we're here?"

Grandy looked stunned at my insensitivity.

"Eve." Grandy used that tone of voice that said I'd done something socially inept.

I ignored her. "Why don't you and Nappi get us some of that instant coffee? I think we could all use a pick-me-up."

With Grandy and Nappi off raiding Shelley's cupboards, I had Shelley to myself.

"Okay, no more of this nonsense. You have something you want to tell me, despite what your so-called friend Darrel might think. Blow your nose and wipe the snot off your face and tell me. Now."

"You know Mom's ring?"

"The one found among Grandfather Egret's collection in his work area? You identified it as your mother's, right?"

"It was Mom's ring. I've no doubt of that."

"So what's the problem?"

She hesitated.

"Shelley. Talk to me."

Before she could say anything, her only friend Darrel slammed through the door.

"What's the bitch doing here?" he yelled.

Nappi appeared in the kitchen doorway.

"And the goon's here." Darrel nodded at Nappi.

I caught a look of annoyance flit across Nappi's face, but I knew Darrel hadn't a clue what it signified. Nappi crossed the room and confronted Darrel. "We met once before. That time you were also without manners. I'm sure your mother taught you some, but perhaps you need a refresher course." There was no inkling of threat in Nappi's voice unless you counted smooth as the satin lining of a coffin a threat.

Darrel snorted. He caught sight of Grandy, who held a tray of cups and the coffee pot. "I think you two," Darrel nodded at Nappi and me, "should take Betty Crocker here and skedaddle."

"Says who?" I asked.

"C'mon in, fellas!" Darrel yelled out the door. Three young men, larger and more muscular than Darrel, shoved into the living room.

"Says me and my friends here. We was just saying to one another about how bored we were tonight with nothin' to do. And here you are. Let's take 'em out into the swamps and leave 'em."

"No thanks," I said. "I've already done that once, and it was with better company than you."

Darrel signaled to the guys behind him, who moved toward Nappi. Darrel grabbed my arm. I slugged him in the side of the head, a move he was not expecting. It certainly had an effect, but not the one I hoped for. Instead of yelling "ow" and dropping to the floor, he tried to shove me backwards, but I held on and pulled him with me. The couch broke our fall for a moment; then we tumbled onto the carpet.

Out of the corner of my eye, I saw Nappi grab the guy in the lead, spin him around, pin his arm behind his back and rest the barrel of a very large pistol against the guy's temple.

Darrel had managed to get on top of me and was trying to land a punch on my head and shoulders. Through deft arm movements, I managed to block him with surprising effectiveness.

"Darrel, stop it!" shouted Shelley. He ignored her and continued his surprisingly inept attack. I could smell the fumes rising off him and was just glad he wasn't in top form. Or I might have a concussion by now.

"Darrel, let her go! Or this guy is going to shoot me," said the fellow Nappi had grabbed.

"No. Don't be silly," said Nappi, smoothly, "I intend to shoot all of you."

I didn't know how long I could keep up my defense. My arms were getting battered pretty good. He actually managed to land a blow to the side of my head, though he seemed to be pulling his punches now as if he knew the jig was up. His companions stumbled over one another trying to back up. Nappi let go of the one he was holding and threw him toward the others.

"Get off her, Darrel," said Nappi.

Darrel paused with his fist raised. Before it could connect again, Nappi strode across the room and placed the pistol's barrel against his head. "Like you and your companions, I get a little bored down here. I don't think I've killed anyone for several days."

Darrel uncoiled his arm and dropped his hand onto my shoulder. He patted it and stood up. "Just a joke. No hard feelings. Okay?"

For a minute, I thought Nappi might shoot Darrel. His eyes were so cold I feared I'd never see the warmth in them again.

Nappi took the gun away from Darrel's head. "Go. Now."

I'd never seen a guy jump up so fast. I hardly had time to blink before I heard a car engine start and the sound of spitting gravel as the tires spun out.

Nappi reached down to help me off the floor. "Are you okay? Do we need to get you to the hospital?"

"I think I'm fine." The thought of another visit to the emergency room made me certain a few Band-Aids, several Scotches, and a lie-down in my bed would do the trick.

Shelley looked as if she was about to cry again.

"Don't you dare," I said, "at least not until you tell me what you were going to say before Darrel and company interrupted."

Grandy had placed the tray she was carrying on the coffee table. "Are you sure you're okay, Eve?" She touched my head.

"Ow. Leave it alone. It's my head, the hardest part of my body. I've taken worse blows there."

"Well, at least sit down," she said.

Nappi helped me to the couch.

I patted the cushion next to me. "Sit here, Shelley. And talk to me."

She gulped. "About the ring they found at Grandfather Egret's … I'm pretty sure it was sitting on Mom's bedroom bureau after they found her dead that morning in the mud bog."

CHAPTER 15

——

"WHY DIDN'T YOU tell the police that the ring was on your mother's bureau after her murder?" I said, anger boiling up inside me.

"They didn't ask. They wanted me to identify it, and I said it was Mom's. I tried to explain, but they didn't seem interested, so I kind of … shut up." Tears ran down Shelley's face once more. This gal was producing enough water to raise the level of the lake by several inches.

"Well, now you're going to open up. Call Frida." I held out the phone.

"I told Darrel, but he said it didn't matter, that the old Indian could have broken in here and taken the ring."

Nappi stepped forward to confront Shelley. "Didn't you think with Darrel around here all the time that it was just as likely he took the ring?"

Shelley stopped sobbing, and her eyes widened in disbelief. "Darrel wouldn't do such a thing."

"Yeah, right. Like Darrel would never come in here and threaten us and beat the hell out of Eve." Grandy leaned over and shook Shelley. "What is wrong with you anyway? That man is bad news, and he's trying to run your life by intimidating you. Your mother was a strong woman, and she raised you to be one too. Now do the right thing."

Shelley sensed she had no allies in this room for her support of Darrel. She took the phone and punched in the number I gave her.

Shelley explained why she was calling, listened intently for a minute, then hung up.

"Detective Frida said she'd relay the message to her captain. She'll be here as soon as she can.

Twenty minutes later Frida arrived. I thought she would be almost as excited as we were to learn about Jenny's ring, but her face was glum.

"Tell me again." Frida took out her notebook and scribbled notes as Shelley repeated her story about the ring.

"So when will Grandfather be released?" I asked. "This does mean he didn't kill her."

"My captain and the assistant DA, who happened to be in the office when I told them about the ring, said it didn't make any difference."

"What? Why not?" I was stunned.

"Because Grandfather could have stolen the ring out of the house. Jenny's body was found near his airboat business. They think the motive for the murder was anger over how she was using her land."

"So he just wandered into the house and took the ring? Why would he do such a stupid thing?" I could feel the fury begin to work its way up my body. I thought the top of my head might blow off.

"See," said Shelley, "Darrel was right about Mr. Egret stealing the ring."

Frida's gaze slid from me to Shelley. "What?"

"Darrel said the Indian broke in here and stole it," Shelley said.

Frida didn't reply, but the look on her face gave away what

she was thinking. Like me, she figured it was more likely Darrel took it.

"Does Mr. Lightwind know about this development?" I asked.

"He will, just as soon as you tell him." Frida flipped her notebook shut and stood. "Got a minute, Eve? Could you walk me to my car?"

"This is all bull slobber, you know," I told Frida once we were outside.

"I know, I know. But I thought I'd slip you some good news— something I'm not supposed to tell anyone."

"So why tell me?"

"As angry as you are, I know you'll do something foolish. You always do, so maybe this bit of information will convince you we're doing our job, and you'll back off a bit. But you can't pass this on to anyone."

I wasn't certain if she'd insulted me or complimented me. "So?"

"The hand we found wasn't Jenny's."

"Do you know who it belonged to yet?"

"I kind of knew when I got a good look at it."

"Are you some kind of an expert on dead hands, or is another person missing one?"

"It's a fake. A good one."

My mouth dropped open.

"There's more. It's likely the body was moved to the location near the airboat business."

"Moved? How do you figure?" I asked.

"This is kind of gross for a civilian's ears, but you're a big girl with some, uh, dead-body experience. The body was in bad shape for only being outside and in the water for a few hours."

"Explain. Frida. I don't understand what you mean by 'in bad shape.'"

"An alligator had been working on it. We believe Jenny was killed near the mud bog event, shot in the back, and her head severed from her body by a blow from a large knife, probably a machete. There's no way to confirm that's where she was killed because by the time we searched the area, it was torn up by all those huge trucks. We do know the murder took place early in the morning before the event. We also speculate from the tooth marks on the body that a gator, probably upset by all the activity around his hole, dragged the body off to a location less disturbed by humans. You know how gators like to bury their kill before they dine."

I gulped. That was more than I needed to know. The hamburger in my stomach threatened to come up.

"We did find a machete when we searched Grandfather Egret's shed for the hand, but it turned out not to be the one used to sever the head from the body." Frida paused in her story, looking up at me for my reaction, but then hurried on, "So the captain and the DA's office are keeping the information under wraps, thinking we might be able to track down where the hand was purchased—probably some costume store on the coast. Linc's over there now looking into it. And we don't have ballistics back on Grandfather's rifle."

I batted the rifle issue away as if swatting a fly. "And you have to know buying a fake hand is not something Grandfather would do. It was deliberately planted by someone too stupid to know the cops would figure it out quickly."

"Maybe so," said Frida, "but we're hoping that finding the person who bought the hand will give us a lead on the killer."

"You don't think that lead will point at Grandfather any more than I do. This is ridiculous." I felt my anger ramp up again. Frida must have noticed it too.

"Let it go for now, Eve. We'll sort this out soon."

"You already know this hand prank wasn't something the killer did, don't you? You said it yourself. Either someone was intimidated into doing it or paid to do it." A name crossed my mind. *Darrel.* Frida smiled as if she shared the same thought.

"He may not be a killer, but he might know something. He and Shelley are tight, right?" Frida asked.

I sighed. Who knew if Shelley would forgive Darrel for his attack on me tonight? He seemed to be able to twist things around in such a way that she believed he was only defending her.

"You're thinking he might confide in her?" I asked.

Frida nodded. "Maybe. She likes you, Eve. You plunged in and helped her when she had no one. You could find out what Darrel said to her. You're good at wheedling information out of people."

"Wheedling?"

"Well, you know what I mean. People seem to confide in you."

Taking Frida's comment as a compliment, I nodded in agreement.

Maybe I wouldn't have to "wheedle" anything out of Shelley. If Nappi, Grandy, and I talked with those ranchers interested in mud bog racing tonight, I might have some leads into Jenny's murder and know if Darrel was connected to it or if he was simply a very bad boy with a lousy sense of humor.

I walked back into the house with a plan.

SINCE WE WERE right next door to Clay Archer's property, and he was one of the ranchers who had expressed interest in a mud bog event, his ranch was our first stop. I told Shelley we were paying a visit to the men interested in mud bog events.

"Yeah, Mom told me he looked into the mud bog event. We both thought that was kind of odd. The man runs about a thousand head of cattle on his property. He's one of the wealthiest ranchers in this county, so why would he be interested in mud bog racing? That's money to us poor folks, but not to him."

I had mixed feelings about Clay Archer. He certainly was handsome, and he could be charming, yet in my few brief encounters with him, I'd observed that he had an unpleasant edge. Or was it simply that he didn't like me and my stance on mud bog racing, and I found that unacceptable? I'd give him a chance tonight to change his mind about me, and in the process perhaps determine if he had reason to kill Jenny.

"I guess Mr. Archer has been through a lot lately," Shelley said.

"Oh?" I was interested in any background I could get on these ranchers. Perhaps Shelley might have some information that would help me see Mr. Archer in a clearer light.

"His wife left him last year. He's got no kids, so he's there all alone. Mom felt sorry for him, so she took to inviting him over for dinner every now and then. Of course, that stopped when she got engaged. I thought for a while he was sweet on Mom." There was a hesitancy in Shelley's voice.

"Maybe he was the one you heard arguing with your mom? Maybe a kind of lovers' spat?"

"I don't know. Maybe." She shrugged.

Hmm. Was he sweet enough to feel jilted? Maybe Jenny reconsidered Archer's attentions and dumped George. Archer had money and George did not, and if Archer found out he was being used for his money, then …. But Shelley said nothing about Jenny taking up with Archer after she ended the engagement. My line of reasoning was a stretch, with little to support it. Shelley looked as if she had more to say, but she dropped her glance and turned away.

I had a lot of questions for Mr. Archer.

I wondered at the wisdom of leaving Shelley alone again, but what could we do? Take her with us? This was her home, and if she chose to let Darrel back into her life, I couldn't stop her. Maybe tonight's events had knocked some sense into her. Anyhow, I doubted Darrel would attempt to return this evening. He'd be too worried about encountering Nappi again. Shelley promised to lock up when we left and not open the door to anyone other than the police. Or me.

*

ARCHER HAD COMPANY when we pulled up to his house. A car sat in the drive, a racy little Porsche convertible. For a brief moment I was jealous, but then I considered the repair bills on such a vehicle and was grateful for my Mustang. I had barely planted my feet on his front walk when I heard shouting from inside.

"It doesn't belong to you, and that's final." A tall woman with red hair a darker shade than Madeleine's slammed open the front door. Under other circumstances, I might have found her features beautiful, but at the moment they were ugly, distorted by anger. Archer stood in the hallway behind her, reaching out in a gesture of supplication.

"It was Daddy's, and now it's mine," the woman hissed.

She rushed down the steps and pushed past me, throwing herself into the driver's seat and laying rubber as she sped out of the drive.

"That's no way to treat a classy car like that," I said to Archer. He frowned when he saw me, but my remark must have caught him off guard because the scowl was replaced by a grin and then by laughter.

"Ms. Appel, to what do I owe this visit?" His laughter stopped when he caught sight of Nappi and Grandy getting out of the car behind me.

I introduced them, and since I wasn't certain his good will toward me would hold up for long, I decided to get right to the point.

"How keen were you to get that contract for the mud bog event?"

He shrugged. "Not very. Not upset that Jenny got it, so if you're asking if I killed her, the answer is why would I?" He gestured toward the large herd of cattle grazing on his property.

"So why even look into the possibility?"

"It was my wife's idea. I thought it was an unnecessary intrusion into the way we were using the property, but she insisted we find some way to utilize the swampy area near Jenny's land. Audra—that's my wife—doesn't like to see potential go untapped."

I'd been thinking Jenny was murdered by a man, but could a woman have done her in? Decapitated her? Audra was as tall as Jenny.

Archer wrinkled his brow in disbelief. "If you're thinking Audra might have killed Jenny, you're off the mark. Audra lost interest in the mud bog idea, like she loses interest in a lot of things."

Like she lost interest in you?

"I told your detective friend all this when she questioned me." There was that defensive edge to his voice again.

"This is a big ranch, Mr. Archer. You must need a lot of hands to work it," said Nappi, his gaze taking in the cattle as well as the house and the outbuildings.

Archer chuckled. "At one time I employed several men, but now I work it alone. If I need help, I hire temporary. I've got time on my hands now that my wife—actually my about-to-be-ex-wife—lives in Boca Raton." He hesitated, then added by way of explanation, "She used to keep me busy with charity and volunteer events. Now I spend my time with the cattle. I find them better company." Although he wore a grin, this last sentence sounded bitter.

"You must have had to sell off some of your cow ponies since you don't need all of them now," observed Nappi.

"Yep, I did. I still have three good little cracker horses left. You know about cracker horses? Their bloodlines go back to the horses the Spanish conquistadors brought over here. You interested? One of them is about to foal."

"Could be," said Nappi.

"Come this way, and I'll let you see. Ladies." He gestured us ahead of him toward one of the barns.

He flipped on the barn light and walked down toward the end stall. A chestnut mare raised her head at our approach.

"Sadie is her name."

The horse blew gently as Archer reached out and stroked her nose. Her sides bulged out, showing her pregnancy. I thought of Madeleine and worried that she was too little to manage a pregnancy.

"This gelding might interest you, Mr. Napolitani. He's a clever little cow pony, but he rides like a dream. He just needs a firm hand. He's probably not a good horse for a woman, unless she can command him. He's picky about who holds the reins. He can read hesitancy and will give you a ride you'll never forget if you let him."

The gelding's ears went back. I knew just enough about horses to keep my hands away from his teeth.

"Maybe you could handle him, Ms. Appel. I hear you're not one to back down from a challenge."

I shook my head. "Horses and me, we're not a good match. One did save my life once, however, so I have a soft spot in my heart for her."

"Sounds like there's a story there," Archer said.

Before I could reply, Grandy said, "I might try a ride on this fella sometime." We hadn't noticed her approach the gelding and begin stroking his nose and neck. The horse seemed to like it.

"You, Grandy?" I laughed.

"I rode almost every day when I was in Connecticut. Don't you remember, Eve?"

I had forgotten that when I was growing up in Connecticut Grandy was friends with a woman and her husband who ran a riding stable. Grandy had tried to get me interested, but my tastes ran more to cheerleading, basketball, and hanging with Madeleine, and as I grew into my teen and young adult years, shopping and fashion. I knew Grandy spent time at the stables, but I didn't consider that she might have been doing more than chatting with her friends.

"I even tried a little jumping," she said. "I'm too plump for that now, but I'd love to come out and ride this guy sometime, maybe consider buying him if he's for sale."

This was too much for me to wrap my mind around. The image of Nappi, fedora and silk suit, mounted on a cow pony accompanied by my chubby grandmother, white curls blowing in the breeze as they wrangled a herd of cattle, was more than I could handle.

"What would Max think? Where would you keep a horse on your boat?" I asked.

"We're not going to run that boat forever, Eve," Grandy replied. "We'd like to buy some land, maybe around here where you are. Get a few horses."

Now my mind's eye added Grandy's husband Max to the picture: a man who looked like Ernest Hemingway—white beard and stocky build—sitting in the saddle with his short, sunburned legs wrapped around his mount. I shook my head.

"It looks like you'd better learn to get along with horses, Ms. Appel, or your friends and relatives will leave you in the dust, so to speak." Archer smiled at me. I was beginning to like him a bit more than I had the evening at the Biscuit he told me to mind my own business.

Grandy and Archer talked a bit more about horses. Nappi said he was interested in the other horse in the barn, another gelding.

"Give me a call and you can come out and ride," said Archer.

Back at my car, Archer shook hands goodbye with me and said, "I apologize for my rudeness before. Perhaps we could start over."

"That would be nice," I said.

"I'll give you a call. We could have coffee."

Driving away from Archer's ranch, I mulled over the conversation. I was beginning to change my mind about Clay Archer as a possible murder suspect when Nappi said, "There's something odd about that situation. It's as if he's selling off his ranch."

"He's downsizing now that he has time on his hands," I said.

"Is he? Maybe," Nappi replied.

I looked over at him, but he said nothing else.

"Where to now?" asked Grandy.

"Let's stop at Jay Cassidy's place. He's the second name on the mud bog list I recognized. So while we're examining possible suspects—" I began, but was interrupted by Grandy.

"And setting up coffee dates with admirers …."

"And gathering information pertinent to this case," I continued, ignoring her. "And who acted interested in buying a horse, anyway? You two."

"We *are* interested in buying horses. Those were wonderful animals," Grandy and Nappi said in unison.

I snorted in derision. "Right. Now let's see what Jay has to say about mud bog racing. And try to keep your feigned interest in horses under control 'cuz he's got lots of them."

As we headed toward Jay's place, I realized that the most direct route was to skirt the western edge of Sabal Bay.

"Tom Riley, the other rancher interested in the bog-racing event, has his small ranch near here. Let's pay him a quick visit. It's on our way to Jay's."

I saw the driveway to the ranch on my right, up ahead, but I also spied something else—a For Sale sign at the turn-off to the Riley ranch. As I pulled off into the drive, my lights caught the "sold" sticker pasted across the sign. The gate across the drive was closed, and no lights shone from the house.

"It looks like Mr. Riley isn't in residence any longer," Nappi said.

"This is a dead end. We'll ask Jay about Riley and get the story." I backed into the road and turned around.

JAY'S HOUSE STOOD back from the road, as did most of the ranch houses in this area, but the drive leading to Jay's place was more impressive than most around here. Live oaks lined both sides, and the large single-story ranch house perched on a small rise, unusual for the area. The change in elevation was surely not natural, but it directed the eye to where the architect wanted it to go—the wide veranda running the length of the front. I'd been here several times before, but the place still impressed me with its simple, understated classiness. Like Clay Archer, Jay once had a wife who left him. I wondered what it was about ranch life, ideal on the face of it, that resulted in so many marital split-ups. Or was my sample somehow skewed?

Jay's black SUV was parked in front of the house. As we drove up, the entryway light came on, and Jay emerged from the door. The light silhouetted his lean figure and created russet highlights in his brown hair.

I waved at him as we got out of the car. He didn't acknowledge my greeting. *Not good.* Was Jay still angry at me for the stand I took on mud bog racing?

"I see you brought reinforcements," he said, stepping off the porch step and confronting us before we got to the house. "Knowing you, I assume you're doing your own investigation into Jenny's murder."

Jay knew my snoopy nature well. He and his foreman Antoine had helped me when I was searching for the person who killed a West Palm matron found on the floor in one of the dressing rooms in our consignment shop.

"I'm trying to help out a friend of mine who's in jail for a crime he didn't commit," I said.

"That Miccosukee, Mr. Egret," Jay said.

"You're not one of those folks who would make him guilty because of his race, are you?"

I watched his face darken in the porch light. "You know me better than that, Eve."

"Do I? I thought you were my friend, regardless of my political views."

"And I thought you knew better than to step on my toes."

Grandy moved in front of me. "Your toes? No one stepped on your toes, Mr. Cassidy. Eve was executing her right of public assembly."

Jan might have been willing to be nasty with me, but he wasn't used to confronting a woman who looked as if her picture belonged on a cake-mix box.

He chose to ignore her and addressed his words to me. "I don't like your views, Eve. You're a Yankee who's interfering with the peoples' right to use their land in any way they want."

"You need to get over thinking of me as an outsider. I may have been at one time, but now I'm as much a part of this community as you are."

"It was Jenny's right to set up mud bog races on her private property. Listen, Eve, the people around here love the life they have." He crossed his arms over his chest.

"You love this land. I get that. And that's why I'm trying to make certain this area stays the way it is, untouched by overzealous developers or companies trying to make money at the cost of wildlife. I get that people around here need money, too. There has to be a middle ground. I'd like to help look for that place. But for now, I'm concerned about my friend, Mr. Egret."

Jay dropped his arms and toed the dirt with his boot. "Okay, let's talk. About everything." He gestured for us to come into the house.

Jay acted almost like his old self—friendly, flirtatious, and welcoming. He offered Nappi and me Scotch and Grandy her favorite wine, a California merlot. We sat in his living room with Nappi and Grandy on his leather sectional, Jay in a distressed-leather recliner while I sunk onto the floor at Grandy's feet.

He took a sip from his Scotch while we waited for him to speak. With Archer, I had gotten right to it, but Jay seemed to be tossing something around in his mind, and I wanted him to work it through before he spoke. Besides, it was great Scotch, and I figured I could sit here sipping it all night if that was what it took to get him talking.

He set his glass on the table beside his chair, a signal he was finally ready. "I talked to Frida."

I nodded.

"I left out a few things. It's about Jenny and me."

CHAPTER 16

—

"I ASSUME YOU got my name through some ingenious deception you played on the bogger guy in West Palm. I won't ask for the details," Jay said.

I nodded, eager for him to get on with his story.

"I don't know what he told you about the selection process, but you have to apply. You submit a bid, which includes the money you're willing to put up front for the event and the amenities you can provide. You also describe your property with respect to its boggy and swampy terrain, parking facilities, electrical and water hook-up. Some venues can offer camping. The company comes out for an inspection of the property and examines your paperwork to make certain everything is in line. While you can make a lot of money doing one of these events, the bogger company takes a percentage of the fees you charge, and you have to provide the land as well as good-faith money up front in case something happens at the event."

"You mean something like a murder?" I said.

Jay gave me a disdainful look. "I mean something like you fail to provide the services you contracted for. The folks in West

Palm aren't willing to lose their shirts. They want a guaranteed return on their investment."

"Like what? It sounds like you do all the work."

"They pull permits and get the necessary insurance. They also provide the machinery to sculpt the area into a challenging bog-racing venue."

"But Jenny didn't have any money. How was she going to put up the cash needed?"

"That's where I came in. I liked Jenny. We helped each other out at times. I know she got a bad deal with her husband's death. That property he bought and bankrupted their savings with was garbage land. Mostly swampy. No pasture for grazing cattle and too expensive to fill areas for sod farming." Jay took another sip of his Scotch.

"I submitted my papers, but I had reservations about using the property for the event. Once I gave it further consideration, it seemed foolish to destroy wildlife habitat that way when I had the means to just let it sit and keep it wild. I was about to withdraw my bid when Jenny approached me. We'd talked about doing a mud bog event, so she knew of my interest. I told her I'd submitted my application but was thinking of withdrawing it. She was desperate for money, and she knew I wasn't, so she asked me what my application looked like. She wanted to put in a lower bid, ensuring she'd get the nod from the bogger company."

"Why didn't you just withdraw your bid once you let her know what it was?" Nappi asked.

"We were worried the bogger company would go looking for other bidders. We knew there were folks around here who were interested but hadn't submitted papers. If they had, Jenny wouldn't know what their bids were. We talked, and I said I'd go along with her plan. I also promised to loan her the upfront money."

"That's very generous of you, and probably illegal, too," said Nappi.

"I know, but as I said, I felt sorry for Jenny."

Nappi looked as if he didn't quite believe Jay's story.

"Okay, okay. For my generosity, Jenny promised me a cut." He set his glass down on the table with a thud. "It was stupid, I know. And I really had no intention of taking her money, other than to recover what I loaned her."

"But what about the other people interested in doing the event? They could have made their bids sweeter than either yours or Jenny's." Suddenly I saw clearly what Jenny had in mind. "She must have gone to the others interested and tried to make the same deal with them. And you'd never know. If she did approach anyone she knew was interested in the event, she'd know the money amount and other features of a proposal."

"I don't think so. Tom Riley had already put up his property for sale. He just hadn't let the mudder company know."

"What about Clay Archer?" asked Nappi.

Jay shrugged. "He's a good businessman. He would have put together a package to make money. Jenny's would have been absurdly low, but knowing what I was willing to provide for the event, she would have made a bid too sweet to reject. The woman was desperate for money. If she hadn't done something quick, she wouldn't have been able to pay the taxes on her crummy land this year or send her daughter to school."

Grandy said, "If you were really so concerned, why didn't you just loan her some money? You certainly appear to have enough." She waved her arm at the room and furnishings. "Instead you tried to make money off the poor woman by taking a share of her profits."

Yep. I came by my in-your-face stance honestly. Grandy was telling it like it is.

"I wouldn't have taken any of the money she got—I told you." Jay sounded defensive.

"But she didn't know that, did she? And she never found out how generous you intended to be," Grandy added.

Jay ran his fingers through his hair and looked down at the floor. Maybe he *had* meant to be big-hearted, but he must have heard the obvious subtext as he repeated his story: that he had entered into a shady deal to make a buck for himself.

He raised his gaze to Grandy's. "You're right. Looking back on it, I'm not really proud of myself, but Jenny wouldn't hear of my loaning her money. She wanted a business deal."

"Yeah, well you both behaved in an underhanded and unethical manner. You should be ashamed." Grandy set her wine glass on the coffee table in front of her. "I believe I'm ready to go home now," she announced.

I held up my finger to stop her from getting up. "One more question. Clay told us it was his wife's idea to go for the mud bog event, not his."

Jay smiled. "Well, it could have been. That woman pushed Clay around all the time. No one could figure out why he put up with it. I guess he worshipped her. To be honest, I think he's better off without her. I don't know if he sees it that way."

"Shelley said Clay and Jenny had a thing going for a while," I said.

"Hmm. Unlikely, but as you suggested, maybe she also approached him about the mud bog event and worked out some kind of deal. It could have included a little romance, I guess."

"Shelley seems to think Clay had a crush on Jenny. She could have used that, I suppose."

"Money troubles make people do all kinds of things they might not ordinarily consider," Jay replied.

"But then Jenny fell for George, who had no money, and that was the end of Clay." *Love trumps money*, I thought. *Or does it?* If she had set up the deal with Jay when she met George, she wouldn't need Clay. She'd have had both money and love.

"I don't blame you for what you think of me," said Jay, taking Grandy's hand as he walked her to the door. "I keep worrying about what role I might have unwittingly played in her death."

Grandy nodded. "You may never know. You'll just have to live with it."

Before I got into the car, I turned to ask Jay a final question. "Do you own a machete?"

"Of course. Everyone around here has one. They're a necessity for cutting through brush or taking down a snake."

"As common on the ranch as a thirty-thirty, right?"

Jay nodded, a look of confusion on his face.

I THOUGHT BACK on the events of the evening as I drove home. Romance and money … they were somehow intertwined in Jenny's death, I was certain of it. No, that wasn't right. Why sugarcoat it? Lust and greed were the more likely motives for Jenny's murder.

I wasn't happy with what I'd learned from the other individuals who had submitted proposals for the mud bog event. It didn't appear to me that any of them had reason to kill Jenny. One had dropped out of the competition, the second—my friend Jay—had worked a deal with Jenny, and the third was Clay Archer's wife, who lost interest in the event. I had gotten nowhere in tracking down the killer, and Grandfather Egret still sat in jail, the authorities convinced he was connected to the murder.

Back home, after Grandy had gone to bed, I thought back to my earlier assessment that lust and greed were responsible for Jenny's death. I seemed to have ruled out greed, so that left lust. I needed to talk once more with George, Jenny's fiancé. I set my alarm for six in the morning, intending to get up early and revisit the fish camp where he lived.

At two in the morning, Grandy knocked on my door. "Eve, honey. I need your help."

I jumped out of bed just as Grandy threw open the door. A sob escaped her as she ran into the room and threw her arms around me.

"What's wrong?" I asked.

"It's Max. The captain of the boat next to ours just called. The ambulance took Max to Reef Hospital. It looks like he had a heart attack."

Any plans I'd made for solving this murder were put aside. Right now all I knew was that Grandy needed me. Everything else faded into the background.

"Let's go." I shoved her toward the guest bedroom to pack what she needed while I tossed a few essentials into an overnight bag. Minutes later we were on the road to Key Largo.

"Did your friend say how he was doing?" I asked as I sped out of Sabal Bay and headed toward the turnpike and West Palm.

"He didn't know too much, just that Max was alive and had been admitted. I called the hospital, and they couldn't tell me much more."

"Well, don't you worry." I patted her hand. "He's a tough old bird. He'll pull through this."

"It's so hard not knowing what's happening."

I pushed down on the accelerator. It was important to get there as soon as possible. If I got a ticket, so be it.

The Florida State Troopers must have been busy with other criminals because we set a record driving to the hospital in Tavernier, shaving a half hour off my usual time, and I am not a slow driver.

I dropped Grandy at the emergency entrance, knowing she'd want to be by his side right away, and parked the car. I was directed by the people at the desk down the hallway and into another smaller waiting room. Grandy was talking with a tall, thin man in a white coat. I ran up to them.

"Oh, Eve. This is Dr. Grant. He admitted Max and says it was a moderate attack."

"When can we see him?"

The doctor turned to me and Grandy introduced me as her granddaughter.

"I know both of you are anxious to see him, but right now he needs rest. First thing tomorrow morning, you can talk with him. I'll let him know you were here and that you'll be back. He's a lucky man. We haven't yet assessed the damage to his heart, but we're hoping it was minimal." I was relieved that he appeared confident Max would recover. He gave Grandy a pat on the shoulder and me a smile of encouragement. Although also reassured by the doctor's report, Grandy wanted to stay in the hospital and wait until morning.

"I know we won't sleep," I said, "but let's go to the boat and at least get comfortable. We can be back here early." I looked at my watch. It was early in the morning, already after five.

I lay down in the berth in the stern while Grandy took the one she and Max shared in the bow. I surprised myself by sleeping until the smell of coffee woke me at around seven.

"Did you sleep at all?" I asked Grandy as she handed me a cup of coffee.

"No. And don't ask me if I'm hungry because I couldn't eat a thing. Let's gulp this down and go."

"We can take it with us in the car." I threw on a pair of shorts and a cotton tee. Before we could get into the car, the guy on the boat next to Max and Grandy's stopped us.

"I heard you arrive early this morning. How's Max doing?" he asked.

Grandy introduced us. "Oh, Rob, tell me what happened."

"Max came over to my boat around one in the morning, saying he was having chest pains. He got that something serious was going on. I don't know why he didn't call for an ambulance."

"He didn't call because he's a stubborn old cuss," Grandy said.

Rob smiled his agreement. "I called and the ambulance was here within five minutes. I followed in my car. I couldn't get much out of the people at the hospital, but Max asked me not to call you. He didn't want to worry you."

"Damn, stubborn cuss," Grandy repeated.

"So I promised I would keep my mouth shut, and that's when I called you."

"I'm glad someone around here has some sense. Thanks, Rob. I'll just lie and tell him the hospital called me. We talked with his doctor when we arrived, and he told us Max is doing well. We'll find out more this morning. We're headed there now."

"I've got a morning charter or I'd come with you. Tell the old goat I said to get well."

"Will do." Grandy waved and we got into the car.

At the hospital we ran into Dr. Grant.

"He's doing well—so well that he thinks he can go home this morning. He asked if you had been notified and threw a fit when I said you had been. He thought he could keep this whole thing from you. I told him we were recommending inserting a stent in the area that was partially blocked. He asked if we could do it right away so he could get out of here. He's something else. With his up and at 'em attitude, he should recover quickly."

Grandy snorted. "Unless I bop him alongside the head for trying to keep this from me. Will a concussion retard his recovery, do you think?"

The doctor laughed. "I understand your attitude, but hold off on the bopping until we've got him back on his feet. Then you can bop him all you want."

"I'll tell him that," said Grandy. "Now where is the old curmudgeon?"

The doctor led us to the room where Max was sitting up in bed and regaling several nurses with a pithy sailing tale.

"Hi, hon," he said, a flush rising on his cheeks. "You shouldn't have bothered coming down. This is nothing. As I told the doc, I feel good enough to go home now."

Grandy rushed over to the bed and hugged him, her face turned to one side. I saw her fight back the tears. Joining her, I gave Max a kiss on his leathery cheek.

"I know, I know, but I had to come home to pick up some clean underwear anyway, so it was no bother," she said.

Well, aren't they cute? I thought. *But someone has to cut through this dance of prevarication.*

"Okay, you two. Max, I got the word from the doctor that you'll be here for a few days, having some tinkering done on that ticker of yours. Then you're coming back to Sabal Bay with me to recover. Pack plenty of clean undies, both of you. You'll be there for a while."

Max insisted he was going to stay in Key Largo after he got out of the hospital. He even swore he would begin taking out charters the day he got out. Grandy vowed she'd leave him if he didn't cooperate and take at least a week off before they decided what the next step would be.

As WE WHEELED him out of the hospital several days later, Max said, "We're not discussing 'next steps' again. My next step will be back here, chartering this old tub, that's what it'll be. I'm a man who needs water. What would I do with my time up there among all those cattle, cowboys, and horses? I don't even know how to ride."

"There's lots of water where I live, a huge lake. You could go fishing for your own pleasure there. You might like it." I opened the door to my Mustang, and he got in.

"That water is brown. I'm not taking any fish out of brown water." He slammed the door before I could close it.

"The fish there are used to brown water. They like it," I said as I got into the car. Grandy was already in the backseat making harrumphing sounds.

"I'll blow up your damn boat. What do you say to that?" she said.

"Well, there's no way you could do that, is there?" he shot back.

"I've got friends who know how to convince people to do what they don't want to do," Grandy rejoined.

The look on Max's face spoke for itself. He knew she meant Nappi, and he wasn't certain how serious she was about having the mob boss help her blow the boat out of the water.

"Well, okay then, since you insist. But I'm coming back here in a week. We need the money."

I looked in the rearview mirror at Grandy, who shook her head no and mouthed, "We do not need the money."

Madeleine called me in Key Largo to tell me Jenny's body had been released and the funeral was scheduled for the next day. "Shelley called. She said she'd left several messages on your cell but you never responded, so I told her about Max."

"Thanks for letting her know. I've been too distracted to check my messages."

"There was something else. She said it would be better if we didn't attend the funeral, given the local feelings about the protest the day of Jenny's death."

"She's probably right. The funeral is about Jenny, her daughter, and her friends. I don't want the attention taken away from that, do you? But I have an idea. Would David be willing to attend?"

"You mean to represent us?"

"Kind of," I replied.

"You mean as a spy of sorts," Madeleine said in that astute way of hers. "Is there anything specific he should look for?"

"I want to know who comes to the service, and I'd particularly like to know if Darrel accompanies Shelley."

"Oh, surely not. Not after that incident where he hit you."

Love's a funny thing, I said to myself. I ignored Jerry's unfaithfulness for years. Why? I guess I thought it meant nothing to him so it should mean nothing to me. With Alex, I'd found someone who I knew would never cheat on me. *Is that all there is to love?* I wondered. *Simply find someone who curls your toes and is kind, intelligent, and faithful?* How did Alex feel about me? He said he loved me—I knew that meant I made his toes curl too—and he liked my sassy attitude. Or did he? I was beginning to think he did not find that quality endearing, but rather something he'd have to learn to overlook. And just where did that sass come from? The question brought up an image of my parents on their boat, the wind blowing through their hair, smiles on their faces. I missed them like crazy. Was that it? My sass was a way to deal with inner pain? I wiped away the tear already trickling down my cheek. *Naw. That's silly. Alex doesn't dislike my sassiness; he just doesn't understand me.* I wanted to leave it like that, but I had a niggling feeling that I was missing something that had to do with love. I let the feeling drift away, to be replaced once more by concern for Shelley. She'd said it herself: Darrel was her only friend. Whether she was right or not, friendship was a powerful component of love.

I ARRANGED FOR one of the fishing guides at the nearby park to take Max out on his boat the day after we returned to Sabal Bay. When he arrived back at my place that evening, he tossed a string of speck on the kitchen counter and launched into a fishing tale that went on and on until Grandy finally put a stop to it. She told him to get out back and clean the fish or there would be no dinner.

"Okay, gals. But you'd better be prepared for a lot more of the same tomorrow, because I've scheduled another tour with Captain Mike. This time we're going after some bass." Max slammed through the back door, taking the stringer of fish with him. We could hear him singing some song out of tune at the top of his lungs. He sounded happy.

"I thought he didn't like fish from a brown lake," I said to Grandy.

"In principle, he doesn't, but the challenge and fun of catching them is another matter."

"Looks like we'll be on a fish diet for the next week or so, until he gets bored with the sport. There's enough there that

I'd better invite Madeleine and David over for dinner. Maybe Nappi, too."

"Invite Jerry. You know he's been helping Madeleine out in the shop while you've been with us in Key Largo," Grandy reminded me.

I sighed. She was right. I had debts all over the place. And while I was issuing invitations, I got ahold of Sammy at the airboat business. I had talked with him when we got back yesterday, but only for several minutes. Grandfather Egret still sat in jail. My calls to Frida to find out what was happening with the case weren't returned.

Tonight Sammy picked up the call on the first ring.

"Alex is here, and we've been going over the case. I'll have to call you back, but I don't think I can make dinner tonight."

I couldn't help asking, "Are you and Alex following up on some hot lead tonight then?"

Part of me hated the idea that Alex might be close to breaking this case, but the other part of me wanted him to be successful. With Sammy's help, he might be on to something I hadn't thought of.

Sammy hesitated. "No. In fact, I think Alex wants to talk with you. Hold on a minute, would you?'

Alex came on the line.

"I understand that you knew Jenny's fiancé years ago and that you and Grandy visited him after the murder."

"We did, and he told Frida I was harassing him."

"Would you be willing to harass him some more?"

Would I? You bet.

CHAPTER 17

I
T SEEMED OUR little crew of friends got along best when there was food to gather us together. Grandy fried up the fish with a flour and cornmeal coating, the way I remembered her doing it when I was a kid, and served sides of tangy cole slaw and hush puppies. Sweet iced tea, a Southern favorite, accompanied the meal, which was followed by pecan pie and a lot of sighs of satisfaction and groans of, "I am so full."

I slumped down on the couch after the meal, Alex beside me. I decided I should pump him for why Sammy couldn't be here tonight. He had seemed so odd on the phone earlier.

"I don't know what he was up to tonight. He said he had to get home, take a shower, and change his clothes. He usually goes right from working on the airboat and the ranch to visiting Grandfather in jail. I'll bet he had a date." Alex gave me a sideways glance, a sly look on his face. Was he outright lying or only trying to get a rise out of me?

I changed the subject. "So what's your plan for talking to George? And what makes you think I'd be any more successful this time than I was last time?"

"This time I want you to be friendly, not confrontational. Do you think you can do that, just this once?"

If I'd still had a plate of pie in my hand, I would have beaned him with it.

"I'll give it a try," I said as I bit back a snarky retort.

Alex looked surprised, as if he'd expected sass in my response.

"Help me with the dishes?" I asked, getting off the couch.

Alex nodded, still wide-eyed.

The two of us gathered up plates and glasses and carried them into the kitchen.

"I thought you were going to get in touch with me after my foolish proposal at the Biscuit," he said as he loaded plates into the dishwasher.

"I meant to, but I didn't know what to say."

"It's over between us, isn't it, Eve?"

I nodded. "It's not your fault."

"Oh, yes, it is. There's something about you that I'm missing, isn't there?"

I thought about that and nodded again.

"You're crazy about sleuthing, aren't you? It just brings out your competitive side, and then we fight. The making up is always good, but that's no way to live. And it's not the kind of relationship either of us needs."

I opened my mouth to tell him he was only half right, but the words wouldn't come out. Maybe I didn't have the words yet.

"I love you, Eve, but not the way you need to be loved. And I know you care for me, too." He reached for me and gave me a hug. I hugged back.

We both wiped at wet eyes, but he spoke first. "Now about this George guy. You don't mind buttering him up?"

"Not at all."

"Good. You know, Eve, you would make a damn good private eye. You've got the drive, the intelligence, and you can ferret out clues. You just need one thing."

"A license?"

"Nope. You need to listen better. You jump in with your own conclusions too soon. Let people talk. You'll get more out of them."

I thought back on my conversation with Shelley. I'd labeled the harsh words between Clay Archer and her mother a 'lover's spat' and thought Shelley agreed, but maybe I had jumped the gun. Maybe Shelley would have called it something else. What?

"Good advice," I said.

Alex laughed. "Really. I can think of a time when you would have told me to go suck an egg."

"It's good advice, and now go suck an egg."

We both laughed.

"Can you take some more advice?"

Well, maybe I'd had enough, but Alex seemed eager to play the part of mentor now.

"There's a guy, name's Crusty McNabb. He's been a PI for years now. He's rented the small office front next to your shop. You should go talk to him."

My mouth dropped open in surprise. "I think Sabal Bay may have its share of PIs. They don't need one more and a Yankee woman to boot."

"Just go chat with him. He's older and wanting to retire soon. He might consider taking you on as an apprentice. I've told him all about you."

I could just imagine what Alex had said.

"I run a consignment business, and I'm happy doing that. It takes up all my time."

"Does it? No time for snooping into crime, huh?"

We finished loading the dishwasher together; then Alex left.

I was about to go back to join everyone when Grandy came in.

"I kept everyone out of here so the two of you could talk," said Grandy.

"Thanks."

"It was time, you know."

"Yep."

"But he was only half right, you know."

I looked at her, curious about what she had to say.

"You do need to develop better listening skills …."

I was about to say something, but I snapped my lips together.

"Yeah, like that. And you were pretty competitive with him when it came to ferreting out clues and chasing down the bad guys or girls."

I simply nodded.

"What he doesn't get is that you do all this because you're a rescuer."

"A what?"

"You heard me. A rescuer. Like with Shelley. Think about it, Eve. If you do, you'll realize I'm right."

"Who else do you think gets this about me? I mean, if it's true, and I'm not saying it is."

"Well, honey, you just think about that too. You need a man who gets that about you."

I knew someone like that.

"Meantime, while you're digesting all this, you might want to think about what Alex told you about Crusty McNabb."

I snorted. "Me? A PI? What about Madeleine and my business?"

"Things have a way of sorting themselves out. Now come and say good night to your friends."

Before I left on my errand, Madeleine whispered in my ear, "We haven't had time to talk. I do have information about the funeral."

I pulled her and David onto the porch and shut the door.

"Tell me."

"Darrel was at Shelley's side, as you suspected would be the case," said David. "All the usual players from the ranching community were there. Jay Cassidy looked particularly upset."

"As well he should be with that shady deal he made with Jenny," I said.

"George was there too, David said," Madeleine interjected.

David added, "Most people weren't happy at that, given he was one of the protesters, but I guess he was tolerated out of respect for Jenny, because of their engagement."

"Anything else interesting?'

David hesitated. "Clay Archer showed up with his wife, soon to be ex. I thought that was kind of odd."

"Maybe they're reconciling," I said.

"Everyone around here hopes not. We think Clay would be better off without her telling him what to do. I thought Clay was beginning to see it that way too. Maybe not," David concluded.

"She probably knew Jenny well since she was her nearest neighbor, the years before she and Clay split," Madeleine said.

BECAUSE WE'D EATEN early, it was not quite seven in the evening when I pulled up in front of George's trailer. I had a perfect excuse for visiting him again. I had forgotten to give him the clothes and items he'd left at Jenny's house. I pulled the bag out of my trunk and approached the door. It opened and George stood there, his arms crossed over his chest, a look of dislike on his face.

"Now what do you want?" he asked. "Say, what happened to your face? It looks like you got hit with shrapnel."

"Someone took a shot at me. You wouldn't know anything about that, would you?"

He shook his head.

I remembered my assignment wasn't to interrogate him, but to get him to tell me what he knew about Jenny, so I gave him one of my best Eve smiles, a bit of womanly friendliness thrown in. "I forgot to drop these off the other day." I handed the bag to him.

"What's this?" He took the bag tentatively, opened it and peered in.

"Some of your stuff from Jenny's house. Shelley was going to toss everything, but I told her I'd take it to you. I forgot about it last time."

He looked more carefully into the bag, then glanced back at me.

"What do you want?" he asked, his tone no friendlier than it had been before.

"For heaven's sake, George, it's just your stuff, not a bomb I built to blow you up. We were friends once, you know."

He continued to stare at me, only with less suspicion. "Might as well come on in then."

"You sure I'm not disturbing you and your girlfriend?"

"What girlfriend?"

"There was a woman here who didn't show herself last time I visited. I thought she might be permanent."

He smiled. "You know me better than that, Eve."

I laughed. "I do indeed, so I'm wondering what possessed you to want to marry Jenny McCleary. You must have thought she had money."

He didn't answer my question, but walked over to the kitchen counter and held up the coffee pot. "Coffee?"

"Sure."

He extracted a cup from the cupboard, filled it, and handed it to me, gesturing toward the plaid couch in the living area.

I expected him to take the recliner across from the couch, but once he refilled his own cup, he joined me on the sofa, sitting a fraction too close for me to believe he saw me as anything other than a possible conquest. I wanted to shift away from him and say something smart, but I was here to obtain information.

"Just like old times, huh?" George said.

"Yep, but then we were drinking cheap wine, not coffee."

"I got some of that, if you'd prefer."

I shook my head. "This is fine."

He leaned back into the couch and slid his arm onto its back. His fingers slipped down to touch my shoulder.

"Now about Jenny. At first I thought she had money, but then she confessed she was doing the mud bog event to get some. That woman was dead broke. Did you know that?"

I nodded.

"I thought I was gonna talk her out of the event, but I couldn't move her even when I proposed and told her I'd find a way to help her out. I think for a minute she believed me, but after several weeks, she seemed less interested in me and any money schemes I had for us. She broke off the engagement. I think she found someone else and came up with some way to get the money she needed to enter the mud bog event."

"She got Jay Cassidy to front her the money."

"So I found out later from her."

I was surprised that Jenny had been so up front about that with George.

"You're not telling me everything you know, George." I was guessing, but my probe was worth a try.

"I think she and Clay Archer got friendly."

"I thought they got friendly before you came along."

"Yeah, but I think they never really broke it off."

"Are you saying that Jenny used you, George?"

"Maybe she did, but I used her too."

Well, of course he did. George always had ulterior motives when it came to his relationships with women. Some he let believe he loved while he was only after sex. Others he slept with for political advantage. And no matter whom he had a thing with, he had some other women on the sly. George might have been on the correct side of environmental issues, but he had no respect for women. I was secretly pleased that Jenny had used George for money until she found out someone else had more to offer. It wasn't something I could admire in Jenny, but the woman was desperate and wanted to finds funds for her daughter's education. I found Jenny more admirable than George, with his belittling attitude toward women and using ways. I wondered if George really intended to help Jenny find some money, and I was also curious about what schemes he might have cooked up to get it. I decided to go slow instead of plunging in and putting him on the defensive.

I was missing something here, and it was the timeline for Jay's arrangement with Jenny, Jenny's engagement to and subsequent rejection of George, and Jenny's friendship with Clay Archer. Clay told me his wife was interested in the mud bog event, but then lost interest. What about Clay? Had his interest outlasted his wife's? Jay said she dominated him. Did she just tell him to forget the event? And was that before or after they separated?

I needed to talk with Clay again. That was the interesting thing about trying to wheedle information out of someone. The more you knew, the more you could find out. People often didn't outright lie to you, but you had to know the right question to ask or they kept important information to themselves. I had a great reason to visit Clay again because Grandy and Nappi were interested in his horses. Grandy had to cancel the time she'd arranged to ride Clay's gelding because of Max's heart attack, but maybe she and Nappi might like to visit again for a ride. We could take Max with us and see how he took to equine events.

While I was ruminating about the events leading up to Jenny's death, George had slipped his hand down over my shoulder and began working his way under the neck of my blouse. Once I became aware of his actions, I jumped off the couch.

"George! Keep your hands off me."

He jumped up too and moved toward me. "You came here to be friendly, didn't you? Now you're giving me a hard time, Eve. You're a little tease. You always were." His face reddened as he reached out for me.

I backed away. "You really don't like it when women reject you, do you, George?"

"Not when they first say they want me, then they toss me aside."

"Like Jenny did." I maneuvered my way across the room toward the door, but George was close enough to grab my arm and pull me toward him. My body slammed against his, and I could feel the hard muscles in his chest. He pulled my face to his and pressed his mouth on mine. I bit his lip. He roared with anger and let me go for a moment, holding his hand over his bleeding lip. Before I could stumble to the door, he recovered from the shock of my bite and hit me opened fisted in the head. I fell to the floor.

He was not only strong, but quick, and on me in a second. His knee came down between my legs, and he reached for the zipper of my jeans. The blow to my head was hard enough that I couldn't think clearly, but I rolled to my side. He grabbed my hips and slammed me onto my back once more.

"Help!" I yelled, even knowing no one would hear me, or if they did, come to my rescue. Suddenly I knew George was one of those men who didn't understand that not getting a woman's cooperation was rape. He didn't care if sex was consensual as long as it was sex. It was likely that the residents of this fish camp had heard similar sounds from George's visitors and chosen to ignore them.

"Shut up, bitch. I've been wanting to do this for years, but I never got the chance until now. You know you want this, babe."

Maybe if I let him believe I was simply being coy in my rejection of him, that I really didn't mean it …. "You're right, George, but this won't be any fun for either of us unless I help out a little. Just let me—"

"No."

I looked into his lust-crazed eyes, and I realized something else about George. He preferred his sex this way—mean, hard, and with the woman resisting. His physical strength was too much for me. He didn't want my cooperation. Now I knew what to do.

I went limp.

"Hey. What the hell are you doing? Wake up." He shook me,

but I remained as immobile and loose as a piece of overcooked linguine. He let my head and shoulders fall to the floor, then stood over me, legs on either side of my body, and leaned down to peer into my face.

He slapped me, and I let my head fall to one side with the strength of his blow. Nothing. Out of the corner of my eye I saw his hand come back to deliver another slap, but before he could, I pulled back my foot and slammed it into his little boy parts. I'll never know if that blow would have rendered him helpless—it certainly produced a wonderful effect, his holding his crotch and whimpering—because just then the outside door was flung open and a woman entered.

"What the hell is going on here, George? And who is this blonde bitch?"

George could only roll around on the floor, the sounds emanating from his mouth more animal than human.

I got to my feet, still dizzy from too many blows to my head, but in far better shape than George. Tears ran down his cheeks, and he began producing huffing sounds.

"I don't think he'll die on you, but you are certainly welcome to seek medical help. As for me, I'm calling the cops."

"Georgie, honey. What did she do to you?" The dark-haired woman bent over him, scattering kisses across his face and wiping his tears with her blouse.

Despite my threat to summon the police, I knew I'd have one heck of a time making a case for attempted rape, so I left them together on the floor and walked out. On my way home, I phoned Frida and explained what had happened.

"I know this isn't much, Frida, but I've no doubt that George is capable of great violence, especially when a woman rejects him. And that's just what Jenny did. It could have gotten out of hand."

"He's always been my favorite suspect. There was just something about the guy. But we've got nothing on him."

"I know."

"Do you want to file charges?"

"There's no way to make them stick, is there?"

"Your word against his, but let me pay him a visit right now while that gal is there. Let's see what he says ... or what she says. Maybe she's jealous enough she might give us something more on Georgie. Are you going to tell Alex what happened? You said it was his idea to get you out there again."

"No! Alex would go ballistic."

"I'll let you know what I find out."

Frida's visit to George didn't take long. As I was pulling into my driveway, she called me back.

"I talked with George and his woman, Mary Holbrook. I kept it casual and told them you registered a complaint. They both said you came to the trailer and were drunk and seductive and he had to get physical with you to get you out of there."

"I'm not surprised. What is it with some women's taste in men? She's completely duped by him."

"Maybe, but perhaps not for long. She supported the story, but she didn't look happy about it. I'd bet their relationship is on its way out and soon." I heard her sigh. "You really didn't find out anything much from George before he attacked you?'

"Well, no I didn't." It was true. George didn't tell me anything I already didn't know, but his comments about Jenny got me thinking about when Jenny talked with Jay, when she broke up with George, and when Clay was in and then out of the picture. Unfortunately those were simply the jumbled thoughts of an amateur detective. Nothing I wanted to share with Frida. She'd probably laugh herself off the phone with the absurdity of my suspicions.

"Let me know if you think of something. Anything." Frida ended the call.

Of course I'd let her know if I thought of anything—if I thought of something I thought was worth thinking of.

When I pulled into my drive, I looked into my rearview mirror. There was a fresh scratch on my cheek joining the other fading scratches and my blouse was unbuttoned. My punked hair looked about the way it usually did—punked. I hid the scratch as best I could with foundation and dotted blush on my cheekbones. I buttoned my blouse and tried to look calm. Sammy's truck was in my drive, and he wasn't visiting by himself.

Grandy and Max sat on the couch and turned to look at me as I entered. Sammy got out of the easy chair and smiled. In the other living-room chair sat a woman with long black hair and gray eyes. She also got up. She was as tall as me and wore faded jeans, a black tee shirt molded over large breasts, and black stiletto heels. I admired her fashion sense. I felt the finger of jealousy tickle my neck. I took in the high cheekbones of her face, her olive skin, wide mouth, and even, white teeth. She was drop-dead gorgeous. Her only flaws were the laugh lines around her mouth and the fine lines at her eyes and on her brow. It was clear this woman was far too old for Sammy. But how could you blame a man—any man, no matter his age—for being taken with her? She would be the center of attention in any room.

She crossed the room and held out her hand to me. "I've heard so much about you."

I ignored the hand. "Funny. I haven't heard a thing about you."

Sammy looked shocked, but the woman laughed, a warm, friendly sound. There was no hint of reproach in it.

"Sammy, you bad boy. You didn't even tell Eve your mother was coming for a visit."

Oh crap.

CHAPTER 18

"**O**H, STUPID ME, Mrs. Egret. Sammy did tell me about your coming to visit, but I've been so wrapped up in, uh …."

"She's a bit of a snoop, Mom. She's working on this murder like Alex and me. I told you all about her curious side." Sammy got up and stood by his mother, his arm around her shoulder.

"Sammy told me you liked to, uh, look into things a bit, but he didn't tell me you were also a private detective like his friend Alex."

"She's not, Mom. She's just a woman who—" Sammy didn't get to finish his sentence because Grandy interrupted him.

"Like me, she sticks her nose into things that aren't any of her business. It runs in the family. I must say, however, that we've been wildly successful at tracking down some bad dudes around here."

"Yeah, well, she had a lot of help," Sammy added. "Alex and Jerry and Grandfather Egret helped out too. And, don't forget Nappi."

"It's been a collaborative effort, a sort of amateur swamp posse," Grandy said.

"I can hardly wait to meet the other members of this group." Sammy's mother seemed genuinely impressed by our motley crew of snoopers.

"Now wait just a darn minute," I said. "Most of the sleuthing was mine. I had some help … mostly incidental."

"Incidental? We're incidental, Eve?" said Grandy.

"Most of the ideas were mine."

"True, and then we all have to ride in and rescue you because you go off like the Lone Ranger."

Sammy's mother laughed. "Oh, dear. Does this mean you're her Tonto?" She tapped Sammy on the shoulder.

He reddened and smiled.

"In fact, Eve was off on an information-gathering mission just now. Right?" Grandy said.

Alex must have told her he was sending me back to George's place.

"He didn't have much to say. A dead end." I didn't want anyone but Frida to know about my encounter with George. Everyone would be so concerned for my safety that I'd have a babysitter at my side each time I left the house or the shop or town. I intended to leave town for Boca Raton the next day. I just had to figure out how to do it without anyone knowing. And after the Boca trip? I wanted Grandy, Nappi, Max, and me to do some riding.

"Max and I are going to turn in. Listen, Eve, I told Madeleine that Max and I would take over the rig tomorrow. She's been working hard while we were in Key Largo."

"I think that's my responsibility. I owe her for being willing to step in and run everything for almost a week." I was telling the truth about Madeleine's generosity. How was I going to manage the business and find out who killed Jenny?

"Don't be silly. You supported us through a bad time. Now that Max is better, it's the least I can do to repay you, my dear."

Max got off the couch and leaned down to give me a kiss. "You were a rock to me and Grandy. Besides, I think it might be fun."

"Tell you what, then. You two sell at the rig tomorrow, and I'll call Clay Archer to see if he'll host us on Sunday. How do you feel about doing a little riding, Max?"

"Riding on what?" he asked.

"A horse. Grandy saw a horse at Clay's ranch. She told him she was interested in riding it. What do you say?"

Seeing his sudden pallor, I worried he might be having a heart episode.

"Are you okay, Max?"

"I'm fine. It's just that I'm not really certain how I feel about horses. The only thing I'm interested in riding is my boat. Cantankerous as she is, at least she listens to me."

"Just come along with us and get to know the horses," Grandy said. "When you're feeling more fit, you might want to give it a try." She steered him toward the spare bedroom. "You might like it as much as fishing this lake."

Max looked back at me and rolled his eyes.

As they headed down the hallway toward the bedroom, I heard him say, "I like fishing this lake fine, but I don't want to do it forever. I belong in salt water. Those alligators are frightening."

"And sharks aren't?" I heard her say before the bedroom door closed.

"You've got the day free tomorrow then," Sammy said. "That's great. The three of us can do something together. I'll get Jerry to take care of the airboat business. What will it be?"

Uh-oh. He seemed so anxious to get his mother, himself, and me together that I felt as if he was taking me home to meet the family.

"You two decide. I've got to go to the West Palm area tomorrow because we haven't had time to visit our clientele there lately. They expect us to stop by now and then and pick up clothes. I hate to disappoint them."

"West Palm?" asked Mrs. Egret.

"Yep. If Sammy didn't tell you, Madeleine and I sell high-end secondhand clothes in our shop. We get them from the wealthy matrons in West Palm. It's kind of our unique niche here."

"Maybe I could ride with you and help," offered Mrs. Egret.

I groaned inwardly. *No, no*. You could not do that. It would mess up all my plans. I also feared she'd try to pick my brain about Sammy and my relationship, and I wouldn't know quite what to tell her since I wasn't sure myself what our relationship was all about. Good friends, soon-to-be bed partners?

"I, uh, well …. That's very nice of you, but my convertible doesn't hold much, and I'll be needing all the room in the car and the trunk for the clothes and whatever else I might find."

"Come on, Mom. You know there are family members here that want to see you. And you're staying such a short time. We'll visit the family tomorrow morning, and when Eve returns from the coast, the three of us can go out to the state park for a late lunch."

Her expression darkened. "You really think the family wants to see me?" she asked.

"Of course they do," said Sammy, but his words lacked conviction.

She turned to me. "The family never really understood my marrying Sammy's father. And no one was surprised when I left Sammy with Grandfather. Of course, they also disapproved."

"They've forgiven you," said Sammy.

"There was nothing to forgive," she insisted.

This sounded like the beginnings of an age-old family dispute.

Sammy was quick to smooth things over. "Think about it, Mom. It's really your call. But let's spend the afternoon with Eve. I'm covered. David will be at the ranch and Jerry at the airboat business. And I'll be with the two most important women in my life." Sammy gave me a pointed look as if daring me to deny the truth of what he was saying.

*

I'D TOLD EVERYONE I was on my way to West Palm to pick up consignment items when my real destination was Boca Raton to speak with Clay Archer's estranged wife, Audra. What I remembered about her was that she was a striking woman, almost as tall as me with auburn hair and classic features. And according to Clay's friends, a domineering manner and an acid tongue. I'd handled tough women before. And I was one.

Before I took action, I needed a cover story, so I called Frida.

"You interviewed Audra Archer, right?" I asked when I connected.

"Okay, Eve, what are you up to now?"

"I'm going to be in the West Palm area, so I thought I could travel south a few miles to Boca Raton and have a little chat with her."

"You're free to talk with anyone you want. So what's the problem?"

Oh, she was the coy one.

"I need a way to convince her to cooperate. I thought I'd tell her I was with the Sabal Bay Police Department."

"As what? A nosy friend?"

"How about as a consultant needing to question her about irregularities in the papers filed for the mud bog event."

"I didn't know there were irregularities or that you were interested in them." Frida was spinning me around in the wind.

"Maybe I can get something out of her that you didn't." I crossed my fingers, hoping Frida might agree.

"Give it a try. I'll cover your designer-clothed butt. Don't break any laws, try to be civil, and call me as soon as you finish." She disconnected.

For Frida to agree to my scheme meant she was desperate for a break in the case. I knew she had been optimistic about finding who bought the hand; obviously that had not come through yet. I was glad to help my police pal out.

Somehow I'd have to find the time to pick up donated clothes as well as question Mrs. Archer. Locating her was easy enough.

She was in the phone book. She lived in one of the wealthier gated communities in Boca, so I called first and told her what I wanted.

"You can call my co-worker Frida Martinez, and she'll verify my credentials," I told her on the phone. I gave her Frida's number.

"Well, I don't understand it, but come to the house. I don't want any loose ends impeding the divorce."

"Righto," I said. "Loose ends are never good for a divorce."

Mrs. Archer's house was like every other mega-mansion in the area—landscaped front lawn, mature plantings of royal palms, and a walkway made of coral. Once inside, I saw the usual high ceilings, and in the living room, white leather couch and chairs, marble floors covered with expensive Persian rugs, and art that could have been original and probably was— though not selected by Mrs. Archer. The place had the feel of design by paid consultant—costly and a bit cold. This was her pied-à-terre between marriage and divorce, a temporary place until she could arrange for better.

"I checked with your boss, Detective Martinez. She said you were a real bulldog for following up on leads. I'm not sure I understand. Why am I a lead?"

"Your husband, Clay Archer—"

She interrupted, "My soon to be ex-husband."

"Yes and that's just it. He said filing the papers for the mud bog event was your idea."

"Did he? Well, it wasn't my idea."

"Really? He indicated that you were initially enthusiastic about booking the event, but then lost interest."

"In a way he's right. I let him file the papers and then I did lose interest. However, he was the one who withdrew the papers."

"He did? Hmm. That's not what he told me."

"Well, you can't always believe Clay. He's a bit of a liar."

"For example?"

She leaned forward on the couch. "He said he loved me. It just wasn't true."

"Oh."

She shrugged her shoulders. "I married him anyway, thinking he'd changed and that I could change him more. I thought I could make him love me."

Oops. Somehow I'd gotten myself dead center in a marital issue that was totally unrelated to Jenny's murder. Or was it? I plunged ahead.

"Someone told me he was interested in Jenny McCleary."

She opened her eyes wide in surprise, then leaned back on the couch and laughed. "Did Jenny say that? If she did then she was denser than I thought. Let me tell you something. If Jenny McCleary thought she could handle Clay Archer, she was dead wrong." Her words must have echoed in her head because she stopped talking for a moment. "Sorry about that. What I meant to say is that Jenny didn't have a chance with Clay."

"You didn't like Jenny? But you attended her funeral."

"It was the appropriate thing to do. Besides, I was curious."

"About what?"

"I thought you were here to inquire about the mud bog event, not Jenny McCleary's funeral."

"Right. I think she might have been trying to make some kind of a deal with him."

"Using her charms as bait? Not likely. She had nothing that would charm Clay."

"It appears she was going to have Clay withdraw his papers so she wouldn't have any competition. She would then offer him a cut of what she made for the mud bog event if he would put some money up front."

Again, laughter erupted from her. "Now that's almost as funny as the idea of her trying to get him into bed. If you're here thinking Clay might have killed Jenny because she took the mud bog event away from him or reneged on some deal they had, you are wrong, wrong, wrong."

"How do you know that, Mrs. Archer?"

"Because Clay doesn't have a nickel to his name. That ranch belonged to my father, and he gave it to me. The only way Clay could use it for any event would be if I signed off on it. I wouldn't do that unless there was a guarantee that I got the mud bog event. I like to get my own way, Miss Appel, and I don't like competition, especially from some cracker woman in Sabal Bay. Jenny got the event, and there was nothing Clay could do about it. If she had dropped out of the competition like the others, then maybe I would have looked at it. But she didn't, did she?"

So Clay had no money and didn't have the right to use the land for the event. I watched Mrs. Archer's face. While her words sounded honest and revealing, her expression remained shuttered. She was hiding something. What?

"Why are you so certain Clay wouldn't have been interested in Jenny? As I understand it, you had left him. Maybe you misjudged him. Maybe he liked a self-sufficient, opinionated woman from the country."

"Oh, please. Are you kidding me?"

"What then?"

She arose from the couch. "I think this interview is over."

I CALLED FRIDA as soon as I left the house. "I probably don't know any more than you do, except I do find Mrs. Archer quite unpleasant."

"Everyone does. No one can understand why Clay put up with her for so long."

"Money, of course."

"You found out about that, did you? Well, keep it under your hat. I don't think anyone around here knows Clay doesn't have a penny to his name and doesn't own that ranch and won't get it once they've divorced."

"Keeping his secret, huh?"

"Let him keep his pride. He had no reason to kill Jenny that

I can see and spreading gossip about his marital difficulties won't change that."

"I got the feeling Audra Archer was keeping something from me."

"Good sense on her part, I'd say." With a chuckle, she ended the call.

I HEADED NORTH to West Palm and dropped by several of our best patrons to pick up items for consignment in the shop. It had been several weeks since either Madeleine or I had visited. I came away with clothes, jewelry, and household items such as candlesticks, paintings, glassware, and high-end cookware. I hadn't lied to Sammy's mother. The inside of the car and the trunk were piled high with merchandise. I had about twenty minutes to unload my car at our store on wheels before I was to meet Sammy and his mother at the park.

I hadn't been near the shop we were renovating since I came back from Key Largo. I looked at my watch. I had just enough time to stop by. Madeleine told me the Miccosukee crew Sammy recommended had been working this past weekend. She said their work was excellent, and they had nearly completed the rewiring and replumbing of the shop. I hadn't expected any workers to be there since it was a weekday, and they were only scheduled to work on the weekends or evenings. Sammy had arranged for the work to be done during off-hours. Thanks to his "in" in the tribal business, we were still being charged the lower weekly rate.

A Miccosukee tribe member from the work crew was at the shop when I arrived. I remembered meeting him at one of the local arts and crafts festivals selling tribal art.

"Ms. Appel, how are you? I heard about your grandmother's husband. I hear he's up here, and you and your grandmother are taking care of him at your place. I wish him a speedy recovery."

I shook my head in amazement. I'd only been gone to Key

Largo for a week and already the entire Miccosukee tribe seemed to know about Max. How did they manage that? I was certain Grandfather Egret read minds, but did all tribe members? They certainly had a way of finding out what was happening in Sabal Bay. How they did it continued to baffle me.

"Max is recovering nicely."

"I understand he's pretty good at catching fish."

"How did you know that?" I asked suspiciously.

"Oh, everyone knows that." He gestured toward the walls. "We got the walls up where you want them, but now we need to choose colors for them. Madeleine was by here yesterday and said a light sage would be good, but to check with you. Should I bring by some samples or do you want to just buy it from the hardware store?'"

"I'll talk with Madeleine, and we'll buy the paint. I'll drop it by tomorrow morning."

"Good. I'll be in this weekend to finish up then."

"Really? That was fast."

"Yes, ma'am. Once I get the paint on the walls, just see to it that you don't get any more wildlife in here to ruin my work." He grinned.

So he'd heard about our alligator visitor. Why wasn't I surprised?

"And I recommend you stay out of the shop until you get someone to do the cleansing."

So everyone knew about the evil invading the shop as well.

"Aren't you worried about it?" I asked.

"No, ma'am. As I understand it, these spirits are the work of the previous owner and directed only at you. You must have really gotten to her."

I WAS ONLY a few minutes late getting to the park. Sammy and his mother were already there unpacking the food—pastrami on rye sandwiches, chips and root beer, a watermelon for dessert.

"I hope you didn't expect something Miccosukee, but I love pastrami on rye," said Sammy's mother.

"Anything food is fine with me, Mrs. Egret," I said, and to show it was, I took a big bite out of my sandwich.

"Call me Renata."

We had just finished our lunch when my cell rang.

"Eve? Hi, it's Jerry. I know Sammy and you are having lunch together. Could I talk to him? The airboat broke down, and I can't get it started. We have a line of unhappy women here wanting a ride."

I gave Sammy the phone. He listened for a while, then disconnected and handed it back to me.

"Sorry, gals, but I've got to get back to the airboat business. Boat's down."

"You go on ahead, honey," Renata said. "Eve can bring me back to Grandfather's house later. We'll stay here and soak up the sun for a few more minutes." She turned to me. "You don't mind, do you?"

I knew what she really meant was that we could have a private chat. I was certain it would be about Sammy and me, and I was not eager to be interrogated by Renata Egret concerning my relationship with her son. However, I smiled and said, "No. I could use a little sun."

We watched Sammy drive off in his pickup, and an uncomfortable silence fell between us.

After we both stared off into the lake for several minutes, I finally decided it was best to get this over with.

"You must be curious about Sammy and me."

"Not at all."

I was shocked.

"I may not have the sixth sense of a Miccosukee like Grandfather, but there's nothing puzzling about Sammy and you. He's obviously in love with you."

"That can't be. We're just friends." Were we? After that hot encounter on Grandfather Egret's porch, we were certainly more than friends.

"Oh, don't worry. He doesn't even realize it yet. He knows something is different about his feelings for you, but he'd never label it 'love.' He's telling himself you're interesting, different, and he'd like to get you into his bed. Still, as honest a man as he is, my son is not honest with himself about his emotions. I thought you might like a heads up. Please don't break his heart. If you can't feel the same about him, then be good enough to back off from this involvement. I don't think Sammy has ever felt this way about a woman."

Since she was being so honest with me, I owed her the same.

"I just got out of a relationship because, well, I think I'm relationship-phobic. My marriage was a disaster. I trusted Jerry for no good reason. The only positive thing to come out of it was that now I'm better at telling the good guys from the bad guys. That doesn't seem to help me make a commitment."

She sipped the last of her root beer and placed the bottle in the garbage bag on the picnic table. "Sammy told me about Alex. He seems like one of the good guys, like my son. And Sammy likes him, respects his work. Sammy has some trust issues also, so if you decide to get more involved with him, it won't be easy."

I thought about Sammy's reluctance to talk about his father and wondered if that's where the problem was.

"Sammy won't answer any of my questions about his father. Why not?"

She hesitated. Was she going to stonewall me also?

"He can't."

I waited.

"He doesn't know where his father is. None of us do."

CHAPTER 19

—

"How can that be? How can no one know where Sammy's father is?"

Renata sighed deeply. "This isn't easy to talk about, but I guess it's my fault. I was a rebellious teen. I hated school, hung out with a bad group of kids who were into petty theft, shoplifting, stuff like that, and of course, drugs. I stayed out late, played hooky from school, never studied, and bad-mouthed my teachers. My parents couldn't control me. I wasn't a bad kid really, but my mom and dad were very conservative. They thought they could set up strict rules, and I should obey. I ran away at age sixteen with a boy who was only a year older than me. He abandoned me when we got to Kissimmee, and I never heard from him again. I worked as a waitress in a diner for over a year until this tall, dark Miccosukee came in—Lionel Egret, Sammy's father. I think I was looking for someone to rescue me from the dead-end life I'd gotten myself into. In my book, he was an exotic Native American I couldn't wait to take home and shove in my parents' faces. I knew they'd disapprove." She paused and laughed.

"Yeah, I'd stayed in touch with my parents, who had all but

given up on me. I hadn't given up on them. I needed something to rebel against. They were still it, so I dragged him back home with me to Iowa. The reaction of the small community I was from was even more dramatic than my parents'. My new husband and I stayed there for one night, then headed back to Florida and the tribe. By the time we'd been married for half a year and I was five months pregnant, it was clear to both of us that our marriage was a mistake—we were too different. We hung in there anyway. The day after Sammy was born, his father took the airboat out into the swamps, and no one ever heard from him again. The tribe blamed me for his disappearance. Sammy has somehow blamed himself for his father leaving."

"Do you think he's—"

"Dead? I don't know. You know Grandfather. He says the swamp takes things away and sometimes returns them. He also believes that to be true of people who go into the swamp. If Lionel is not dead, I wish for Sammy's sake he'd show himself. Then maybe Sammy could off-load his guilt."

"And then you left, too?" I couldn't keep the disapproval out of my voice. How could she do that to Sammy after he'd lost his father? Did Sammy blame himself for her leaving too?

"I wasn't happy here, and the tribe wasn't going to help me adjust to being an outsider. I knew I should leave for Sammy's sake. I was making my son unhappy with my own misery. When Sammy turned five, Grandfather came to me and told me he had a dream about a desert and a tall, white woman living there. He said it was a message—that the woman was me, I was content there, and Sammy's face was once again filled with laughter."

"So Grandfather's dream led you away from the tribe and Sammy?" I wondered if she was telling me the truth or if she wanted to make it appear that her leaving was not only her idea but condoned by Grandfather.

"I don't know if Grandfather really dreamed that or used it to

make me finally exit without remorse, with a clear conscience."
She shook her head. "You know Grandfather. He's a mixture of
the old and the new."

I showed her the amulet I wore around my neck. "He gave
it to me to wear for protection. Maybe I'm just lucky or I only
think it works, but the one time I got into real trouble—and
that was with a Cape buffalo—was when I didn't have it on me.
Since then I've never left it behind."

"Grandfather may only be lucky with his pronouncements,
but I always listen to him."

"You like him, then? You don't blame him for making you
leave?'

"I knew he wanted me gone. He was right in what he said
about Sammy's unhappiness. Sammy is at home here, and he
wouldn't have been if he'd gone with me or if I'd stayed here.
Do I like Grandfather? He's kind and wise, and he sees through
into my soul. I had a very angry and untrustworthy soul back
then."

"Is it better now?"

"Much. But Grandfather knows I was responsible for his
son's disappearance. Though he's forgiven me, he still doesn't
trust me. It's hard to like someone who knows how capable
you are of evil."

"I wouldn't call what you did 'evil.' You were hardly more
than a kid."

"I knew what I was doing. It was adolescent rebellion. For
Sammy's father, it was love, a love I couldn't fully return." She
stared into my eyes as if trying to determine if I understood
what she was telling me. It wasn't just about her and Sammy's
father. It was about Sammy and me. He was in love while I was
trying to work out who I was, whether I loved anyone other
than Grandy. If I could trust anyone. Who did I trust and
love—really love? There was Grandy and Madeleine, people I
knew inside and out, people I tried to treat well. Even if I sassed
them, I always felt bad later. And always had to apologize. I

should learn to think first before I hurt people I love. Renata saw herself in me. She was right, but I knew I wouldn't be able to blame an adolescent identity crisis for anything that happened between Sammy and me. I was an adult and responsible for my actions. I got it. I needed to be careful with Sammy's tender heart.

CHAPTER 20

—

RENATA AND I visited Grandfather at the jail, bringing along a pastrami sandwich and a bottle of the root beer. He seemed to be in great spirits, chanting his native songs as we entered the visitors' area.

"He's a happy old man," said the guard who escorted him into the room. "He's been entertaining us with songs and telling tales from the past. It gets real boring around here. I'll be sorry to see him go."

"But we want him home," I said.

"I understand. Sorry." The guard nodded to us.

"Give those to Clem next door," Grandfather said to the guard when we handed him the food. "He's always hungry. The food around here isn't bad, but there's not enough to fill him up."

I could see why. The last time I'd visited, Clem had just been leaving the visitors' area as I came in. He was over six foot four and had to weigh in at over three hundred pounds.

"Clem says being in jail is like going to a fat farm," Grandfather said. "He claims he dropped ten pounds in the first two days. He'll make short work of the sandwich. I've seen him polish off one in four bites, and he likes to upend a bottle in one long gulp. The guy is a good eater."

"We should have brought more," I said.

"You're looking your usual lovely self," Grandfather said to Renata. "Las Vegas agrees with you."

"It's the dry weather. I mildew around here," she replied.

Their exchange was friendly enough, but not really warm. I could feel the distance between them.

"Why did you come back here?" Grandfather was getting right to it. So much for friendly. His tone of voice said he was worried and somewhat displeased by her appearance.

"I came to see Sammy."

"You see any of the other tribe members?"

"This morning."

He nodded at her reply, then turned his gaze on me.

"I thought Sammy might be with you."

"He's off repairing the airboat. It broke down when Jerry was squiring some women from West Palm through the swamps."

He sighed. "I miss two things being in here: the smell of the swamp and your store, Eve. I sure did like selling to those ladies."

"You can do it again real soon, I'm sure."

"Only if whoever killed Jenny feels safe enough with me sitting in here to believe he's off the hook."

"Frida told you about the fake hand?" I was surprised she'd shared this detail with Grandfather.

He chuckled. "She did not. She's too professional to give that away. I figured it out for myself. I got a look at that hand and saw it wasn't real. The rest just fell into place."

Of course Grandfather knew what was going on. The cops may have seen him as some dumb old Indian off the rez. Frida knew better, even though she couldn't do anything about it.

As we turned to leave, Grandfather called after us. "By the way, Eve. We do not think of Miccosukee land as a reservation. It's our land. We fought for it. Some say we won."

"I know." But how did he know what I was thinking about the cops?

I looked back at him. He waved and smiled. "Tell Sammy the airboat needs a new ignition switch, that's all."

"How do you do that?" I asked.

"He reads more than minds, I guess," Renata said.

Grandfather heard her. "Nope. That switch has been bad for months, that's all."

As we were getting into my car, Frida pulled up in her police SUV. She was smiling.

"You got Jenny's killer?" I asked.

"Not yet, but we're close on his heels. I think we may have arrested one of his accomplices."

"Who?"

"Your favorite friend and Shelley's beau."

"Darrel? Darrel killed Jenny. But why?

"I don't think he killed her, but he may know who did."

I wondered if Frida knew how much I ached to put my hands around that little weasel's throat and squeeze until his eyeballs popped out. Or better yet, grab him by the back of his shirt and toss him into the slough near the Fifty-five-and-older RV park. Or perhaps I should …. I stopped myself.

"Where is the little shit?' I asked.

"He's at police headquarters in our interview room. Linc is talking with him while I grab a bite to eat for both of us. We've been at this all morning without a break."

"What evidence do you have?"

"I can't tell you that."

"Oh, come on, Frida."

"You remember Linc was headed to the coast to see if he could track down that phony hand?'

"Yep."

"You do the math." She grinned.

"Darrel," I said.

"You didn't hear it from me." Grinning, she rolled up her window and drove off.

I dropped Renata at the airboat ride. Sammy had finished the repairs on the boat. Was I surprised it was the ignition? I shared with him the news about Darrel.

"That's good news. Maybe Grandfather will be freed today," he said.

"I wouldn't get your hopes up. You know how the cops work. They'll want all the t's crossed and i's dotted. Better yet, they'll be looking for a confession."

His happiness grew less pronounced. "Still," he said.

I watched Sammy and Renata drive off to meet with other relatives, then walked over to the airboat chickee to have a few words with Jerry. A line of women stood in front of the stand, waiting to buy tickets. They didn't look happy.

I recognized one of them as a consigner.

"Delays, right? Kind of frustrating when you want to get out into the swamps."

"Listen, Eve. A delay is just fine with me and my friends if we get to watch your Miccosukee friend repair the engine—especially when it's as hot as it is and he takes off his shirt." She fanned herself with her airboat brochure, and I was sure it was to wave away internal heat and not the outside weather. "Now we've got that other guy, who told us he's part Miccosukee. He sure doesn't look like it. He sounds more like he's from up North. Do you know him?"

"I've seen him around."

As much as I wanted to drop by police headquarters and insist upon being let in to see Darrel, I knew Frida wouldn't allow me access. I feared she'd told me all she was going to. I was out in the cold. Or was I?

I punched in Alex's cell number.

"Hi there," I said, as cheery and friendly as if we'd never parted ways. "How's it going?"

"Hi, yourself. I know what you want, but first could you let me know where Sammy is? I tried to get him at the airboat business, but Jerry answered and said he was unavailable."

"Right. He's with his mother. They might be visiting more relatives. Maybe I could get a message to him."

There was a pause.

"No. I can wait."

"It's about Darrel, isn't it? I told Sammy he was being questioned. What do you know?"

"Let's meet at the Biscuit for a drink."

"What time?"

"Around five? Have everyone who's free meet us, too. They'll want to hear what I found out."

Good. I had just enough time to stop by the rig and thank Grandy and Max for lending a hand today. I could give Madeleine a call also.

I ARRIVED EARLY at the Biscuit, so I grabbed a table and ordered a drink before the crowd came in and took all the seats. Alex strode in, looking like the cat that ate the canary. He knew something I didn't. What was it?

"Okay, give."

The waitress set the drink down in front of me.

"I'll have the same."

"Great. You got a table." Grandy plopped herself down in the chair across from me. Max followed, carrying two mugs of ice-cold beer.

"No sense waiting on service when you can get it yourself from the bar." Max wiped his forehead with a handkerchief. "A hot one out there."

The waitress returned with Alex's drink just as Madeleine and David entered. She ordered iced tea and he a draft.

"Nappi not free?" Alex asked.

"Right here," said Nappi, walking up behind him.

Before Alex could tell us whatever he was hiding so happily,

Frida appeared. She looked as if she could use a drink. The makeup she'd applied this morning had slid south, and she had eaten all her lipstick off her lips. She'd obviously been rubbing her eyes because her mascara was smeared under her lower lashes.

She signaled the waitress. "Double Scotch on the rocks, hold the rocks. I drove by the rig and Eve's house. When I found no one at either place, I reasoned you'd all be here."

"I was just about to tell the gang about Darrel," Alex said.

"Go ahead with your end of the case, then let me hop in with what I know."

Alex shrugged. "All I really know is Linc went to the coast to see if he could find who bought that fake hand."

"Oh, you know more than that, by the look on your face," I said, but before he could speak, Frida held up one finger, asking me to wait for the answer while she took a sip of her drink.

"Ah, that's better." She sat back in her chair. "I needed someone to let Darrel know we'd found out he bought the hand and were about to move on arresting him for murder. So I had Alex tell him he was doing him a favor because of his relationship with Shelley by letting him know before we got there. Alex also gave him a piece of advice that helped us. 'Give yourself up voluntarily and you can work a deal with the cops if you tell them what you know.' " Frida laughed. "No one believed Darrel put together any of this on his own."

"So what did you find out from Darrel?"

"Well, not what we thought." Frida signaled for another drink.

"What then?" I wanted to shake her to get on with it.

"Here's what we know. It concerns you, Eve, as well as Grandfather Egret. Darrel bought the hand and planted it. He stole Jenny's ring and called us to say we should search Grandfather Egret's shed."

"We all knew Grandfather didn't have anything to do with Jenny's murder," said Nappi.

"I knew that too, but it's not the way we decided to do things. And I thank you for your help on this, Alex," Frida added.

"I could have done that, you know." I was a little hurt she hadn't asked me.

"Oh, Eve, honey, think about it. You going to Darrel and telling him you're doing him a favor? I don't think that would have worked. I needed someone with whom Darrel didn't have bad blood. Besides, as it turns out, Darrel told us something that made it clear how much he disliked you."

"What was that?"

"He and his buddies were the ones who put that alligator in your shop."

"He must have taken a shot at me also, then?"

"Nope. He said he didn't have anything to do with that," Frida said.

"You believe that?" I asked.

"I don't think Darrel has the stuff for killing, and that was a situation that could have resulted in your death."

"He didn't confess to the killing then?" said Alex, sounding disappointed.

"No, but we can free Grandfather Egret now that we know how he was set up and who did it. Sammy's at the jail right now, picking him up. He said he was taking him home and would talk with all of you later."

"If not Darrel, then who killed Jenny?" I asked.

Frida finished off the rest of her drink. "We are back to square one on this case. Darrel doesn't know who set him up to play these pranks. He just responded to phone calls. He didn't recognize the voice."

"You mean Darrel simply enlisted his buddies to play jokes suggested by a voice over the phone?" I asked.

"It wasn't just for the fun of it. He was paid," Frida said.

"How much?" asked Alex.

"Not as much as you'd think."

"That fits in with what we know of the jerk," Madeleine said.

"Jenny said it herself at our shop. He shoplifted from the cut-rate stores, merchandise of questionable quality, so it's not surprising he would settle for a miniscule payoff."

"He got fifty bucks for the hand and split a hundred bucks with his buddies for that gator in your shop."

I gave a snort of disgust. "I would send him the bill for cleaning the alligator poop and disinfecting the place so it didn't smell like the swamps, but it cost me more than he made off the trick." I wondered if I should take my case to small claims court. I'd ask Mr. Lightwind when I saw him next.

"I get the feeling Darrel would have done both deeds for free. He just seems to like making trouble for folks," said Frida. She got out of her chair. "Jenny's murder case is ongoing, and I need some sleep. Let me know if you think of anything." She trudged to the door, her shoulders slumped in defeat.

"The poor woman," said Grandy. We all nodded.

And what about Shelley? I wondered.

"Shelley," I said. "She called Darrel her best friend. We may not agree, but she's suffered the loss of her mother, and she has no one else except for Darrel." *And me*, I added to myself. Alex gave me a warning look.

"What?" I asked.

"Shelley McCleary is not your responsibility," he said.

"Then whose is she? She trusts me. I'm not about to abandon her now." I got out of my chair. "I'll be back at the house later. I'm going to the McCleary ranch."

Although she was older than I was when my parents died, Shelley was like me—alone, confused, looking for comfort after the awful blow the world had dealt her. I couldn't leave her with Darrel as her sole support.

"No dinner?" asked Madeleine.

"I'll grab some takeout," said Grandy. "It'll be waiting for you when you get home, Eve."

I nodded, feeling not at all hungry, although my stomach did let out a growl as I rushed to my car.

Before I could open the car door, Alex was at my side. "I'm coming with you."

"You? Why are you concerned about Shelley?"

"I'm not. I'm worried about you. Shelley had every reason to kill her mother. She didn't try to talk her out of the mud bog racing."

"She changed her mind about that once she hooked up with Darrel."

"Darrel certainly has been a bad influence, and he may have talked Shelley into seeing the situation his way: with Jenny out of the way, she and Darrel could use the property any way they wanted. Shelley has already signed an agreement to do a mud bog event in a few months. What does that say about her?"

"That's she's desperate."

"She might be desperate enough to kill again, and her target could be anyone getting in her way, like you."

I hesitated. Could Alex be right? My gut said no, he was wrong about Shelley, but I didn't want to fight with Alex.

"Come along if you want."

He got into the passenger's seat. Before he could say anything, I held up my finger to stop him. "Please don't say, 'I'm glad I talked some sense into you.'"

"How did you know I was going to say that?"

I shrugged. Maybe the "sight" that Grandfather Egret and Grandy had was catching. *Huh*.

As it turned out, I need not have worried about Shelley. She was being taken care of by her next-door-neighbor Clay Archer, whose sentiments about Darrel turned out to be the same as my own.

CHAPTER 21

———

When Alex and I entered the house, Shelley rushed into my arms, sobbing.

"I know Darrel didn't kill Mom. I just know it."

"Perhaps not, but he may know who did kill her," I said. "That's why the police are holding him." I glanced at Clay, whose expression I found hard to read.

He said, "I know you care about him, Shelley, but think about it. He did some pretty mean things to Eve and to the elderly Mr. Egret. Darrel's been in all sorts of trouble before too."

"But he was playing a joke, that's all," she wailed.

"Did you know about all this before he was arrested today?" asked Alex.

"No. No!" She dropped onto the couch and buried her face in her hands.

"Of course she didn't," Clay said. "Darrel hid it all from her. Trying to win her trust. I can't understand why the police haven't arrested him for murdering Jenny. He was just angling to marry Shelley. After he removed her mother, he could take over the property." Clay's voice was hard, his face contorted with anger. He moved toward Shelley and placed an arm around her shoulders. Instead of leaning into his comforting embrace, Shelley leaned away. The expression on her face changed from distress to repugnance. What was that all about?

"Mr. Archer is right, Shelley. You might have been his next target," Alex said.

I didn't believe it for a minute. As much as I disliked Darrel, I knew he wasn't clever enough to develop a plan to kill Jenny, win over her daughter, then engage in tricks to aggravate me and implicate Grandfather Egret in the murder. Darrel didn't plan all this. He was just an opportunistic criminal. A shirt in the store? No one looking? Steal it! And if he was so smart, why had the fake hand been traced so easily to him? Putting the alligator in my shop and hiding the hand in Grandfather Egret's shed were actions not designed to leave anyone physically hurt. But shooting at me? As Frida pointed out, I could have been killed.

"I don't know if you should be alone, Shelley. Why don't you come home with me?" I offered.

"Or me. I'm right next door," Clay said. He saw the look of shock on my face. "Oh, don't worry yourself, Eve. It'll be all proper. I have a housekeeper who lives in. What do you say, Shelley? It's up to you."

"I want to stay here. This is my home. I'll be fine."

"I can drop over and check on you," said Archer.

Shelley shook her head. "No." Looking at me, she added, "Eve, I'll call you if I need anything."

"ARCHER SEEMS GENUINELY fond of Shelley," observed Alex as we drove away.

"I'm not certain she feels the same way about him, but anyway, he's a guy. I think female company is what she needs right now."

"Unless it's Darrel," Alex said.

"He's more her age. I'm sure she sees Archer as …." I stopped to think about what I was about to say. What did she think about Archer? I hadn't gotten the feeling she saw him as a father figure. In fact, thinking back to her reaction to his attempt at comfort, I had the distinct feeling she felt ill at ease with him.

"You're off the hook, Eve. Archer can look in on her if she needs someone."

"Maybe."

"What are you thinking?"

"Archer is wrong, you know. Darrel is responsible for the alligator and hand stuff, but not for killing Jenny. He's just too limited. But who was giving him orders to set up those scenarios and who paid him? Was it the person who killed Jenny?"

"I have to admit I've got no idea."

"I wonder if George knew Darrel?"

"Your George?"

"Not mine. George, who's now with another woman. George, who likes to force women to …" I stopped. I hadn't told Alex about my encounter with George. Me and my big mouth.

"You never told me much about the conversation you and George had when I sent you out to his place. Did something happen you're not telling me about?"

"Kind of."

"It did or it didn't. Tell me."

So I did, and I knew it was a mistake.

"I guess I need to have a little talk with George." The look on his face was terrifying.

"Don't you dare, Alex. Frida knows what happened, and she thinks George's current live-in may change her mind about supporting his story. Just let it go. Please. There's murder on our plates, and that's more important than George's proclivity for hitting women."

"Unless it's behind Jenny's murder."

He was right, but somehow George didn't track as the killer for me.

We drove on in silence, both thinking our separate thoughts. I hoped Alex's weren't still focused on George.

"Have you ever met Darrel's father? What do you know about him?" I asked.

"You think he might have been Jenny's killer? What would be his motive?"

"I don't know. I'm just looking for someone who could have worked out this scheme and had Darrel do some of the dirty work."

"You busy tonight?" asked Alex.

"Why do you ask?" What was Alex up to now?

"Let's pay a visit to Darrel's pappy and see what he has to say."

Wow! I guess I'd graduated into the ranks of acceptable sidekick.

DARREL'S FATHER, DARREL Senior, was a large man with a reddish complexion and broken blood vessels decorating his cheeks and nose. He answered the door with a bottle of beer in his hand.

"Yeah? Who the hell are you?"

We told him. He slammed the door in our faces. We decided to play on his sympathies.

"We know your son has been arrested, but we can't believe he's responsible for Jenny McCleary's death. We'd like to talk to you. Maybe you can help us figure out who put him up to the pranks he copped to." It looked for a minute as if Alex was wasting his breath, as if his words couldn't penetrate the door.

"Okay, come on in then." Darrell Senior opened the door to a living room that looked as if it hadn't been cleared of the rubble left from the last hurricane. Empty food containers occupied every horizontal surface. A stack of empty pizza boxes formed an end table for the recliner chair, and a pile of beer cans sat next to a plaid couch, its two seat cushions indented by deep butt depressions. From his bleary eyes, I knew we'd come to the wrong place to find Jenny's murderer. The only planning this man seemed capable of was sorting his way around the trash in his living room and into the kitchen, where I assumed the beer was stashed in the fridge. It was a case of the apple not falling too far from the tree.

I tugged on Alex's sleeve and whispered in his ear, "This is a dead end. Let's go."

Alex shook his head.

"So, can you think of anybody who'd want to hurt Jenny McCleary and set your son up for it?"

He set down his beer can on the pizza-box end table. It teetered there momentarily, then fell onto the rug. Luckily the rug was so filthy that once the beer stain dried, probably no one would be able to tell there was another spot in the pile. Now that was clever decorating. Maybe I had misjudged Darrel Senior's planning capabilities.

"Damn. Be right back. Can I get you folks a cold one?"

We shook our heads.

We heard him open the refrigerator door. "Damn."

He came back into the living room. "Good thing you didn't take me up on that. I only got one more left. Gonna have to make a beer run."

On second thought, if the guy hadn't prepared for his beer needs, he was no planner. I took him back off my suspect list.

He flopped into the recliner across from the couch. The chair's leather was cracked in several places, but someone had mended it with that great American fix-all, duct tape. The pattern of the tape almost made it match the couch—mustard yellow and silver.

"Anyone?" Alex said, reminding him of the question.

He popped the top of the beer, took a deep slug, and gave the question some thought. It looked like thinking, but he might have passed out.

He reentered the world with a loud belch. "Well, here's something to ponder," he said. "I think one of the ranchers vying for the mud bog event kind of put all his eggs in one basket, so to speak. He needed the money from the event bad; otherwise his ranch would go into foreclosure. As it turns out, it did."

"You mean Tom Riley?" I said.

And there it was, sitting in front of us all the time. Tom Riley had needed money, Jenny beat him out of the event, he killed her, and then the ranch was put up for sale. A revenge murder that didn't net him a dime.

But where was Tom Riley now?

WE'D FORGOTTEN FRIDA was off duty when we called her at the station, and both Alex and I wanted Frida to be the official with whom we shared our information about Tom Riley. Neither of us thought it necessary to disturb her at home. We said good night and arranged to meet early the next morning at police headquarters.

THE FOLLOWING MORNING at police headquarters, I let Alex tell Frida what we'd learned from talking with Darrel Senior.

"Riley isn't around here anymore," Alex said. "I checked when we were looking into the applicants for the mud bog event. I never followed up with him because he had given up on the event and left his ranch when the bank foreclosed on it. That was weeks before the event, but he might have come back here that morning."

Frida sat in her desk chair, feet up on the edge of the desk, arms linked behind her head. "I'll find him. Nice work, guys."

Alex left the station before me. Frida and I continued to talk about Jenny's murder.

"I'm worried about Shelley. That poor young woman has suffered two losses, one right after the other. I mean, if you can consider Darrel's arrest a loss. I don't understand what she sees in him."

"Male company," Frida said. "And there's little enough of that going around in this place, especially when some consignment-shop owner hogs her share of available men by taking two instead of the allotted one." She smiled, taking the edge off her remark.

"I don't have two men. I don't even know if I have any."

"Oh, right." She laughed so hard she began to sputter. The phone on her desk rang, and she recovered enough to say hello. She listened for a minute, then disconnected.

"Well, I guess that solves part of Shelley's problem."

"What do you mean?"

"Darrel's father just posted his bail."

"I can't believe that. Where would he get the money? What was bail set at anyway?"

"Two hundred and fifty thousand."

"Mortgaging his house and all his possessions wouldn't net him more than a few thousand, would it?" I asked.

Frida shrugged. "I'm told he paid in cash. He must have resources we don't know about."

"I can't believe it."

I walked out of the building, trying to reconcile Darrel Senior's trashy house with two hundred and fifty thousand dollars. Someone had to have loaned him the money, and I wondered who and why.

If Darrel tried to see Shelley, he was probably out of luck. Clay Archer was right next door and would probably see Darrel's car and take some kind of action. Darrel would have a difficult time getting to see Shelley if Clay had anything to say about it.

I decided to call Clay to let him know Darrel was probably coming his way and to see if I could set up a time for Grandy, Max, and me to visit the ranch for a ride on his horses. There was no answer. Maybe Clay already knew about Darrel and was at Shelley's house. The thought should have comforted me, but I wanted to check on Shelley myself. Right now I needed to help Madeleine open our rig.

When I got to our shop on wheels, Madeleine was already there.

"I stopped by our new place this morning on my way here and found that everything is almost finished. We have a decision to make, Eve. Do we run both places or move everything into the new place and operate out of there?"

"If we do both places, we'll be stretching ourselves thin, especially with the baby on the way," I said.

"Need I remind you, as I have David numerous times? I'm pregnant, not ill," Madeleine said. "We could each work one place and set up a schedule to alternate weekly or daily, whichever we want."

"Better yet, let's operate the shop during the week and on Saturday. One of us can take the rig to the coast on the weekends."

"Even better." Madeleine clapped her hands together. "We're gonna be rich."

"Maybe, but first, we have to pay off our loans."

I touched the amulet around my neck, convinced it had brought us this good fortune.

Out the window of the rig I watched Frida's cruiser pull up. She got out of the car with a smile on her face and gave a wave.

"I thought you should be the first to know, Eve. Thanks to Alex and your lead, we found Tom Riley and brought him in for questioning. He wasn't saying much so we executed a search warrant for his ranch. There we turned up a machete that looks like it has dried blood on it. When we presented him with that evidence, he lawyered up. But we'll get him."

"That's great news. Is it Jenny's blood?"

"Preliminary results say the same blood type, but the lab is backed up, so the DNA analysis will take time. He claims he didn't do it, of course. Though he was and is one furious man over Jenny getting the mud bog event. He blames her for his losing the ranch. And he admitted coming back here to meet with Jenny near the bog early on the morning of the event. Everything is falling into place."

"Did you find a rifle?"

"No, but we haven't finished searching."

"Have you told Shelley the good news?"

"I tried to call her but she didn't pick up. The machine kicked in. This is not something I want to leave on an answering device. And thanks again for leveraging that information about Riley out of Darrel's father."

"I don't think we did much leveraging. It was just a matter of his remembering about Riley between beers."

Frida laughed and said goodbye. I hadn't seen her so happy since before the murder. I was happy for her, although a little disappointed I hadn't been more involved. Or was that it? Something was bothering me, and I couldn't put my finger on it. *Really, Eve*, I told myself. *Deal with it. You can't solve every murder in Sabal Bay. Be happy for Frida*. And I was, yet that feeling ….

The morning slipped by with few customers.

"I thought by now people around here would have forgiven us for being in that demonstration, but business is still down," said Madeleine.

I dismissed her concern. "It'll pick up." If it didn't, we would be hard put to pay our bills.

I was about to go on a run for lunch when a middle-aged woman—tall, thin, her brown hair streaked with gray— stepped into the rig.

"I'm looking for something to wear to an interview. I don't really know what would be appropriate because I've worked at the same ranch for many years. Maybe you can help me?"

"Sure. What kind of work do you do?" asked Madeleine.

Madeleine had this one in hand, so I decided it was time to re-dress our two mannequins with outfits we'd just taken in on consignment. I was checking our shorts and knit tops when I heard Clay Archer's name mentioned.

"Hi there. I'm Eve. Madeleine and I own this shop together. I couldn't help but hear you mention Clay Archer."

She held out her hand. "Daisy Goodhelp. I'm looking for an

outfit I can wear to an interview for a housekeeper. That was my job for Mr. Archer."

"Was? I was led to believe you still worked there."

"No. I left." She seemed uncomfortable, as if she wanted to change the subject.

"Really?" How interesting. I bit back a barrage of questions and for once simply let her fill the silence.

"Well, I don't want to tell tales out of school, but I was cleaning his desk the other day and I found ... something." She stopped talking and seemed reluctant to continue.

Again I simply smiled and nodded encouragement.

"I'm no prude, but ...." She contorted her face as if viewing something disgusting.

The words tumbled out. "Pictures of girls, teenage girls, some even younger. They were all nude. I can't work for someone like that. I just can't." Mrs. Goodhelp began to sob.

CHAPTER 22

I RUSHED TO get Mrs. Goodhelp a glass of water and help her into a chair.

"No, of course, you couldn't continue to work there. Did Mr. Archer know you had found the pictures?"

She shook her head.

"Could he have suspected?"

She shook her head again.

I breathed a sigh of relief. Archer wouldn't want his secret blabbed around town, and I worried what he might do to someone who knew about his interest in illegal pornography. Once Madeleine and I had helped calm down Mrs. Goodhelp, I suggested she might want to report what she knew to the police.

"It's against the law to have child pornography—to buy it, sell it, or download it off the internet," I said.

She gathered herself together and left, indicating she was headed to the police station.

I'd promised myself I would call Shelley earlier, but I'd gotten distracted with business and then by Mrs. Goodhelp. After the housekeeper's visit, I felt a renewed urgency to contact Shelley.

I worried for her safety. Maybe I was being foolish, but I would feel better after talking with her. I tried her house again and again got no answer, so I called Clay Archer.

"I tried to call Shelley but she's not picking up. Have you seen or talked to her today?" I asked, keeping my tone matter-of-fact.

"Yep, but I think she stepped out to get some groceries. She should be back soon."

"Do you know if Frida got in touch with her?"

"No. What does she want with Shelley?"

I paused. I didn't want to give anything away.

"It has to do with the case. If you see her, could you have her get in touch with me? I left several messages on her machine, but it's important."

"Will do," he said in a cheery voice and hung up.

I called Darrel Senior, who answered after five rings. "Is Darrel there?"

"Nope. I bailed him out, and he went off to see Shelley. What business is this of yours, anyway?" He hung up.

I checked my contacts on the cell, hit connect, and then turned to Madeleine. "I may need you to mind the shop for a while."

"Is that a while as in hours, days, or weeks? And what are you up to now, Eve?"

"Don't be so suspicious. I'm making a trip to Boca."

"So we're talking five hours—two and a half down, the same back if traffic cooperates."

"The rest of today then."

My call connected. "Hello?"

"Mrs. Archer? This is Eve Appel. I need to talk to you."

"You've got me. So talk."

"I think this is something we should talk about in person. It concerns your husband."

"He's no longer of interest to me."

"Let me ask you this. If you knew Shelley McCleary was alone at his place, would that trouble you?"

There was silence at the other end and for a minute, I thought she had hung up on me.

"I'm going out shopping in West Palm, at City Place. There's a small brewpub there. Meet me in an hour."

An hour to get to West Palm. That was cutting it close, but I had no choice. It was far better than going to Boca.

"Gotta go, Madeleine. I'll be back as soon as I can."

"What are you up to, Eve?" she asked again.

Waving goodbye, I ran out the door, jumped into the car, and was off.

I arrived in West Palm in an hour and ten minutes—record time, given traffic on Okeechobee Boulevard into the city.

It took less than half an hour for Mrs. Archer to tell me the story of Clay and her. To her credit, she had married him convinced that he could change. To his credit, he made an effort to change, to be a good husband to her, but after a few years she was forced to make two payments to keep Clay's secret out of the press and out of the courts: he had sexually assaulted the teenage daughters of two couples they knew, and Audra paid to keep the parents from going to the police.

"He went into therapy, then we went into therapy together, but I could see it wasn't going to work. I filed for divorce. Clay needed money, and I wasn't about to settle any of mine on him. I'd given him more than he deserved. I guess he thought he could talk Jenny McCleary out of the mud bog event. It appeared for a time that he had, but he told me one night, 'She betrayed me.' Clay might have been able to dig up money from our joint accounts to fund an event, and maybe I would have taken pity on him once again and fronted him the money, but since the event went to Jenny, it was a moot point."

"So that's why you laughed at the idea of Clay and Jenny."

"Jenny had to be delusional if she thought Clay was after

her. Of course he could have faked it. He did with me. And probably for the same reason. Money." She looked up from the coffee she was sipping.

"How did Clay act around Shelley?"

"I never saw them together."

"Weren't you worried, given his predatory behavior with other young girls?"

"I kept an eye on him. He didn't have much opportunity to be alone with anyone."

"He did once you left him." I know I sounded accusatory, as if I'd blame her if Clay assaulted Shelley.

"Look, you don't know how it was living with him and his … perversity. There wasn't a thing I could do."

"You could have let those parents go to the authorities instead of covering for him."

She seemed ready to stalk off, but instead she leaned back into her chair and struggled for control. For the first time since we'd met, Audra Archer dropped her haughty attitude and let me see the fear and guilt beneath.

"Maybe. I guess I was too much of a coward to face public humiliation.

"He was the predator, not you."

She nodded. "I know. I handled it badly. Look, all I know is this, and it's why I agreed to meet you today. If Jenny was half as bright as I think she was, she would have noticed something wasn't right when Clay was around Shelley."

"And Jenny might have confronted him. Correct?"

"Yes," she replied in a whisper.

"And what would have happened then, do you think?"

"Clay had kept his perversion under wraps for years. He wouldn't have wanted anyone to know. I can't imagine what he might have done if confronted by Jenny."

I slid out of my seat. "Thanks for the information, but I've got to get back to Sabal Bay as soon as possible. Three lives are at stake."

"Three?" She looked surprised. "Who—?"

"Shelley, Darrel, and Clay. They're all up against the wall with no way out."

Maybe I should have included myself. I had no plan for how to diffuse the situation, and I needed help. I tried to call Alex, but his cell went to voicemail. I left a message telling him what I had found out. I also called Frida, Grandfather Egret, Sammy, and Nappi. No one was available to take my call. I was on my own, and this time I doubted the pair of red patent stilettos I was wearing would be much help. Stilettos could be useful, in a pinch, almost as handy as an ice pick.

ON MY DRIVE back up the Bee line Highway to Sabal Bay, I kept turning over in my head what I now knew about Clay Archer. Clay liked young women, *very* young women, women who were naïve and trusted easily, like Shelley McCleary. Shelley was only sixteen and knew little about men, especially men like Archer, a sexual predator of the worst kind. He had used his wife as a cover and used her money to keep him out of jail, paying off parents so they wouldn't report his behavior with their daughters to the police. In many ways, Audra Archer was as naïve as Shelley, thinking she could change the man and believing she was helping him by keeping him out of jail.

Clay must have been enraged when Jenny went ahead with the mud bog event, leaving him with no way to make money. I had every reason to believe Jenny had picked up on something unsavory in him and suspected he was not after her, but her daughter. That could have been the argument Shelley heard the morning of her mother's murder. If Jenny accused him of lusting after her daughter, his rage would have been boundless. The result was murder.

I thought back to Shelley's reaction to Archer. She, too, felt uncomfortable around him, and I was too blind to see it because, like everyone else, I thought Clay Archer was charming. Oh, he was charming, but also predatory when it came to very young women and girls, an urge he found impossible to keep in check.

I kept trying to reach someone, anyone who could help me. I knew it was foolhardy to confront Clay alone with what I knew, but I had no time. I needed to get to Shelley's place *now*. Yes, I could become his next target. Still, Darrel was looking for Shelley. Maybe the two of us could reason with him. I heard the bitterness in my own laughter. As if reasoning was something Darrel was good at or even considered a tactic …. I continued to focus on what I would say to Clay when I got to the ranch. It kept my mind off what might be happening to Shelley. I was certain she was not out shopping for groceries but in the clutches this horrid man.

When I pulled into the drive, I spotted Darrel's Camaro parked by the front steps. I ran to the door and banged on it. No answer. I banged again, then listened. Nothing. I peeked in the windows on either side of the front entrance, but couldn't see anything. I worked my way around the house, checking each window to see if anyone was inside. When I came to the living-room window, I saw a red sneaker sticking out from behind the couch. From its battered condition, it had to be Darrel's. I tapped on the window—not too hard. I didn't want the sound to carry if Clay was in there. The foot didn't move, and no one responded.

I tapped more loudly and heard a moan. "Darrel, are you okay?"

Another moan. I had to get in there now to see how badly Darrel was hurt. I ran back to the front door, turned the knob, and pushed. It swung open.

"Shelley?" I called. No one answered.

I ran into the living room and over to the couch.

"Darrel?"

He lay face down, blood on the side of his head where he had been hit, but he was breathing.

"Where's Shelley?" I asked.

"Who are—" he muttered.

"Shelley. Where is she?"

"Clay took her out the back door when he heard someone drive up." That was all I got from him before he lost consciousness.

I heard a vehicle start up. I'd have to leave Darrel and hope for the best. Shelley was my concern now.

I dashed into the kitchen as Clay's truck pulled out of the back drive. I could only see Clay in the driver's seat and no one else. Was Shelley with him, as Darrel said? And was she alive?

I ran out to my car, jumped in, and followed him as he drove down the drive and then turned onto the dirt road that ran toward the mud bog, parallel to the main road.

He had to have seen me pursuing him. If he turned onto the main road, I could keep up with him easily, but on this rutted lane, my car might bottom out. I picked up my cell and tried Frida's number again. No answer. I tossed the phone onto the passenger's seat in frustration.

Suddenly I saw Clay's brake lights come on, and he stopped just this side of the mud bog. He jumped out, a rifle in his hand. With this other hand he held Shelley. Her face was sickly white with fear. I got out of my car and moved toward them.

"Don't come any closer, or I'll shoot her," he yelled. He fired at me, but hit my windshield on the passenger's side. He threw Shelley to the ground, and with both hands on the rifle, took more careful aim. He hesitated only a moment, a look of murderous glee on his face. The rifle came up, and I stared down the barrel at my own death. All I could think was that now I was involved in this case, but not the way I'd hoped.

Neither of us had counted on Shelley. She got to her feet and flung herself at him. Archer's shot went wide as I rushed at him, my fists raised to pound his face. Now too close for a shot, he used the rifle as a club, swinging it at both of us. He landed a blow on Shelley's collarbone, and I heard a sickening crack. I jumped out of the way of the rifle, knowing the same could happen to me. I didn't want to put too much space between us for fear he'd get off another shot at me. Realizing his dilemma, he spun around and opened the truck door, obviously intending to flee. I grabbed his shirt and hung on.

"You want to come with me, ya little bitch?" he said. "Fine then. I can use a hostage in case any of your police friends decide to come after me." He pulled me up by my arm and shoved me across the seat into the truck, then put the vehicle back into gear and stomped on the accelerator, taking us along the edge of the bog toward the main road. I grabbed the door handle and tried to open it. He lunged across the seat and pulled me away from the handle. His attempt to control me made the wheel slip through his hand, and the truck veered toward the bog, its driver's-side wheel catching on the muddy bank. The truck slid into the bog and turned on its side, slamming into a cypress at the water's edge.

The impact threw me against the dash and knocked the air out of my lungs. Clay's head hit the steering wheel with a crack. Limp, his body started to slide toward the door and into the water that flooded his side of the cab. Once I caught my breath, I realized that Clay would drown if I didn't pull him out of the muddy water. My side of the cab was clear, and I could roll down my window and escape. Or with more difficulty, I might open my door. First I grabbed Clay's shirt and tried to pull him toward me. He didn't budge. He was dead weight. I felt around in the water to get a better grip on him and realized that his arm had been thrown through the open driver's side window and was now pinned beneath the truck.

I needed help to move him. I rolled down my window and crawled out, then ran for my car. Where was my damn cellphone? I remembered tossing it onto the passenger's seat, but it wasn't there. Maybe it had fallen onto the floor. I leaned over the seat and across the center console. There it was, just out of reach. Damn! I rushed around to the other side of the car, opened the door, and grabbed the phone. I called 911 then dialed Frieda's cell again. This time she answered.

"Where the hell are you? I got your messages, and I'm at the house, but there is no you. We found Darrel."

I ran over to Shelley, who still lay on the ground where Clay had thrown her. "I've got no time to explain, Frida. I need you here. Now!" I explained where we were and the situation with Clay. "I think Shelley's in bad shape."

I assured Shelley help was coming.

"Don't leave me, Eve."

"Just for a minute, honey." I ran back to the half-submerged truck and looked into the cab. Clay lay where I had left him. His entire body was submerged in the murky waters and vines. Water lilies, water cabbage, and water hyacinth had rushed in, green and yellow, purple and white blossoms. A macabre funeral wreath encircled his head where it still rested against the steering wheel.

This wasn't the mud bog experience Clay Archer had planned. I felt a momentary sense of regret at his death, but remembering what he had done to Jenny, Shelley, his wife and those other young women, I decided it was only right that he should die in the bog.

CHAPTER 23

—

I HEARD SIRENS and looked back toward the house. Frida's cruiser pulled up near my car, and she jumped out. An emergency vehicle followed hers. My primary concern was Shelley, who lay on the ground without moving. I ran to her and kneeled at her side. Her skin was white and covered in perspiration. I worried she was going into shock and signaled the EMTs over.

"I think her collarbone has been broken."

Frida had walked over to Archer's truck, opened the passenger's door, and crawled in. A few minutes later she backed out, shaking her head.

She joined me at Shelley's side. "Tell me what happened here. Why did you suspect Archer?"

I told her the story in detail, paused to take a breath and then shared some of my feelings about Archer's death.

"Don't waste a teardrop of grief on that man, Eve. Once we check his rifle, I'm certain we'll find it was the one used to shoot your rig. He would have killed you, too."

I couldn't think about that now. I wanted to focus on the

living, even on Darrel, the little weasel. "You found Darrel at the house?"

"Yup. Linc is with him."

"I guess Archer put Darrel up to those other pranks, right?"

"Probably, but Darrel can't identify who hired him. He only heard a voice over the telephone and picked up the money at a drop-off destination. At least that's what he told us before he bailed out. I don't think he was any threat to Archer, who wanted him out of the way just in case."

"I think he had another reason for wanting Darrel out of the picture."

Frida looked puzzled.

"Shelley liked Darrel," I said.

"Right. And Archer was worried enough about leaving Darrel as a loose end that he gave Darrel Senior the money for bail so he could lure him out to the ranch and kill him. He targeted you and the shop because he saw you as Shelley's protector. He wanted her to himself, but there you were playing mother hen."

"Darrel's going to be okay?"

"Yeah. I guess your arrival got in the way of Archer's plans to finish him off. He gave him a good crack on the head, thinking that would do it, but Darrel seems to have an extraordinarily hard skull. I'll bet he was hatching some kind of plan to make it look as if Darrel killed Shelley. What the next step was, I don't know—maybe to put a gun in Darrel's hand and shoot Shelley, making it look as if Darrel did it. Your timely appearance saved her life." Frida shook her head. "Audra Archer was crazy to have covered for him all these years."

"She was in love with him. I think she still is. Something went wrong with Archer's plan. I don't think he wanted to kill Shelley, at least not originally. He wanted her to be his, as he did those other girls."

"We'll question Shelley when she's in better shape. I think she could use some therapy to get over this."

"Be back in a second," I said. I walked over to where the EMTs were loading Shelley into the ambulance.

"How are you feeling?" I asked.

She gave me a wan smile. "It hurts."

"I know, but they say you'll be fine after they reset your shoulder."

"I doubt I'll ever be fine."

"It's not your fault, you know." I wanted to ease her gently into reliving what Clay had done to her today. Recovering from all this was going to take time.

"He wanted to sleep with me. He even said he'd marry me. He's so old. What a creep!"

Wow. I was shocked at her response—not horror but anger and disgust.

"Did he force—" I couldn't help asking.

"He did not. He came to the house this morning and grabbed me, but I fought hard, kicked and screamed. He finally locked me in one of the bedrooms. He thought he'd wear me down. He placed flowers, candy, and other gifts outside the door and begged me to come out. That was even creepier, his begging. I told him he was a sicko, and I'd rather die than give in to him."

"You thought something was wrong with him, didn't you? Or did your mother warn you?"

"She told me he wasn't what he seemed to be and to keep my distance. He was always touching me, trying to be friendly. It made my skin crawl, so I avoided him."

When he finally confronted her outright, Shelley had refused him, fought him off, and hate replaced desire. Shelley was not the naïve and compliant girl he thought she was or needed her to be.

"He was a sick man," I said.

"Yeah, I know. And I think Mom guessed about him, too. I wish she would have said something more direct to me. People think I'm too fragile to handle the real world. I'm not."

From the way she threw herself against Clay to prevent him

from shooting me, I knew she was a lot tougher than anyone thought. She was more like Jenny than I realized.

I patted her hand. "I'll visit you in the hospital once you settle in."

"Let's go, guys," Shelley said to the EMTs. "Shelley could use some big time pain killers. Chop, chop."

Hmm, ordering the EMTs around. Reminded me of her mother. If Darrel wanted to remain in her life, he would need to do some revamping of his character, especially with respect to his sticky fingers and his pushy attitude. On second thought, I guessed she'd soon reject an accused felon as poor boyfriend material.

"I've got to leave," I told Frida.

"Maybe you should have a doctor examine you too," she suggested.

"For what?"

"Shock maybe?"

I laughed. "Not a chance. Given my past experiences with murderers, I think I'm getting used to them meeting with justice of one sort or the other. I expect it."

"But dying as he did with you right there? That's not easy to deal with. Cops are used to these situations, and even we have trouble with the aftermath."

"Maybe it will be delayed. I'll keep a lookout. I need to do something."

"Now?"

"Yes, right now."

I drove directly to Jay Cassidy's place. The horror of what might have happened to Shelley and Jenny's death, all related to this mud bog business, plagued me. I wouldn't get beyond it until I took some immediate steps to remedy what I had been thinking was wrong with mud bog racing, and even what wasn't right with our protesting it. Mud bog racing wasn't going away, but the competition for the money it brought in had resulted in one murder and had led directly to the foreclosure on Tom Riley's ranch.

Jay welcomed me with a return of the warmth he had for Madeleine and me before we joined in to protest the mud bog event at Jenny's.

"Scotch?" he asked.

I nodded. After my day, I could use it. I held up my fingers, indicating a double.

"I've come to talk about mud bogging," I said. "I know everyone finds the topic unpleasant, given Jenny's death and the protest, but I think it's time the community got together and worked something out, especially now." I explained about Clay Archer.

"I'm shocked. Good old Clay. Are the police sure?" He watched me slug down the Scotch and added, "Are you all right?"

"Just dandy, or I will be, once I've had another of these."

He poured me another, smaller than the first. I gave him a hard look before he gave it to me. He caved and added another shot.

"So talk." He settled back into the couch.

"With Nappi I referred to it as crop rotation."

He laughed. "And what does that mean?"

"Why don't all the ranchers who like the idea of mud bogging get together, create a cooperative, and rotate from year to year where the event is held? Everyone makes out, each site goes back to its natural state for a number of years, and here's the best part: if the cooperative pays the insurance, does publicity and arranges support services at the event, you can cut out the middle man—the bogger guy in West Palm."

He thought for a moment. "Sounds good. It might be worth a meeting with some of us. You want to be there?"

"I absolutely do not." I looked at my empty glass. "Time for me to go home. I'm beat." I tried to get up from my chair and fell back. "Whoopsie!"

"I think you're too drunk to drive."

"I'm too drunk to move. Or think." That was good. I didn't want to think anymore. Maybe not for a few days. Maybe never. I nodded off.

I AWOKE BACK in my own house, in my own bed. Grandy hovered over me, holding a hot cup of something.

"How did I get here?" I asked. "The last thing I remember is being in Jay's place." I tried to sit up. "Oh, man. My head hurts."

"That's what too many Scotches will do to you. Jay drove you here and carried you in." She handed me the cup. "It contains hot chocolate. It'll settle your stomach. And we need to get something solid down you."

"A big rack of ribs would be good."

"I'll order take-out from the Biscuit."

"Where's my cell? I owe a lot of people calls."

"I already took care of that. If you're able, we can invite some of them over later. If not, it can wait until tomorrow. Your friends are concerned about you. Frida told us what you went through."

I remembered Shelley in the hospital. "I suppose I'm not in good enough shape to drive?"

"Right."

"So could you drop me at the hospital while you get the ribs?'

"You're concerned about Shelley." Grandy reached in her pocket. "Here's you cell. Give her a call. She's probably been admitted and has a room now."

"I owe her a visit."

"You owe yourself a break. Call her." Her tone had a note of finality in it, and I knew better than to fight it.

I was connected with Shelley's room immediately. "I'm sorry I haven't gotten to the hospital yet."

Her voice sounded groggy. "It's okay. I just want to sleep. Come visit tomorrow." She disconnected.

I flopped back down onto the bed and fell asleep until I awakened again to the delicious smell of barbeque, fries, and creamy slaw wafting in from the other room. Grandy opened my bedroom door and stuck her head in.

"Food and people?" she asked.

"Yes to both."

I had just finished my ribs when folks began to appear at the door. First, Madeleine and David, then Sammy and Grandfather Egret, and finally Nappi and Jerry. Grandy told me Alex had called while I was sleeping to say he had wanted to drop by, but had a case in Miami and was on his way there.

"Mom had to catch a plane back to Vegas," said Sammy. "Otherwise she would have been here too."

Frida arrived last with news. "Is this a good time to talk about the case?"

Everyone looked at me. I nodded.

"We released Tom Riley, of course. He claimed the machete we found on his property wasn't his and his son verified that, bringing the machete that did belong to his father into the station. There was a partial print on the handle of the one we found, and it matched Clay's thumb, not Tom's. We're trying to expedite the DNA analysis of the blood on it. I'm sure it's the blade Clay used to remove Jenny's head."

CHAPTER 24

A MONTH WENT by before Frida got the results on the DNA. It was Jenny's blood on the machete identified as belonging to Clay Archer.

A lot happened in that month.

Interested ranchers under Jay's direction formed a mud bog cooperative. Shelley joined them and was able to rescind the contract she had signed with the firm in West Palm. The cooperative awarded her the location for later this year. She told me she would put the ranch on the market after the event.

"Then what will you do?" I asked. Before she could answer, I asked her to consider what we had talked about earlier: "Finish high school, take evening and weekend fashion and design classes, and work at the shop as our seamstress, designer, and fashion consultant."

"Really?"

"Madeleine and I have talked it over and we think it's a great idea. We can use the help, and who knows, maybe eventually you can come in as a partner."

Shelley was excited at the proposal.

I don't know if she and Darrel ever talked about that awful

time at Clay's place right before he died, but whatever romance they'd had appeared to be over. I never heard of her visiting him after he had been charged with his gator and hand "pranks," as he called them. Darrel Senior admitted that he got the money to bail Darrel out of jail from Clay. Where Clay found that money was never determined. I suspected Audra, not knowing what it was for, gave it to Clay. She wanted to let go, but as I said to Frida, she still loved him. If Clay were alive to face charges, Audra might have paid for his defense.

The horses at Clay's ranch were being boarded at Jay's place, and when their schedule would permit, Grandy came up to ride them. The best she could do was get Max to lead one of them around. He said they were "getting acquainted." Max wouldn't talk about retirement, but he was feeling more and more at home fishing on the lake, eating ribs at the Biscuit, and talking with David about property for sale around Sabal Bay. For now, it was just talk.

There was still the matter of cleansing the new shop. I hadn't been into the location since I'd talked to the construction guy from the tribe who warned me away until I'd followed Grandfather's advice. While others could enter the place with no immediate harm, Grandfather worried the foul spirits in the place might eventually build up and bring harm to them also. Grandfather was adamant that evil prowled its rooms. Madeleine and I weren't convinced.

"It was an alligator put there by Darrel," I insisted.

"What about all those plumbing and electrical problems?" asked Grandfather.

"Shoddy workmanship from the previous owner," I replied.

"I'm free this Saturday," said Grandfather. "I can do it for you then."

Madeleine and I shrugged. "I guess if we're going to move anything in there soon, we'd better listen to him or he'll post tribal members at the door and refuse us entrance," I said. "And he could be right about the evil in there."

"This Saturday then," Madeleine agreed.

Saturday found all of us—Madeleine, David, Grandy, Max, Alex, Sammy, Nappi, Jerry, and me—waiting outside the front entrance to our shop while Grandfather roamed from one room to the other. He held a feather in one hand and a smoke bundle in the other.

"If it's so evil in there, why is he safe?" asked Jerry.

"Shhh," I said. "He's got a special dispensation from badness or something."

We couldn't hear much coming from within the shop, just an occasional whisper followed by low chanting.

After several minutes, Grandfather stepped outside. "That's about it for now. You probably need to reinforce it every year or so. I'll send you my bill in the mail."

"You're charging us?" I was shocked.

"I may not be cheap, but I'm the best around here. Do you know of anybody else who would work on the weekend?"

I thought I caught him wink as he turned away to usher everyone into the store.

"He's not serious, is he?" I asked Sammy.

"Next time I could ask around to see if anybody can do it for you cheaper," Sammy replied, his expression deadpan.

We stepped into the shop. All the work had been completed—partitions, paint on the walls, and the air conditioner humming away quietly. Everything seemed to be working. I walked down the hallway and stuck my head into our small bathroom. No water, except what flowed out of the faucet when I turned the handle. Oddly enough, the place smelled sweet and clean, and I felt an overwhelming sense of happiness surround me. *Hmmm, maybe this cleansing thing does work.*

TOM RILEY CAME by the shop the following week to thank me for taking down Clay Archer.

"I wasn't responsible for 'taking him down,' Mr. Riley. He took himself out."

"Yeah, well, you did hang in there, and I thank you for exposing him. Whatever I can do for you, let me know."

I hesitated. "I understand you've moved back to this area, so you might spread the word around town that Madeleine and I are not such bad sorts, and that we do want to be part of this community. And you could send your wife in to shop here and bring her friends."

"Done!" he said.

Alex's words kept coming back to me, so as I returned from grabbing lunch that day, I took a quick detour and on impulse entered the shop next to ours.

The sign over the shop door read, "Crusty McNabb, Private Investigations." I pushed open the door and entered. The area was small, only a nine-by-twelve-foot space. It housed a desk with a chair in front of it. Behind the desk sat a man who had to be in his late sixties, dressed in a plaid shirt and khakis. His face, what I could see of it hidden behind a white beard and mustache, was ruddy. His bright blue eyes gave me a quick appraisal from head to toe.

"I know you," he said, getting out of his chair. "And I bet I know what you want."

His voice was so loud, I looked behind me, thinking he was talking to someone who had just entered.

I'd never met the man before—believe me, I'd remember him—and I was about to say so, but he gestured to the chair, and in his booming voice, told me to sit. I sat.

"How do you feel about guns?" he asked.

"What?"

"Guns. If you're gonna be a PI, you need to carry. So you like guns or not?"

"Uh, I don't know. I've never given it much thought. I suppose it might be easier to take down a bad guy armed with a gun rather than a black patent-leather stiletto sandal."

He roared with laughter.

"Could you tell me how you know who I am?"

"Your friend, the other detective around here. Alex."

Alex.

"He said you were a real snoopy kind of gal, one who liked to get involved in criminal stuff. So are you? Snoopy, I mean?"

I thought about that for only a moment. Yes, I was snoopy. I nodded.

"Sit down. You need to fill out this application." He pushed a paper across the desk at me, as if expecting me to start work right away.

"I haven't decided what I'm going to do for now, but thanks." I got up and left. What was I thinking. Me? A private eye?

"You'll be back," I heard him call out as the door closed behind me.

MADELEINE HAD A doctor's appointment that same afternoon, so I managed the shop. She and I had decided to put off final decisions about the rig and the shop. We both liked the idea of splitting our time between places, although it would mean we wouldn't be working together. I'd miss that, and I knew she would too, but we could take the rig to the coast on Sundays and sell there together. I was certain Grandfather Egret would want to take over one of the shops on an afternoon or two. With his help and Shelley's, we'd do just fine.

"Eve, Eve!" shouted Madeleine, running into the shop from her doctor's appointment. "Look at this." She waved a grainy black-and-white photo in front of my face. I couldn't make out the image.

David trailed behind her, the silliest smile on his face.

"Our first baby picture," she said. "It's done by ultrasound. Isn't it wonderful?"

I looked at it more closely and still couldn't discern much but a lot of shadows. "Sure. I guess."

She looked hurt at my reaction. "Don't you see?"

"You tell me. I'm not good at these baby things."

"Twins. I'm having twins."

"*We're* having twins," David repeated, the loony smile still in place.

"Maybe you better sit down," I suggested.

"I'm fine," Madeleine replied.

"No, I meant David. He looks like he's in shock."

Twins it was to be, and so we began the naming thing. First, a list of girls' names and a separate list of boys' names. Then from those lists, a list of girls' names, each paired with another girl's name, a list of boys' names each paired with another boy's name, and finally a list of boys' names, each paired with a girl's name.

"Why so many lists? Why can't we simply generate a list of girls' names and a list of boys' names?" I asked that same evening when we sat down at my kitchen table with pads and pencils in front of us. Of course everyone had to be there to help: Grandy and Max, now back in Key Largo but in Sabal Bay for the weekend, Alex, temporarily back from Miami, Sammy, Grandfather Egret, and even Nappi and Jerry. Madeleine was *that* happy.

"We have to make certain first that we like the name," she explained as if she thought I had the mental capacity of a three-year-old turtle. "Then we have to make sure the one name goes with the other."

"Huh?" I said, proving I did have the IQ of turtle.

"Oliver, for example," she said.

"You like the name 'Oliver'?" I asked.

"It's just an example, Eve." She began again, "Oliver couldn't be used with Olive now, could it?"

I didn't like either name, so I kept my mouth shut for the rest of the evening. I wondered how long this naming thing would continue. I feared it would go on until the actual day of the birth.

MOST OF THE month I spent waiting—I couldn't put into words for what. I was certain I'd know it when it happened.

Then the day arrived, almost a week after the shop cleansing. I was home by myself, Grandy and Max having returned to their boat. I stepped out onto my back patio.

He was standing there, washed in the light from a full moon. His dark eyes were like soft velvet when he turned and looked at me. I reached out my hand, and he took it and placed it on his chest. I remembered his mother's words cautioning me against taking his feelings too lightly, but I knew now that I would never do that. I felt the strength of his heartbeat, and I leaned into him. My heart took up the same rhythm as his.

He whispered into my hair, "A ride in my canoe to our place in the swamps?"

"Yes, yes," I said.

"This time I have no pound cake."

We both smiled.

Pound cake was not what we yearned for.

Creations in Fotografia by Rafael Pacheco

LESLEY A. DIEHL retired from her life as a professor of psychology and reclaimed her country roots by moving to a small cottage in the Butternut River Valley in Upstate New York. In the winter she migrates to old Florida—cowboys, scrub palmetto, and open fields of grazing cattle, a place where spurs still jingle in the post office and gators make golf a contact sport. Back north, the shy ghost inhabiting the cottage serves as her literary muse. When not writing, she gardens, cooks, and renovates the 1874 cottage with the help of her husband, two cats, and of course Fred the ghost, who gives artistic direction to their work.

She is the author of a number of mystery series and mysteries as well as short stories. *Mud Bog Murder* follows the first three books in the Eve Appel mystery series, *A Secondhand Murder*, *Dead in the Water* and *A Sporting Murder*.

Visit her online at www.lesleyadiehl.com.

Now catch up on the first three Eve Appel Mysteries

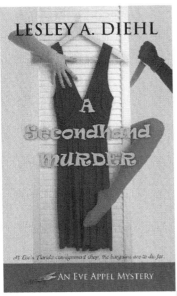

Spunky Eve Appel moves from Connecticut to rural Florida intent on starting a new life as the owner of a consignment store. But Eve's life, and her business with it, is turned upside down when a wealthy customer is found stabbed to death in a fitting room. As accusations fly and business slows, Eve takes matters into her own hands.

During an airboat trip in the Florida swamps, Eve's Uncle Winston is shot in the head. Eve soon discovers that Winston was "connected," although this was no simple mob hit. The Sabal Bay consignment shop owner vows to find his killer, even after her car is wrecked, she is left to the mercy of the alligators, and her best friend is kidnapped.

LESLEY A. DIEHL

A Sporting Murder

A hunter is killed, and Eve and her gang are in hot pursuit. But who's gunning for whom?

AN EVE APPEL MYSTERY

Madeleine's new beau, David, has been framed for murder. Who's the real culprit? What about his nasty neighbor Blake, whose rival hunting lodge features illegal exotic animals? Who kidnapped the nephew of Eve's Miccosukee Indian friend Sammy? Can Eve and Madeleine rescue their consignment shop from Blake's horrid wife Elvira? Gators are not the only predators stalking rural Florida.

Also check out three short stories featuring Eve and Madeleine.

LESLEY A. DIEHL

The Little Redheaded Girl is my Friend

AN EVE APPEL MYSTERY SHORT #1

LESLEY A. DIEHL

Thieves and Gators Run at the Mention of her Name

AN EVE APPEL MYSTERY SHORT #2

LESLEY A. DIEHL

Gator Aid

AN EVE APPEL MYSTERY SHORT #5

Made in the USA
Charleston, SC
19 September 2016